Praise for the Novels
of Lacey Alexander

D0205386

What She Needs
Winner of the HOLT Medallion Award

"Lacey Alexander has created a book which literally 'wows' the reader. Buckle up and hold on tight. Impossibly hot!"
—Fallen Angel Reviews (5 Angels)

"One very hot, sexy, and erotic book. Full of sexual fantasies that will have you flipping the pages to see what will happen next!"
—Fresh Fiction

"Prepare to be swept away on an erotic journey of sexual awakening . . . very sensual, erotic, and will open your mind to infinite possibilities!"
—The Romance Studio (5 Hearts)

"An ultraheated erotic romance. The heat is on."—The Best Reviews

"This book sizzles. . . . Ms. Alexander explores the spectrum of the human sexual experience without embarrassment or ridicule."
—Erotic Romance Writers

"Each sex scene is more varied—and hotter—than the last in this delightful read. Fans of heroes with tragic pasts will swoon over Brent."
—*Romantic Times* (4 Stars)

The Bikini Diaries
Write Touch Award Winner and Colorado Award of Excellence Finalist

"Hot, sizzling, and sexy! Lacey Alexander definitely will scorch your senses."
—Romance Junkies (5 Blue Ribbons)

continued . . .

"Ms. Alexander sweeps away her readers in a sinfully erotic yet surprisingly nongratuitous manner." —*Sacramento Book Review*

"With intriguing characters, [a] fast-paced story line, and tight writing, plus a host of naughty sexual adventures, Ms. Alexander delivers a powerful story." —Love Romances & More (4½ Hearts)

"Truly a phenomenal book. Lacey Alexander is a remarkably gifted author who writes exactly what I want to read, pushing boundaries with titillating sexuality, but never going beyond what's tasteful. . . . Do yourself a huge favor and buy everything Lacey Alexander has ever written. You won't regret it." —TwoLips Reviews (5 Lips)

"[The] most erotic book I have read. Lacey Alexander has written a no-holds-barred romp of sexual delights . . . a profound book." —Joyfully Reviewed

"I loved this book. Each sexual act was well written and done extremely well." —Night Owl Romance (5 out of 5, Lifetime Keeper)

"I was completely swept up in Wendy's journey. . . . Lacey Alexander is certainly the queen of what I fondly call 'romantic kink'!" —Wild on Books (5 Bookmarks)

Seven Nights of Sin
Write Touch Award Winner

"Lacey Alexander's books bring out the good little bad girl in all of us. Unforgettable in an 'oh, yeah, do that again, please' sort of way." —Michelle Buonfiglio, myLifetime.com

"Thoroughly tantalizing, with magnetic characters, a sizzling plot, and raw sensuality, this book will have you fanning yourself long after the last page!" —*Romantic Times*

And for Lacey Alexander

"Ms. Alexander is an exceptionally talented author who, time after time, takes us on extremely erotic journeys that leave us breathless with every turn of the page. . . . This author pens the most arousing sexual scenes that you could never imagine."—Fallen Angel Reviews

"Lacey Alexander has given readers . . . hot, erotic romance with no holds barred."   —Romance Junkies

"Ms. Alexander is probably one of the most talented, straightforward, imaginative writers in erotic romance today."
                                    —The Road to Romance

"Lacey Alexander just 'wowed' me! Incredibly hot!"
                        —Romance Reader at Heart (Top Pick)

"Lacey Alexander is a very talented writer."
                            —The Romance Readers Connection

"Lacey Alexander is an intoxicating erotic writer using sensual and sexual prowess to embrace your inner passions and desires. Sexual discovery at its best."   —Noveltown

"Lacey Alexander's characters . . . are so compelling and lifelike."
                                    —Coffee Time Romance

"Sooo romantic and sexy!"   —Cupid's Library Reviews

"Lacey Alexander takes blissful hedonism to a whole new level in this blazingly brazen, passionately erotic love story!"   —Ecataromance

Also by Lacey Alexander

H.O.T. Cops Novels

Bad Girl by Night

Voyeur

Seven Nights of Sin

The Bikini Diaries

What She Needs

Party of Three

A H.O.T. COPS NOVEL

Lacey Alexander

A SIGNET ECLIPSE BOOK

SIGNET ECLIPSE
Published by New American Library, a division of
Penguin Group (USA) Inc., 375 Hudson Street,
New York, New York 10014, USA
Penguin Group (Canada), 90 Eglinton Avenue East, Suite 700, Toronto,
Ontario M4P 2Y3, Canada (a division of Pearson Penguin Canada Inc.)
Penguin Books Ltd., 80 Strand, London WC2R 0RL, England
Penguin Ireland, 25 St. Stephen's Green, Dublin 2,
Ireland (a division of Penguin Books Ltd.)
Penguin Group (Australia), 250 Camberwell Road, Camberwell, Victoria 3124,
Australia (a division of Pearson Australia Group Pty. Ltd.)
Penguin Books India Pvt. Ltd., 11 Community Centre, Panchsheel Park,
New Delhi - 110 017, India
Penguin Group (NZ), 67 Apollo Drive, Rosedale, Auckland 0632,
New Zealand (a division of Pearson New Zealand Ltd.)
Penguin Books (South Africa) (Pty.) Ltd., 24 Sturdee Avenue,
Rosebank, Johannesburg 2196, South Africa

Penguin Books Ltd., Registered Offices:
80 Strand, London WC2R 0RL, England

First Printing, April 2012
10 9 8 7 6 5 4 3 2 1

Copyright © Lacey Alexander, 2012
All rights reserved. No part of this book may be reproduced, scanned, or distributed in any printed or
electronic form without permission. Please do not participate in or encourage piracy of copyrighted
materials in violation of the author's rights. Purchase only authorized editions.

SIGNET ECLIPSE and logo are trademarks of Penguin Group (USA) Inc.

LIBRARY OF CONGRESS CATALOGING-IN-PUBLICATION DATA:

Alexander, Lacey.
    Party of three: a H.O.T. cops novel/Lacey Alexander.
        p. cm.
    ISBN 978-0-451-23574-9
    I. Title.
    PS3601.L3539P37 2012
    813'.6—dc23   2011046535

Set in Centaur MT
Designed by Alissa Amell

Printed in the United States of America

PUBLISHER'S NOTE
This is a work of fiction. Names, characters, places, and incidents either are the product of the author's
imagination or are used fictitiously, and any resemblance to actual persons, living or dead, business establishments, events, or locales is entirely coincidental.
    The publisher does not have any control over and does not assume any responsibility for author or
third-party Web sites or their content.

Party of Three

"There is always some madness in love. But there is also always some reason in madness."

—Friedrich Nietzsche

Chapter 1

"Happy birthday, honey. Ready for your present?"

Mira lifted her cheek from where it lay resting on Ethan's shoulder in the hammock they shared. "My birthday's not until tomorrow," she reminded him with a playful smile.

"Yeah, but . . . don't you want your present *now*?" His blue eyes sparkled as he tilted his head to one side in the netting, and something in his look made the juncture of her thighs spasm, just slightly. Then again, it had been doing that a lot lately. In anticipation of this weekend.

"I thought my present was *this*," she said, motioning around them. He'd brought her to a secluded cabin in the woods on the north shore of Michigan's upper peninsula for her thirty-second birthday. To make up for some things. To start treating their relationship differently. And, of course, for some hot sex, which her body currently hungered for.

"It is," he confirmed. "But . . . there's more."

Hmm. "More? Really?"

He nodded, yet added nothing.

So she leaned closer, lacing her voice with flirtation to ask, "Well, don't you want to save it until my actual birthday?"

"Can't," he told her simply.

And she narrowed her gaze on him. Her boyfriend wasn't usually a man of so few words, so this conversation was beginning to feel downright cryptic. "Um, why not?"

That's when he began to look more hesitant, his expression transforming into a mixture of hope . . . and uneasiness. It was the look a man wore when he'd worked hard to find you the perfect gift but was still waiting to see your reaction when it was opened. Only Mira didn't see any sort of gift bag or box anywhere. "I can't save it," he told her, "because it's sort of . . . *starting* tonight."

Her birthday present was *starting*? Okay, he must be talking about the sex portion of the gift. Yet . . . why would he need to announce it if he was just talking about sex? Because yeah, she was good and ready for that, but . . . they'd had plenty of sex already during their four years together. "The sex, you mean," she said to clarify anyway, though she knew she sounded confused.

"Kind of," he said, and now he . . . hmm, to her surprise

he suddenly looked just as uncertain as she felt. Not nervous exactly—Ethan was never nervous—but he'd slowed down on this present-giving thing and she sensed him wading through it a little more gingerly at this point, and definitely holding something back. What was going on here?

She lowered her chin, met his gaze. "Kind of?"

"Okay, wait," he said, holding his hands out before him. "I should have thought through how to tell you about this, because now that it's time, I don't quite know how to say it. So . . . give me a minute to think about the best way."

Mira just looked at him. How complicated could this present be? He needed a "best way"? He sounded more like someone about to break bad news than a man giving a birthday gift to his girlfriend. "You're starting to make me worry," she admitted, still peering down into his handsome face.

"The thing about your gift," he began, "is that I want you to love it, really love it. But . . . I'm not sure how you'll take it."

She blinked, thoroughly perplexed now, then finally laid her head back on his shoulder, drinking in his musky, masculine scent as she silently provided him that minute he'd requested. A bird twittered in a tree somewhere to her right and the late afternoon sun warmed her face as she looked out over Lake Superior in the distance. Blue skies and unseasonably warm June temps in northern Michigan made the scene complete. And up until a minute ago, she'd felt relaxed, happy, like he really *was* making up for the troubles they'd endured over the past year or so. But right now she didn't know *what* to feel—and the uncertainty turned her thoughts unwittingly back to what had led them here, to this moment.

Ethan had been a workaholic since they'd started dating, and while she admired a strong work ethic—and particularly admired the pro bono legal work he'd embraced—over time she'd started feeling like she came in a distant second behind his career. And when, last summer, he'd canceled their Labor Day weekend boating plans with friends at the very last minute, she'd realized her life with him was starting to be . . . well, not all she'd hoped.

He was hot. Sexy. And great in bed. He was a good guy, a sincerely good man. In fact, Ethan West was the man she wanted to marry, and she'd known that almost from their first kiss. But then things had changed. He'd left the Charlevoix Police Force to study for the bar exam around the same time she'd moved in to his condo. And as soon as he'd passed the bar, he'd opened a small office not far from her shop, and business had been booming ever since for the quaint lakeside town's newest young lawyer. Life had bustled along, and they'd been fine. Until his work had started taking priority over *her.*

And things hadn't improved since Labor Day—and in reality they'd gotten worse. More late nights, more lost weekends. He could spend an entire dinner with her in a nice restaurant looking at his BlackBerry without ever even realizing he was leaving her virtually alone. And evenings at home that used to be spent *together* were now generally spent apart, him behind the closed door of their home office.

The truth was, right up until two weeks ago, she'd been seriously considering moving out. He didn't know that, though—she'd never told him. Because when she did complain about being neglected, he never seemed to hear—except for the times when he threw it back at her, pointing out how hard he was working, that he didn't need her nagging him on top of that, and how nice it would be to get some support. So he hadn't exactly been understanding or apologetic; he'd come closer to making her feel like an insecure shrew and she'd soon learned to just keep the peace by not speaking up at all.

And one day . . . well, she'd even started packing a suitcase. Envisioning the goodbye note she would write. Thinking about the serious logistics of moving the rest of her things.

But then she'd stopped. Because she'd reminded herself one more time that she loved him, and that when he *was* there for her, things were amazing and the chemistry between them—both physical and emotional—was intense. She connected with Ethan in a way she never had with anyone else. Yet lately she'd been asking herself: *Can I give my life to a man who doesn't put our relationship first? Is that what I want forever? And what if we move forward with getting married, having kids? Will he be that dad who never quite makes it to the recital or little league game? Will he be an absentee parent?*

And then—like some kind of miracle—the day after she'd almost left him, he'd taken her to lunch at her favorite waterside bistro and told her he'd rented a cabin upstate for her birthday weekend. He'd said he knew he'd been neglecting her and was going to change. Flashing a seductive grin, he'd told her he wanted to spend her birthday making it up to her by "doing hot, nasty things to you in the sun. Then doing more hot, nasty things to you in the moonlight. With maybe a little sleep in between before we start over again."

She'd bitten her lip, given him a smile across the table, and reached out to take his hand, utterly surprised and happier than she'd felt in a very long time. This was the old Ethan, the Ethan who'd swept her off her feet.

And now here they were, alone in the woods, and she'd begun to think that maybe he really *could* repair what he'd broken between them. He hadn't so much as mentioned a case or a client since they'd left Charlevoix this morning. He'd even left his BlackBerry at home. And he was once again the man who went out of his way to show his affection in ways both great and small—he'd even brought along a few bottles of her favorite wine, one of which they'd opened to drink with dinner a little while ago. Ethan had grilled burgers—saving the steaks he'd brought for her birthday dinner tomorrow night—and they'd eaten at the picnic table on the dock down below the cabin and the hillside where they now lay. "I know wine doesn't really go with hamburgers," he'd said with a slightly sheepish grin, "but . . ."

And she'd just replied with a happy laugh. "Who cares? I like wine and I like burgers. And I especially like how thoughtful you're being, Mr. West," she'd added teasingly.

Normally, she wouldn't have thought of renting a remote cabin as the way she wanted to spend her birthday, but the sentiment had touched her and now that they were here, she realized it was the perfect setting for a weekend of nonstop fucking. Since that was what she suddenly realized she wanted to do. Fuck him from now until Sunday, when it was time to leave. Their sex life had definitely begun to suffer over the past year, along with every other part of the relationship, and she was more than ready to get that back on track, too. And she supposed the wine had her feeling amorous. Even though they were outdoors, no other house was within sight, and the treed landscape added to the sense of isolation, so this felt as private as their bedroom at home—only a little more exciting.

Though she wasn't the sort of girl who usually thought of sex as fucking. A little dirty talk in the bedroom was fun, but it almost surprised her when that particular way of describing it entered her mind. *I must really need this. I must really need to let go this weekend and just let my body have him the way I want him, with no inhibitions, nothing held back.* Because even when they did have sex . . . maybe she *had* held part of herself back lately, due to resentment, not feeling totally connected to him anymore. *Well, this weekend, no holding back. This weekend he gets all of me. Maybe even more than he's ever had before.* She bit her lip, feeling naughty, aggressive.

And as for this mysterious gift of his—well, it would have to wait because she'd just decided there was no time like the present to have her way with her man. She boldly sat up, turned, and moved to straddle his thighs in the hammock. The netting beneath them wobbled and tilted, and for a second she feared it would flip them, but then it steadied, bringing her confidence back at the same time.

"Uh, what's going on?" he asked, clearly jarred—but still a small, sexy smile reshaped his face as his hands came to rest on her denim-clad hips. She liked the feel of his eyes on her.

All of me. I want you to have all of me. The words echoed through her as she spontaneously stripped her tank top off over her head, revealing a pale yellow bra with peach polka dots underneath. "I think I'm ready for some of that hot and nasty I was promised," she replied, taking on a sexy pout.

In response, Ethan's fingers splayed across her hips, then glided smoothly downward to stop high on her blue-jean-covered thighs. She felt every fingertip like a pinprick of electric heat. "Mmm, I like when you get aggressive," he said. "And I hope you still feel just as ready after I tell you about your present."

Oh, so he was back to the mystifying present again, huh? But she refused to let that get in the way of what she wanted right now, so she ran her palms up under his T-shirt, onto his muscled stomach, even as she asked, "Ever gonna end the suspense on that?"

When he squeezed both her thighs, she felt it between her legs. And his eyes twinkled warmly as he said, "Why don't you lie back down with me for a minute and I'll fill you in."

She lowered her chin, slanting a questioning look in his direction. This required lying back down? Stopping her mid-seduction?

A sigh left her, and yet—even as stopping killed a little of her arousal, the strange secrecy going on here kept the spot between her thighs humming with anticipation. Anticipation of sex mingling with anticipation of the unknown.

Ethan eased her back down beside him, cradling her in his arms to say, "Do you remember that night last summer— that night when we had too much to drink and started talking about fantasies?"

She nodded. It had been an evening a lot like this one: warm weather, good wine, and a quiet dinner for two that had led them on a walk to a park, where they'd ended up cuddling on a bench. Intoxication had gotten them laughing at first, and then touching and kissing—and then Ethan had asked her what her most secret sexual fantasy was. "It's okay, whatever it is," he'd told her.

And she'd slowly, quietly admitted that in the darkest, most private parts of her mind . . . she sometimes wondered what it would be like to be with two men at the same time.

He'd asked her questions. "Do you want to have two cocks inside you at once?" "Do you want to be the one in control or do you want to have that taken away?" "How much have you thought about this?"

And she'd answered—with vague replies mostly, because her fantasies had been just that: vague. Not entirely formed. Undetailed. The truth, she'd told him, was that it had started with a dream—she'd woken up remembering she'd dreamed about a threesome with two guys. "And sometimes I think about it because it turned me on, but at the same time, I'm not entirely sure I'm *comfortable* thinking about it—you know?"

He'd grinned, clearly pleased, aroused, by her sharing that. "Think you'd ever really want to do it?" he'd whispered.

"Only . . . under some perfect circumstances that I can't even really imagine," she'd told him honestly. And that had pretty much ended the conversation. Though they'd had really good sex afterward, back at home.

So now, after a long hesitation, she finally answered his question. "Um, yeah, I remember. Why?"

"Well, what if I told you," he answered slowly, reaching to skim his knuckles ever so lightly down her chest, between her breasts, "that for your birthday, I'm giving you your fantasy?"

Mira's mouth dropped open as the blood drained from her face. "You're what?" she whispered.

He spoke low, direct, but kindly. "You heard me."

Lying on her back on the thick netting with Ethan peering down on her, she simply blinked, still not quite able to believe her ears. She felt like someone else, in some other place, time—her whole world transformed into something surreal she didn't quite recognize. "But . . . but . . ."

Yet her lover only smiled—and it was perhaps the surest, most confident and in-control smile she'd ever seen on his face. "Don't freak out, hon," he said softly. "Just trust me."

But Mira suddenly couldn't breathe. And the sun that had lulled and relaxed her all afternoon now began to make her sweat, even as it dipped quietly toward the horizon through the trees to her left. Finally, she managed three words. "I don't understand."

At this, Ethan bent to lower a kiss to her forehead. And despite everything, even just that one chaste little kiss made the crux of her thighs tingle hotly. "Listen, relax," he told her. "Relax and let me explain."

He sounded so calm, so rational, that it *did* relax her. A little anyway. Maybe she'd misunderstood what he was saying. Maybe he meant something else entirely.

"I know I haven't been a great boyfriend lately," he began.

"And I know it's driven a wedge between us. I want to fix things, Mira. I want to make things right. I want to prove that making you happy is my top priority, starting now."

She still just blinked up at him, taking in his features, everything handsome and sexy about him. She'd always loved his olive skin and his dark hair, black as night, traits left over from an Italian ancestry that had faded in name a generation or two ago but showed up in his family's coloring. Now that dark hair stood out in bold contrast to the soft greens and browns above him, the trees that nestled their weekend hideaway and made it feel so deliciously remote. But the moment continued feeling utterly unreal—especially as he went on.

"I thought a lot about how to prove that, what I could give you to make up for how wrapped up in my practice I've been."

She felt the need to interrupt. "You don't have to give me anything more than this, just spending time with—" But he pressed gentle fingers over her mouth, quieting her.

"I know that, but . . . I guess I wanted to make a grand gesture, something big. And so . . . I thought about your fantasy."

Yes, it had been vague, but she'd told him as much about it as she could that night—it *was* about having two cocks inside her at once. It was about being caressed by two pairs of male hands, having her body kissed by two men's mouths. It wasn't about control—keeping it or giving it away. But it *was* about ... maybe being a little overwhelmed. In a good way. With masculine power. With sex itself.

"And I want to make it come true," he continued. "I want to give you that. I want you overcome with pleasure. I want you to have orgasm after orgasm in a way I could never make happen on my own."

Mira blew out her breath, poleaxed by the very idea. Strange how fear and stark desire could mix. And they both swirled inside her now as she tried to wrap her mind around the fact that he was offering this to her. Not as a fantasy, but as reality. Even though they weren't *those* kind of people. They were mainstream, middle-of-the-road; they were dependable and responsible. Yes, a little dirty talk in the bedroom—but that was about as kinky as it got and she'd always been perfectly pleased by what they shared. "We have great sex," she felt the need to remind him. "Mostly, I mean." Maybe not so much lately, but back when things had been good between them, the sex had, too.

"I know we do," he told her, now cupping her cheek in his palm. "But I want this weekend to be ... something beyond normal for us, beyond great. I want it to be something new, something extreme, something that'll bring you more pleasure than you can even imagine."

Okay. It was beginning to sink in that this was really happening, that he was really planning on this. But he didn't know her as well as he thought if he didn't realize ... "Ethan,

I can't have sex with just anybody. I mean, you know I haven't been with many guys." She'd always been in serious relationships. She'd never had a one-night stand in her life. And she'd never been intimate with anyone she hadn't gotten to know first. For her, good sex was about trust, about knowing the person you were with. "So I can't imagine who on earth I'd really want us to . . ."

"Rogan," he said simply—and that was when another tremor shook her world.

Oh Lord. Rogan Wolfe was . . . well, God, what *wasn't* he? Ex-boyfriend, tough cop, bad boy to the bone—and the man who had taught her to love sex. She'd never told Ethan that part about her relationship with Rogan, but while before him she'd liked sex just fine, *with* him she'd found her true sexual being, and she'd loved how much he'd drawn that out of her. In fact, she credited her good sex life with Ethan—well, before its recent decline—in part to her time with Rogan.

Still, she was stunned to hear this was who Ethan had in mind. "You don't even *like* Rogan," she pointed out.

At this, though, her boyfriend just shrugged. "We get along all right."

The fact was, Ethan and Rogan went back a long way, all the way to police academy and the Hostage Ops Team on which they'd been placed and where they'd trained together, both having shown a particular aptitude for handling hostage situations and other similar crises. And she'd always been keenly aware that, in some aspects, the three of them were closely, weirdly intertwined.

She'd met Rogan when he'd joined the Charlevoix Police Force when she'd been in her mid-twenties. She hadn't even known Ethan yet, but he and Rogan had worked together on the force and even now they still played on the same summer softball team.

And what had led Rogan to charming Charlevoix on Lake Michigan in the first place? He'd been looking for a new position and, after reaching out to the other H.O.T. members, who'd kept in touch over the years, Ethan had let him know there was an opening there.

So she'd have never even met or dated Rogan if not for Ethan's involvement in bringing him to town. And maybe she'd have never met Ethan, either—even though they'd both been born and raised in the Charlevoix area—if she hadn't started coming to Rogan's softball games when she'd been dating him. It was funny how much of her world had been shaped by the actions of these two men.

"Getting along isn't the same as liking," she pointed out to Ethan. Because despite the things they had in common, Rogan and Ethan were very different. Almost like night and day in ways. And despite them both being part of a tight-knit group of old friends who got together once or twice a year, apart from the H.O.T. affiliation, they weren't at all close. They might drink a beer together with the rest of the team after a game, but otherwise they didn't socialize with each other.

And so the fact that Ethan was suggesting bringing Rogan into their relationship in such a radical way felt at once ironic and . . . almost fitting. Almost—dare she think?—like a thing that made sense on some level, a thing that was supposed to happen.

"I can like him fine for a weekend," he told her. "And he was the only guy I know who I thought you'd be comfortable with. For this."

This. The mere word brought her back to the matter at hand, the threesome he'd suggested—and she swallowed sharply, the leftover taste of wine in her mouth now turning a bit stale. The fact was, if Ethan had gone so far as to select Rogan, her ex, to join them in his threesome plan, it meant that he'd really, seriously thought this through. It wasn't some off-the-cuff idea he'd concocted a few days ago. And it meant . . . "Um, does Rogan . . . know about this? I mean . . ."

"Of course he knows. He's on his way here right now."

"Holy crap," she whispered. Because this made it . . . real. *Really* real.

And he was already on his way? When there was so much to consider, so many questions to ask?

"Ethan," she began, "what if . . . what if you would think of me differently afterward? I mean, how could you *not* think of me differently?" Because a woman who could do that, who could be with two men at once ... well, Mira had never seen herself as that woman. Even after her dream and the hazy fantasies. Doing it wasn't the same as dreaming it. If she did this, she would be changed, forever. She *would* be different, a different person, at least in ways, than she was now.

"I won't," he told her. Again, as always with Ethan, all confidence. And it assured her once more that he really *had* thought this through, but...

"What if you're wrong? What if I do this and ... and it kills something between us? What if somewhere deep down inside you, it ... makes you think I'm slutty? In some ugly way. What if you can't help it? I mean, once we do this, we can't take it back."

He narrowed his blue gaze on hers and she realized that ... Lord, the fear and desire from a few minutes ago both ran deeper now, fuller. She could almost feel the two conflicting emotions consuming her at once. Was she really considering doing this? *Could* she? And not just from a morality standpoint, but ... could she overcome her trepidation enough to pull it off? To be *that* sexual? *That* self-assured? When deep inside she was scared to death?

"Look, honey," he said, his voice going tender, "I understand what you're saying. But I've thought about this a lot. I thought about it for weeks. And the fact is ... it'll be a gift *you're* giving *me* as much as one *I'm* giving *you*."

She blinked, and her voice came out light, high-pitched. "Huh?"

A solemn sigh left him as his eyes sparkled darkly on her at the precise moment the sun shifted in the sky just enough to immerse them in shade. "The fact is, the more I thought about it, the more it excited me. The more I realized that *I* want it, too." His voice went deeper then. "I want to see you that way. With another man. And with both of us at once." Her skin flushed with warmth at his words. "And once we share that, it'll bring us even closer."

Mira's heartbeat pulsed all through her body. Her cheeks, fingers, breasts, tingled with odd heat. She hadn't thought about it like that—that it could somehow pull the two of them closer together, that it could bond them in a whole new way.

And somehow . . . somehow *that* began to make it feel . . . possible. Like a thing she could maybe, really do.

Just then, he leaned over her, the heat of his body warming hers, his palm curving around her neck as he whispered deeply in her ear, "Tell me you want this as much as I do."

She bit her lip, her pussy pulsing against her blue jeans. Did she? Did she want this? "M-maybe," she heard herself stutter. "I . . . I think," she went on. Then, "Yes. *Yes.*"

She'd heard herself say it. So it must be true.

Chapter 2

Ethan paused from where he stood cleaning the grill to peer down through the trees to the dock. Mira sat there, her back to him, knees drawn up in front of her, looking out on the water. The long brown hair he loved spilled down her slender back in natural waves, and damn, even from behind she was gorgeous. One glimpse reminded him that he was a lucky man.

He wished he could read her thoughts. But hell—maybe it was his own fault if he couldn't. Because it was true that he'd been too absorbed in his work lately and had started taking her for granted. He hadn't been paying adequate attention to her or spending nearly enough time with her. So if he didn't feel quite as in tune with her as he once had, he had no one to blame but himself.

It embarrassed him to remember that it had taken his

mother to point out the problem to him. It had been on Easter at a big family gathering at his parents' house. Mira had been busy playing with his nieces and nephews, hiding Easter eggs, helping the younger ones find them—and he'd watched it all from inside the house, where he'd retreated to block out the noise while he spoke to another attorney on his BlackBerry about a trial starting the next morning.

It had seemed important—it *was* important. But when he'd approached Mira later, after the eggs had all been found and she was helping his mom and sisters in the kitchen, she'd seemed distant, leaving him irritated—something that had begun to feel like a pattern in their relationship lately.

"It's only because she misses you," his mother had said, her voice low as she came up behind him after Mira walked away.

He'd turned to look at her. "Huh?"

"You used to treat her like a princess."

He'd been pretty dumbfounded and even a little annoyed that his mom was sticking her nose into this. "I'm still just as crazy about her," he pointed out, feeling defensive. "But other things matter, too. I work my fingers to the bone, you know."

His mom had simply tilted her head, giving him a long, hard look. It had reminded him of times when he was a kid, times he'd been in know-it-all mode and she'd been getting ready to quietly, calmly set him straight. "She never asked you to."

He didn't get her point, though. "She never asked me to what?"

"To work your fingers to the bone. To change your career. And I'm proud of you for following your heart and working so hard—I really am. But I see it from her side, too. She used to have a man who made her feel special. And I'm not sure she has that anymore."

And when he hadn't answered, just standing there trying to absorb her words, she added softly, "You should be careful, son. Remember, balance in all things. And right now, I'm not sure you have that. If you love her and don't want to lose her, you might want to rethink your priorities."

Until that moment, he'd never really thought about the possibility of losing Mira. They were *that* solid. Or at least he'd thought they were until his mom had piped up and made him start wondering.

He labored damn hard, doing work that mattered to people and affected their lives, and he wanted to be appreciated for that. And if he and Mira had been growing apart lately . . . well, maybe he'd turned a blind eye, just hoping she would adjust to the changes that had taken place since he'd traded in his badge for a briefcase. But the idea of losing her . . . he supposed that had woken him up in a way nothing else could.

And now he was trying to fix what he'd messed up. Trying to fix it in a big way she'd never forget.

But had he gone too far?

Maybe. Maybe this little surprise birthday party for three he'd planned was too much.

But when the idea had hit him, and when he'd thought through it and realized he seriously wanted to bring it to fruition for her, for them both . . . well, he'd just had a feeling that if he suggested it more gently, at home, she'd say no—and maybe not truly mean it. That she'd be too shy to confess she really wanted a threesome, or, as she'd said a few minutes ago, she'd worry that it would change his feelings for her.

And so he'd decided to introduce it like *this*, pushing it on her. Pushing her into the middle of something that was already set in motion. At the time, it had seemed like a perfect birthday present for his perfect woman, so he'd barreled full steam ahead.

And now she sat down there on the dock, thinking . . . God knew what. Did it seem like he didn't cherish her enough if he was offering to share her? Did she get that he honestly felt such an intimate experience could only draw them closer? Was it a fantasy that she wanted to keep *only* as a fantasy?

And had he orchestrated this whole thing solely for her? Or was it just as much for him? He knew it was *partially* for him—as he'd told her, the more he'd visualized it, the more excited he'd become. But had that led him to be selfish here? Because the truth was, he *really* wanted this. Bad.

And did that make him weird—to want to see her with someone else?

It was simply that . . . when they were together, he could see her, but he couldn't *always* focus on her completely since he was *in* it, feeling things, too. This way, there would be moments when he could draw back a bit, simply in order to take in her every response, and he liked the idea that she'd be aware that he was there watching, that those responses would be as much for him as for Rogan.

But at heart, mostly, he just wanted to make her happy—wanted to make them *both* happy. And he'd already asked himself most of these questions along the way and had ended up deciding they didn't matter, that the answers all fell in line with pleasing her, pleasuring her to the fullest, and sealing their relationship in a whole new way.

Just as he tied up a garbage bag and started walking it toward the trash cans behind the cabin, he heard a car engine in the distance, getting nearer.

Rogan was here.

And when he glanced down to the dock and Mira turned to meet his gaze, he knew she'd heard it, too.

Oh God, he was here. Already.

Part of Mira wanted to run and hide. Part of her wanted to rip Ethan to shreds for his "present," because what she'd thought would be a totally relaxed yet sex-filled weekend with her man had turned into something . . . far from relaxed. They'd had a plan, after all. A simple weekend get-away to a cabin followed by a big family birthday dinner at her sister's house on Sunday night after they drove home. And now . . . well, Sunday night sounded light years away.

But get hold of yourself. Do you want this or not?

The real answer: She wasn't sure.

She *wanted* to want it, for Ethan. And maybe even for her-self. But as Mira took one last look out over the vast waters before pushing to her feet, she couldn't quite wade through all her feelings. Her *body* wanted this. There was just no deny-ing that. Her pussy had practically pulsed for the last half hour, and her breasts had become heavy, sensitive. Her whole body felt downright needy.

But again, dreaming it was one thing—doing it another.

And there were things Ethan didn't know.

The truth was, if she desired any other man on the planet besides Ethan, it was Rogan. Still.

Sometimes the old, familiar longing stretched up her in-ner thighs when she watched him on the softball field, grimy and sweating, the muscles in his arms flexing as he stepped up to bat. Sometimes the sight of him, or the mere sound of his deep voice, reminded her how it felt to have his hard cock pounding into her, making her cry out at every rough stroke.

And of course she'd never told Ethan any of that—because why would she? It meant nothing—it was merely human sexual response—and information like that would only hurt him. Or she'd thought that before today anyway. Now it was getting confusing.

Locking gazes with Ethan once more as the sound of Rogan's car drew closer, she suffered the inexplicable urge to rush up the stone steps that led from the dock, to have at least one more minute alone with Ethan before they became a party of three. She wasn't even sure why, but she felt herself moving, leaving the sun for the shade of the trees that dotted the hilly slope, hurrying toward him as if something vital were at stake. Up until now, she'd been basking in the natural beauty of the cabin and its surroundings—the lush greenery of tall trees, the wildflowers that lined the vacation home's foundation and edged the yard—but now she could see nothing but the man she walked toward so briskly.

He'd stopped in place, still holding the plastic bag of garbage he'd been about to tote around the house, but when she reached him, pressing her palms to his chest, he let it drop to the ground. "What is it?" he asked softly, clearly seeing her duress.

"What if . . . what if it starts and I . . . just can't? What if it feels wrong?" She hadn't quite known she was going to ask that, but this had all happened so quickly, and it seemed like something they should address. She wished there'd been more time between his telling her and Rogan's arrival.

But he simply shook his handsome head. "No worries. You just say so. At any time. Whether it's in the first five minutes or right in the middle of things, doesn't matter. If anything feels wrong, you just let us know."

Us. Him and Rogan. The two men planning to fuck her together. She let out a sigh, still trying to wrap her brain around this.

Then she asked him, her voice going a bit lower, "Are you sure? Really sure?"

Maybe *that* was what had sent her flying up the steps toward him. One last chance to make certain he thought this was the right thing to do, certain he believed this wouldn't hurt them or their relationship in any way.

His hands closed warmly over her upper arms as he looked into her eyes. "Completely," he promised. Then said, "Are you?"

She told the truth, the only truth she knew right now. "I don't know. I . . . I want to be, but I'm a little afraid."

"That's okay," he replied. "We'll just see how things go, play it by ear. Rogan knows nothing is set in stone—he knows I'm surprising you with this. So we'll just take our time, see how you feel as the night goes on."

Oh. Well. Okay. Suddenly, the whole situation didn't sound . . . *quite* as daunting as before. Still a little nerve-wracking, but . . . she could still back out. She didn't have to make a decision right this minute. And just knowing that calmed the frantic beating of her heart. A little anyway.

She stood up a bit straighter when she heard the car door slam.

And as Rogan rounded the corner of the house a moment later, a small duffel bag dangling from one hand and a bakery box in the other, her whole body tensed once more. She'd seen him less than a week ago at Ethan's last softball game, but everything was different now. Everything.

As he approached, she took in the jet-black hair she'd once loved to run her hands through, the dark, unshaven stubble on his strong jaw, the barbed wire tattoo that circled one muscular arm.

"Hey," he said. Just that. And the one word made her pussy spasm against her blue jeans. For the past four years, he'd been . . . a distant friend, someone she might chat with casually at the ball field on occasion—even if she did sometimes suffer a sexual response to him. But now, suddenly, he was more. He was . . . someone she was *allowed* to be attracted to again, someone Ethan *wanted* her to lust for.

"Hey," she returned, but getting it out was more difficult than it should have been—as something swelled in her throat.

"Dude," Ethan offered easily, and Rogan gave him a nod.

And Mira decided that it seemed important to say something more, anything at all, before things had a chance to feel awkward—*he's here for sex, we all know he's here for sex, and we're just standing around acting like that's normal*—so she managed a smile and said, "What's in the box?"

"Ethan called before I hit the road—said the one thing he forgot was a birthday cake. So I picked one up."

She spared a quick glance at her boyfriend, who gave a light shrug—she supposed he'd had a lot to organize here and most of it had taken priority over cake. Then she stepped up and took the box from Rogan, her fingers brushing against his as she did, and the mere touch skittered up her arm like electricity.

She peeked through the clear cellophane window on top, expecting to spy swirled icing, sugary roses, and HAPPY BIRTHDAY, MIRA—so it took her aback when instead she saw something much simpler. "Cheesecake," she said, lifting her gaze back to Rogan.

"Of course," he said. "I remember what you like, Mira."

Oh Lord. The words melted all through her because they instantly had her thinking about so much more than dessert preferences. And his dark eyes said he was thinking about more than cheesecake, too. His look locked on hers, so intense that after a few seconds she felt forced to glance elsewhere. But her breasts ached and heat rushed to the spot between her thighs.

And glancing away didn't change the truth. She loved Ethan, but she remained deeply attracted to Rogan. Had Ethan bargained on that? Had he really thought through that aspect of this little arrangement? Had he realized that by involving her ex-boyfriend he might be stirring up old feelings inside her, old responses that suddenly felt way stronger than when she suffered them from a distance, across a softball field?

She let out a breath. So much to think through. Her attraction to Rogan should make this easy. But . . . to be with two men for whom she'd experienced the deepest sort of emotions—that might be harder. Because she wasn't supposed to feel those kinds of emotions for Rogan—but she feared already that being intimate with him might bring them all rushing back. And maybe Ethan knew all that—maybe it was a testament to his love for her that he would risk that, or that he would have enough faith in their relationship to think it wouldn't matter. But what if he *didn't* know all that? What if he'd forgotten she'd once been completely wrapped up in the other man he wanted to share her with?

Thankfully, Ethan and Rogan had started making small talk now about Rogan's drive up, and the bakery where he'd gotten the cheesecake. Which felt . . . almost normal. Almost.

"I'll, um, just go stick this in the fridge," Mira finally said, actually glad to escape the two of them. In one sense that seemed odd to her, but at the moment she might feel a little safer alone. So she started to walk away, heading for the cabin's front porch.

"And Mira," Rogan said, causing her to stop in her tracks, look over her shoulder. "Happy birthday."

And God, even just that—two very simple words, spoken in his deep, slightly rough voice—made her nether regions tremble. For some reason, she found herself answering with the same reply that she kept pointing out to Ethan. "My birthday isn't until tomorrow."

"I know, honey," he told her. "But I figure we'll be celebrating it all weekend long—starting tonight."

Chapter 3

I t was to Mira's great relief and surprise when, after that, things actually started feeling kind of normal. *Truly, honestly* normal. As if she and Ethan were the same couple they'd always been and they were just hanging out with a friend.

Of course, there was no denying the weirdness involved in the way the cabin was laid out. It was a cute but overly simple place—basically one large room divided into areas, like a studio apartment. Which meant it came with one bed, queen size, its headboard pushed against a wall not far from the front door. Fortunately, it also held a couch that unfolded to make a second bed, but the weird part was that even if she put on the brakes regarding the whole ménage à trois thing, the three of them would still be sleeping in the same room. And she hadn't brought much in the way of pajamas, having planned to sleep only in a cami and panties like she usually did at home.

However, Rogan had brought along vodka and orange juice, remembering as well that she liked screwdrivers. He'd mixed up a pitcher of them by the time the sun set, and that was helping her begin to forget about the weirdness. Or to ignore it or something. Because if Ethan and Rogan could act so easygoing about this, so could she.

Now they sat around the small kitchen table, drinking and nibbling on chips, pretzels, and some brownies she'd made for the trip. Music played on the boom box Ethan had brought. And a deck of cards sat untouched near the open container of brownies—so far no one had dealt any, probably because conversation was keeping them well enough occupied.

"Still keeping your nose clean, Rogan?" her boyfriend asked her ex across the table.

Rogan cracked a small smile, and as she glanced back and forth between them, Mira realized for the first time ever the basic physical traits the two men shared. Thick, dark hair, enough muscles to be firm and sexy without looking like overgrown bodybuilders, and that olive skin that harked back to the Mediterranean. Anyone asked to describe them would say they looked similar. Rogan's shoulders were broader—he was a bigger, slightly taller guy coming in at six-foot-three compared to Ethan's six-foot-one—and maybe Rogan's features were slightly more pronounced. But apparently she had a thing for tall, dark, and handsome and had never even recognized it until right now.

"Tryin'," Rogan answered, but the grin implied he might not be completely succeeding. Rogan had garnered a reputation among his Hostage Ops Team friends for skirting the fine lines of cop decorum after a ruckus in Grand Rapids that had involved him roughing up a belligerent speeder. He'd always claimed the other guy threw a punch his way first, and Mira believed him, but she knew not everyone did. And she also knew he'd been in more than a few bar fights while off-duty in his youth, as well. But she thought his attitude now, as always, provided evidence enough that he didn't mind being seen as one of the bad boys of the group.

"To tell you the truth," Ethan said as he tipped a beer bottle to his mouth, leaving the screwdrivers to the other two, "I'm surprised you've lasted this long in calm little Charlevoix. What's it been? Like six or seven years now?"

"About six," Rogan replied. Which sounded right to Mira. She and Rogan had gotten together soon after his arrival and had been a couple for over a year. Then she'd started dating Ethan around six months after their breakup.

She decided to chime in now, too. "Yeah, I keep waiting to hear you're leaving for some big, exciting city, going where there's more action."

At this, Rogan simply shrugged and cast a glance her way.

"Oh, you can find action pretty much anywhere if you're in the right place at the right time."

And heat blossomed in her cheeks. Because his eyes told her he was talking about now, this weekend. *Action.* Was her blush as obvious to him in the low lighting as it felt to her? But then, maybe that didn't matter. Maybe he could read it all in her eyes. The acknowledgment that he'd been invited here for sex—really naughty, dirty sex. Her trepidation about it all. And her . . . wanton desire.

"Still," she said, "I always remember how . . . pumped up you'd get telling me how much you enjoyed the hostage ops training you guys did together. And I always thought you seemed . . . cut out for a bigger place where you could really put those skills to use." It seemed easier to stay on the subject of his work than on what was supposed to happen this weekend.

Yet he just shrugged. "I got to a few times down in Grand Rapids," he reminded her.

"Yeah, and you used to sound pumped up when you told me those stories, too." But as soon as she'd spoken, she wondered if it was weird to be bringing up conversations they'd actually had . . . in bed. Because that tended to be when Rogan had opened up to her the most—cuddling after sex. Oh well, it hardly mattered, given why Rogan was here, and maybe the screwdrivers were kicking in, making it so she didn't weigh things as much as she might normally. "Just seems like your skills are going to waste."

He slanted her a cocky glance and a wink to say, "Not all of 'em, babe."

And despite herself, she felt it in her panties. And found herself swallowing nervously. And deciding it still felt safer to keep discussing police work. So she looked to Ethan, then back and forth between them. "Didn't you guys get into some high-tension situation during your H.O.T. training?"

When the two men exchanged brief looks, she realized that she'd actually only heard bits and pieces of this story from each of them. Finally Ethan said, "There was a little girl being held hostage by her estranged father in a house in Traverse City." That was where they'd gone to the police academy and where their hostage ops training had taken place, as well.

"It was actually the day after we all graduated," Rogan said, "and the locals didn't have any hostage specialists, so they called us in to help. We were the only two who hadn't left town already."

"It got . . . a little crazy," Ethan said, and the quiet in the room made Mira begin to understand why she'd only heard bits and pieces. Clearly, it wasn't a *good* memory.

But she still felt compelled to ask—softly, "What happened?"

"We got the little girl out okay," Ethan said. "I carried her out myself. But . . ."

"The dad almost shot himself on the front porch," Rogan explained then. "Right in front of us all. Ethan had just grabbed the girl and I was moving in on the father with a few other local guys behind me, with our guns drawn. Then he suddenly pulled out a pistol and put it to his head."

Mira gasped. She was sorry she'd brought this up after all.

Still, Rogan went on. "We didn't know he had a weapon at that point. That was where we fucked up," he added, shaking his head.

"But it was literally your first day on the job, so you can't beat yourself up for it," she pointed out. "And . . . you got it away from him, right? He didn't actually do it?"

"Yeah, we got it away from him. But it was . . . damn tense for a while. And it was pretty embarrassing, too. I mean, we'd had the training and passed with flying colors. Only thing was, we were concentrating more on defusing the situation than on some of the technical stuff we'd learned."

"And because we screwed up," Ethan said, "that little girl almost saw the ugliest thing a person could see. So . . ."

"So . . . all's well that ends well, the way I see it," Mira offered, trying for a smile.

And luckily then, both guys seemed to lighten up and let go of the old memory. Ethan released a low albeit self-deprecating laugh, and Rogan said, "It was a long time ago. And a lesson learned."

"And you ultimately saved the day," she reminded them.

"And made damn sure we were more careful after that," Ethan said.

When talk then turned to some of their other H.O.T. friends, Mira was grateful for happier topics. "Think I'm gonna fly down to Miami and see Colt soon," Rogan informed them. Colt, whom Mira had met only once while traveling with Rogan, owned a personal security business in south Florida and had struck her as even more confident and cocky than Rogan could be.

And after a little talk of Rogan's plans for fun in the sun, Ethan told them both what he'd learned from their buddy Jake, whom he'd talked to on the phone just yesterday. "He and Carly set a wedding date. Looks like next April we'll all be getting together in that little town he moved to downstate."

"More to drink?" Rogan asked Mira, gracing her with another sexy smile as he pointed to her mostly empty glass.

"Sure," she said without hesitation. She didn't want to get completely drunk, but a little intoxication would surely help dull her fears.

She watched as Rogan reached for the pitcher, then leaned to refill her glass without spilling a drop. "Basket business still good?" he asked—and she appreciated the shift to another safe-feeling topic.

"Yeah—it's continued to bring in a lot of customers I probably wouldn't have otherwise. In fact, we've been so busy lately that I almost felt bad leaving Lydia alone for the weekend." Mira had owned and operated a bookstore on Bridge

Street, the main thoroughfare through their waterside town, since before she'd met either of the men with her right now. But due to the declining book market, which saddened her in so many ways, a couple of years ago she'd converted the store into Books and Baskets, where she still sold books but also created gift baskets *featuring* books. It was a small shop with only one part-time employee in addition to her, but business had been booming lately.

"I put together a baby shower basket for your neighbor, Mrs. Denby, just yesterday," she told Rogan. This particular basket had featured a baby name book and a reference guide for baby's first year, along with a rattle, tiny socks, a small baby blanket, and a baby brush and comb. Now she recalled how the woman's appearance in her shop had brought Rogan to mind, but she couldn't have imagined being in *this* situation with him just over twenty-four hours later.

Rogan nodded. "I'm glad it's going good for you, Mir." Their eyes met and it made her remember, more than any other interaction they'd shared so far, what it had been like between them once upon a time. What it had been like to be his girl. He hadn't always been the best boyfriend, but at moments, just the way he looked at her could make her feel . . . cherished. Like the center of his world.

She was almost relieved when he moved his attention back to Ethan. "Still working your ass off keeping the people I arrest out of jail?"

Ethan let out a laugh in reply. "Only the innocent ones. Mostly," Ethan added. "You know that's why I gave up the badge—couldn't stand that loss of control after an arrest." Mira recalled Ethan's struggle between the two careers. Before attending police academy, he'd gone to law school, but then he'd wanted to be more hands-on in law enforcement, less caught up in a system that sometimes seemed unjust. In the end, though, he'd realized he didn't like the other side of the equation, either—it had bothered him to have to arrest someone he felt might not be guilty and have no way to affect the outcome. So he'd taken the bar, passed with ease, and turned to litigation, practicing law in a way he felt helped the most honest people.

"Whatever works for ya," Rogan answered easily.

After which Ethan switched his gaze to Mira, lowering his voice slightly. "And actually, now that the practice is pretty well established, I'm trying to slow down, repriori-tize."

And something in her chest warmed. Because yes, the situation they were in right now—it was about sex on the surface, but this reminded her that it was also about something much bigger. Once this weekend was past, she might really have her man back in her life, the way she wanted him. And if she was able to go through with the threesome plan, well, hopefully what Ethan had said would be true: They'd be closer; they'd know each other in a whole new, intimate way. The fact was, to her surprise, this was all starting to make sense to her.

Just then, Rogan pushed back the wooden chair he sat in, the legs squeaking across the hardwood floor, and headed to the bathroom. As she watched him go, then glanced back to Ethan, she realized the screwdrivers were hitting her. In addition to that pleasant, floaty feeling, she found herself having the urge to pick up with Ethan where they'd left off earlier in the hammock; she suddenly suffered the urge to straddle him in the chair.

"Doing okay?" he asked. "About everything?"

"So far so good," she said without even measuring it. Which was a first here. She'd answered easily despite the weight of what he was asking. Again, she could only attribute the fresh comfort to the alcohol. And she didn't mind anything she was feeling. An hour ago, the very idea of admitting she might really want to have a three-way had struck her as too forbidden, shameful. But now, slowly but surely, it had just begun to feel . . . honest. And if Ethan was okay with that honesty, why shouldn't she be, too? "You?" she asked then, just to be certain.

He only grinned. "I've been okay all along. You're the one who wasn't sure."

She widened her eyes on him in playful accusation. "*I'm* the one who had it dropped on me without warning, bub."

He flashed a typical, sexy Ethan grin. "I know, I know. Now that we're in this, I'm realizing that maybe springing it

on you wasn't the best way to go about it. But . . . you're starting to seem more relaxed now."

In reply, she just pointed to the highball glass in front of
her filled with pale, orangey liquid.

Yet that caused him to squint a look of concern. "I hope
it's not just the vodka making you cool with this. Because if
it is, tell me and we'll call this whole thing off. Seriously."

And once more she acknowledged to herself that now was
indeed the time for honesty. "No, it's not just the alcohol
making me cool with it. It's the alcohol . . . making me *comfortable enough* to admit to myself—and now you—that . . . I *do*
want this." Though an unexpected shiver rushed through her
at the confession. Because saying it out loud was different
than just thinking it. And, slowly, feeling each new word as
it left her, she went on to say, "I'm still nervous, yeah, but . . .
I'm turned on, too."

And when her eyes locked with Ethan's, she understood—
in a fuller way than she had before—how this would bring
them closer. Because what she'd just shared with him had
already brought them closer. It was a new openness that
stretched invisibly between them and expanded now, spreading outward through her chest and down. And it was different than the night she'd told him about her fantasy. She'd
been drunker then, actually. And this . . . this was no longer
about sharing a fantasy—this, again, was about reality.

Just then, the door to the bathroom—the only area inside

the cabin that actually *came* with a door—opened, and though Mira almost felt as if there was more to say, it ended their conversation. They were three again. And yet the quiet closeness to Ethan remained. *That's how this will work. Even though we're with Rogan, we'll feel silently connected in a way we weren't before.*

When Rogan sat back down and scooted his chair up toward the table, his knee pressed firmly against Mira's underneath. And he didn't move it.

Oddly, it caught her off guard—just because in most such situations, the other person would shift after bumping into her, give her back her personal space. And when he didn't, it reminded her in a whole new way why. The plan was for her and Rogan to get close again, for the first time in a long time. In front of Ethan. Or *with* Ethan. She wasn't even sure how that part would work, how Ethan *wanted* it to work—or if it was really all about how *she* wanted it to work.

Stop thinking so hard about this. Just let it be what it is, whatever it becomes. Yeah, that sounded like a good idea. But she used the moment to take another big sip of her drink anyway—a little more fuel to help her relax still deeper into this surreal little birthday party Ethan had thrown for her.

"So . . . cards?" Ethan asked, holding up the deck.

"Sure," Mira said for no particular reason.

"What do you want to play?" he asked.

And she blinked, stuck for an answer. But it took only a second for Rogan to suggest, "Strip poker?"

The idea felt almost childish, clichéd, and yet it made her giggle and cast him a look. "That's not exactly fair."

He simply raised his eyebrows as if to ask why.

"I'm"—she glanced down at her tank top and jeans—"not wearing much. Well, not as much as you guys anyway." They each had on socks and shoes, whereas she was currently barefoot. And Rogan wore a denim jacket over his T-shirt.

"Guess that's our gain," he said with a wink she felt squarely between her legs.

And Ethan had just started dealing out cards, announcing, "Five card stud," when an old disco tune Mira loved met her ears. She didn't hold in her response, letting her eyes go wide as she said, "My song!"

Ethan cast her a sideways glance. "'Do Ya Think I'm Sexy?' by Rod Stewart is your song? *Why*? And how do I not know this?"

"I never told you this story?" She started to dance in her chair a little without thought and grew instantly aware that the movement subtly increased and then decreased the pressure of her knee against Rogan's.

"Uh, no. That I'd remember," Ethan said, looking amused.

But she didn't care if loving the old dance song seemed silly—she still moved to the rhythm, and the shift of her legs beneath the table sometimes brought her other knee into contact with Ethan's now, too. "I was a baby when it was popular," she explained, "and according to my mother, I'd never spoken a word—until one day I suddenly sang the whole chorus along with Rod on the radio."

Both guys smiled and Ethan said, "So your first words were, 'If you want my body'?"

She shrugged, still dancing in her seat. "So the story goes. And apparently, it became my theme song after that. I danced whenever it was on, and I'm told I once even danced on a table in a restaurant when my aunt played it on the jukebox and that everyone applauded."

Looking just as entertained as Ethan now, Rogan leaned back in his chair slightly, watching her from beneath shaded lids. "You can dance on the table for us now if you want."

She let out a laugh. "Nope, not getting on the table, but I *will* dance to it. And so will you guys." And with that, she followed the instinct to push to her feet, grabbing onto each of their wrists in an attempt to pull them up from their chairs.

The two men just gave each other are-we-really-going-to-do-this? looks, but when Rogan let himself be guided from his chair, Ethan relented, too. And the next thing she knew, Mira was twirling about the open hardwood surrounding the table with them both.

She and Ethan wordlessly attempted the disco move that involved him spinning her into his arms, then out again, and though it turned out sloppy, they giggled along the way. Mira didn't resist acting a little silly as she moved to the music, letting the pumping beat guide her motions, and she even laughed out loud, feeling just a bit dizzy, a bit giddy during the spins that brought both guys subsequently into view. They were both smiling at her, both thought she was cute, fun—she could feel that. She sang along with Rod without even thinking about it; she still knew the words by heart.

On one rotation out of Ethan's grasp, she lost her balance and whirled right into Rogan, who opened his arms to steady her—and she found her back firmly against his front. Or, more notably, her ass against . . . oh, wow . . . his erection.

She sucked in her breath, her body still plastered to Rogan's as the sexy, upbeat song played on. Again, heat rose to her cheeks, but for a different reason this time. She bit her lip and absorbed the sensation of that hot, glorious hardness pressing against her when she'd least expected it.

Her gaze met Ethan's—he stood just a few feet away—and she knew instantly that he could read her face, see the fresh passion suddenly etched there. And she understood without looking that Rogan sensed it, too—that he knew why she'd suddenly gone so still. He held her hips, yet she could easily dance away from him if she wanted. Only she didn't; she stayed exactly where she was.

And in that moment, the fun-loving mood transformed into something slightly darker—and more profound.

Ethan moved his lips to mouth the words, *I love you. I want this.*

And she felt them in her chest—they were real, he loved

her, and this would be okay. If any doubt still remained, somehow this wiped it all away.

She let out a sigh, more like a heavy breath. And she became aware that Rogan's right hand was leaving her hip and coming up to smoothly pull her hair back off her shoulder, away from her neck, his fingers grazing the tender skin there—even as his other hand snaked farther around her body, his palm coming to rest low on her belly, holding her there, steady and tight against the stiff column behind his zipper.

Still, she reminded herself, *You can stop this. You can stop it right now. You can just spin playfully out of his hold, laugh, make it fun. Then take a little more time to ease into it.*

But she didn't.

Oh God. This is going to happen. This is going to happen and I'm going to let it.

Or at least she thought she was. Maybe when it really began, she'd panic, change her mind, and go running away from it all like a little girl. But for the moment, she was more excited than afraid.

When Rogan's mouth brushed across the tender skin of her neck, she trembled—and pleasure rolled through her. She shut her eyes briefly, trying to absorb it—and oh Lord, it was strange to open them and see Ethan, watching, looking as aroused as if it were just the two of them. At first she felt uncomfortable, like things were colliding here that shouldn't—but then she found herself enmeshed in Ethan's gaze, in that undeniably sexy look in his eyes.

Rogan kissed her neck again, again—each one seeming to explode through her like a starburst. And she suffered urges of her own, the urge to respond, to react, more than she'd let herself so far. Though now that they were doing this, she began to quickly grow more nervous, her emotions ping-ponging back and forth, wild and uncontrollable. Her head swam with alcohol and lust and fear and the last remaining vestiges of the good little girl she'd once been, not giving up her virginity until her twenty-first birthday to her first true love.

That's who I was. A girl who needed sex to come with emotion, who needed to feel deeply close to a guy in order to be that open, that honest, that real. She'd never understood casual sex—she'd never grasped how her girlfriends in college had managed to be naked and writhing and panting with guys they barely knew. But she'd also always known she was in the minority on that. And Rogan was no stranger. Far from it.

So it's now or never. Either you do this or you don't. You can't have it both ways; you can't be in it halfway. All or nothing. What's it gonna be?

And then the hand that had been in her hair drifted to her shoulder, his fingers curling into the fabric of her tank top and the bra strap beneath—and though the touch landed high above her breast, that's where she felt it anyway.

Okay, I'm in it. Completely. And besides, she wasn't sure she had the strength to stop things now even if she'd wanted to.

So with a last fleeting glance toward the man she lived with, she followed her instincts—she shut her eyes and leaned her head to one side so the *other* man in the room could kiss her neck more easily. She absorbed each single, solitary kiss, feeling it fully, accepting the pleasure that dripped all the way down to her pussy like a gift. And then she remembered, it *was* a gift. Her birthday gift from Ethan.

She bit her lip, pressed her ass more firmly against the hard erection she remembered so well. She hissed in her breath at all the sensations, drank in the soft groan from Rogan that came with the shift in her thinking, the shift in her feeling—he clearly understood now, too, that this was going to happen, that she'd started moving past her hesitation.

And then she followed further impulses. To turn, slowly, gently, in his arms. To flatten her palms against his broad chest through the dark T-shirt he wore, the CPD insignia on the front stretching across contoured muscle. She looked up into his eyes. Remembered another relationship, with him, which suddenly felt at once closer in time and farther away than it had really been. He kissed good. He kissed great. She hadn't forgotten that. She wanted him to kiss her.

He must have read the want in her eyes, or on her parted lips, or maybe he was just working on instinct and desire, too—because he lowered his mouth to hers, warm and moist and powerful, the kiss moving all through her like an engulfing wave. For a moment she even forgot Ethan stood behind her watching; for a moment she knew only Rogan's presence, Rogan's heat. Oh Lord, this was going to be more complicated than any of them had probably bargained on.

But that doesn't matter. Stop thinking so much. Just let yourself feel this—two men you trust wanting to bring you pleasure. That was the only way this would work.

Rogan's strong hands molded to the curve of her waist as she sank into him, now letting that hard bulge press against her zipper, right in the spot where she wanted to feel it most. She ground against him without thought, without plan, as they kissed. She wanted him. She wanted all of this.

And that's when new hands closed over her hips, ass, from behind. Ethan. Ending the kiss with Rogan, she instinctively turned her head to look. And he was right there, his eyes meeting hers and twinkling like blue flames. She leaned to kiss him, too.

She couldn't have envisioned how electrifying this would feel, being between these two male bodies, having both their hands on her. She finally ceased thinking, worrying, wondering—now she wanted only to experience this.

She found herself turning fully back again, this time into Ethan's arms, but still cozily tucked in between the two men. Rogan's hands didn't leave her as he lowered a fresh kiss to her shoulder. Lord, she wished she could kiss them both at once—but she had to be content with this, and *this* wasn't bad; no, it wasn't bad at all.

As she continued kissing her boyfriend, his hands rose sensually up her sides until they cupped the outer curves of her breasts, then closed firmly over them. And part of her wanted to suffer some old sort of embarrassment at having him touching her someplace intimate in the presence of someone else—but it just didn't happen, just didn't make sense all things considered. She liked that Rogan was there; she liked the feeling of openness, freedom, beginning to come over her now. And she knew that Ethan had—at least in some ways—been smart to invite Rogan into this situation, because these were the only two men on the planet she could *be* so open and free with.

When Ethan stopped kissing her and took a step back, she instantly missed the nearness, the sense of being so snugly sandwiched between them, but she knew there was more to come. And Ethan wasted not even a second before reaching for the hem of her tank top, beginning to slowly push it upward.

She flashed back to earlier, in the hammock, when she'd so boldly removed it over her head only to have her seduction attempts halted. She couldn't have dreamed that the next time her top came off it would be like this.

Now Rogan had pulled back her hair and resumed raining kisses across her sensitive neck, and she again bent her head to one side to better feel them. She shut her eyes, also drinking in the sensation of Ethan raising her top higher, higher, until she felt the fabric being lifted over her breasts.

That made her reopen them, though, glance down. The two globes of flesh looked pretty to her, plump, the lush inner curves rising from the cups of her pastel bra. And it struck her in that moment that she wasn't afraid anymore of what was happening here. It wasn't that she felt bold or aggressive at all—hints of nervousness still swam within her, but actual fear was gone now.

And that was good.

Because that was when Ethan hooked his fingertips into both cups of her bra and pulled downward on the fabric— and her breasts tumbled out, fully bared.

A soft gasp escaped her as a breeze wafting through an open window passed cool and light over her nipples, turning them harder than they already were.

And it felt to Mira as if . . . well, as if they'd reached a point of no return.

Chapter 4

"Sit," Ethan whispered then.

She wasn't sure if he was talking to her or to Rogan, but it didn't matter because Rogan's hands closed firmly around her bared torso to begin drawing her back—back against him, and then back into the same chair she'd vacated a few minutes before. She'd left it pulled out and at an angle perpendicular to the small kitchen table in her rush to dance to the Rod Stewart song that had long since ended and been replaced by another fast and wild disco song. Rogan sat in the padded chair, thighs spread wide to let her fit in between. And still that glorious erection pressed insistently against her rear.

As Ethan knelt in front of her, the alcohol, the heady music, the unfamiliar surroundings—and, of course, the fact that she was fooling around with two men—all made her feel as if she floated in a dream. A damn sexy dream. A dream she wanted to continue.

When Ethan's hands closed over her exposed breasts, she sighed, watched, liked that Rogan was watching, too. And then Ethan leaned in, flicking his tongue over one turgid mauve nipple to make her gasp again.

"Such pretty tits," Rogan murmured deeply, and something in the simple observation made her breasts swell further against the cups that now framed them so tightly. That's when Ethan moved to the other, licking across the beaded peak, then swirling his tongue around it in circles. A slight, high-pitched moan echoed from her throat as the soft yet intense pleasure radiated through her whole being.

And as Ethan began to suckle her, firm and rhythmic, kneeling between her parted legs, she felt it more than she thought she ever had before. Because of the other hard male body behind her. Because Rogan's presence amplified and multiplied even this one simple sensual affection to wild proportions. Because now that she knew this feeling, nothing inside her would ever be quite the same again.

And when Rogan resumed kissing her neck, her shoulder, she was simply . . . lost to it all. Two male mouths on her flesh at one time—it was like being delivered to a naughty version of heaven. She shut her eyes, drank in the pleasure, felt it pulsating through her veins, as if heating her very blood—felt it flowing thick and heavy down to the needy spot between her thighs like a second heartbeat.

She didn't look at Ethan now, not because she didn't want to, but because her eyes had once more dropped shut in surrender. Yet at some point she remembered she wanted to see this, witness it; she wanted to again watch him kissing and sucking her breasts and at the same time take in the sight of Rogan's touch—now one large hand splayed across her stomach, as if holding her in place for Ethan's ministrations. And when she looked past Ethan's head, past the fingers cupping the side of her breast, she could spy Rogan's forearm anchored around her.

It was when Ethan began to undo her blue jeans that he finally lifted his gaze back to hers, their eyes locking. And she thought he might ask if she was okay, if she was ready for more—but instead all he said was, "Lift up," so he could tug her jeans down. He clearly *knew* she was okay. He clearly *knew* she was ready for more.

So she lifted her ass slightly and let him pull at the denim, watching through the dreamlike haze as her peach-colored cotton panties came down in a tangle along with the jeans. She bit her lip, watching them go, *feeling* them go, feeling exactly how naked she was becoming while still in Rogan's embrace.

And then the song on the radio ended, and for a long

second until the next began she heard nothing but her own labored breathing filling the room, filling all their ears. She hadn't realized until now that she was making any noise.

As Bad Company launched into "Feel Like Makin' Love," Rogan's hands boldly gripped her bare thighs, lifting them, spreading them farther, until each of her legs were stretched across his own, his knees holding her that way, open and exposed. Even more exposed than she would *usually* be if in the same position, she realized, because she'd shaved away most of her pubic hair for the weekend, leaving just a pale brown thatch extending upward from her slit, which she knew turned Ethan on. And yes, Ethan had seen her with her legs opened to him like this countless times, but this was different. *Very* different.

Her breath still came heavy, heated—and when Rogan's finger dipped into her naked pussy, stroking upward, just once, through her wetness, a shocked moan escaped her. And then his hands were closing hard over her breasts at the precise moment Ethan moved back in, pressing his palms against her inner thighs and sinking his mouth where Rogan's finger had just been.

There was nothing tender or gentle about this—Ethan ate her vigorously, clearly as excited as she was now. She whimpered helplessly as the pleasure spiraled through her, Rogan kneading her boobs at the same time, and her arms rose instinctively over her head and behind her to thread through his thick hair as she raised her pelvis against Ethan's mouth.

As before, Rogan spilled hot kisses across her shoulder, then up her neck—one more sensation added to the barrage she now basked in. Then his mouth pressed against her ear and his voice came low, sexy. "You're so fucking hot, babe. Always. But right now more than ever."

The rasped words fueled her, empowered her. *Don't be shy here. Just react the way your body tells you to.* And so she found herself thrusting harder at Ethan's mouth—which he'd now closed over her clit. She bit her lip, then sucked in her breath hard when he thrust two fingers into her below, fucking her with them.

"Oh God, oh God," she murmured. She watched Ethan's face as the pleasure quickly arced higher and higher. She took in the sight of Rogan's hands firmly massaging her breasts. Beyond that, though, she didn't think—she *couldn't* think. She simply followed the ebb and flow of her body's instincts. And when Ethan began to rub his tongue in hot, rhythmic circles on her hungry clit, more high-pitched, uncontrolled whimpers left her.

"Aw, that's right, babe—fuck his mouth. I want to see you come. Come for both of us. I want to see you come so fucking hard."

Rogan's deep voice had always possessed the ability to push her over the edge when he whispered dirty things, and this time was no exception. A few seconds later Mira tumbled headlong into a wild, jagged orgasm that shook her body of its own volition, vibrating through her like an explosion as she cried out her release, over and over.

As she came down from it, trying to catch her breath and recover, she heard herself whispering. "Oh God. Oh God."

When she'd been younger, there had been times while fooling around with boys, not even necessarily having sex, when . . . well, she knew if regret was going to set in, it would arrive now, on the heels of orgasm, when the fever of lust and need had been quenched and sanity returned. And so she looked down at herself, sprawled rather inelegantly at the moment, and tried to gauge her feelings, tried to weigh it all. Yet before she could even begin to grasp her own reaction to any of this, Ethan stood up, ripped his T-shirt off over his head, then undid his khaki cargo shorts and let them drop.

She just watched, sucked in her breath. Why had she thought, even for a second, that her climax was the end of anything?

Self-involvement, she supposed. Which perhaps made sense right now. She'd been the unsure one here, the one who'd needed a little coaxing, convincing. And Ethan had driven home repeatedly that this was *her* birthday present, about *her*.

But now she was remembering that he'd candidly admitted he wanted it, too. And she knew with clarity that Rogan was just as into it, as well. So, yeah, maybe she could be a little selfish here, but at the same time . . . she was being reminded that she wasn't the only one playing, and she wasn't even the one calling the shots.

Ethan kicked off his shoes as he stepped free from the shorts, naked and well-built before her. As a younger woman, she'd of course been drawn to male bodies, but only as she'd begun to get a little older had she really grown to appreciate the full measure of their beauty. Where women were beautiful because they were soft, men were beautiful because they were hard. And Ethan fit her image of a beautiful, hard male body just now. The muscles of his shoulders, arms, were not as pronounced as Rogan's, but they were well-defined, almost chiseled, from working out a few times a week—a habit he'd kept up even after leaving the police force. Dark hair sprinkled his chest, narrowing into a line that led straight down his stomach to the stiffened cock that stood at attention between his legs. And that was where her gaze stuck.

Just looking at it made her pussy surge with fresh moisture, even after having just come. The walls of her vagina contracted with want as she studied the thick cylinder shot through with lines and veins that made it appear almost . . . angry, and certainly demanding, powerful.

Yet as he stepped forward, she realized her pussy wasn't where he was going to put it right now. In fact, it hovered at the exact height of her mouth—which, to her slight surprise, made *that* part of her body yearn to take his erection inside, as well.

And so as he moved even closer, holding the hard, beautiful shaft down level to her, she parted her lips, opened wide. She watched as his cock came closer, a dot of white pre-come having gathered on the tip—yet as he fed it slowly but surely into her waiting mouth, he said, "Look at *me*." So as the erection slid toward her throat, stopping when her lips rested about halfway up its length at the point Ethan knew she could handle comfortably, she raised her gaze.

And even as she began to glide her mouth wetly back and forth on her boyfriend's beautifully solid cock, as she let it fill that part of her to capacity before easing back slightly and then going deeper once more, she thought how strange it was that Rogan still held her. Through all of this. Odd that Ethan was the one doing things to her, yet it was Rogan who cradled her in his embrace. He still caressed her breasts, though slower now, in time with her movements up and down Ethan's shaft; his own erection still pressed firmly to the center of her ass through his blue jeans. And now he whispered, voice low in her ear, "Suck that cock, babe. That's so damn good. Keep sucking it." She wondered if Ethan could even hear the words. And if he couldn't, did he wonder what Rogan was saying to her?

As in their past, she found that his throaty voice spurred her on, compelling her to do more of what already came naturally. She thought of oral sex as sort of . . . an acquired taste, an act she'd assumed was all for the man's pleasure when she was younger, but she had since come to fully appreciate and even relish it. So at Rogan's prodding, now she sucked Ethan's cock a little more vigorously, went down on him a little farther and listened to him moan. And now *he* murmured hot words, too. "God, yeah, that's good. You're so good, baby, so good. And you look so perfect with my dick in your mouth."

She watched him the whole time and felt deliciously dirty to be reminded of how she must appear right now, how obscene with her mouth filled that way. And the fact that Rogan watched, too—Lord, his face was right next to hers and she could smell the musky aroma of him mixing with the scents of sex even as she took Ethan's erection deeper, deeper.

When Ethan began to thrust, she didn't mind—she let his slickened length slide toward her throat and focused on loosening the muscles there, letting him fill her as much as possible without gagging. Because she wanted to amaze them now. She wanted to be their perfect, dirty, sexual plaything. Like before, as she'd neared orgasm, she reached that place of leaving the rest of herself behind for only the sexual being that resided deep inside her. She'd never found that part of herself before Rogan, but she'd experienced it many times since, and now she was experiencing it in a fuller, stronger way than ever before. She was all in this now, completely, and simply basked in the pleasure of having them watch her, these two most important men in her life.

And though she already took ample pleasure in what was happening—oh Lord, much more assaulted her when one of Rogan's hands dropped from her breast to the spot between her still parted thighs. He smoothly thrust two fingers inside her, immediately using the heel of his palm to massage her clit. She moaned wildly around the dick in her mouth—God, Rogan had always known how to use his hands, and he did nothing halfway, his mode of touching her now instantly bold and possessive, as if he were taking ownership of her pussy for a while.

She undulated against his hand without thought as she groaned deeply around Ethan's cock, meeting his small thrusts toward her throat with greater abandon. Sucking him had started out as a slower, less wild thing than when he'd eaten her, but now it had progressed to something ravenous and untamed.

Until finally he drew back, pulled out of her mouth.

Her lips felt stretched, a little sore, well-used.

Rogan's fingers stilled in her, and as she met Ethan's gaze she wondered what he saw in her eyes. So many emotions ravaged her, after all—she could barely process all of them. Was he seeing her as the "girl gone wild" she'd suddenly let herself turn into? Would she become to him exactly what she'd feared—would he have no choice but to see her as a slut, some brazen wanton who'd suddenly tossed her morals out the window?

But that's when he lifted his hands to her face, leaned down, and kissed her. A soft, deep kiss that resonated all through her. And for a second there, she forgot all about Rogan, forgot everything that was going on except for the fact that she felt . . . loved. And she realized what an extraordinary man she had in front of her.

She could imagine that *most* men would promise a sustaining love when trying to talk their girlfriends into extreme sex like this, but she also suspected—even instinctively *knew*—that many of them would feel differently afterward.

And maybe it wasn't even their faults. Everyone was taught certain sexual mores from early in life and they could run gut deep, almost based more on conditioning than on any decisions a person could make about how he or she wanted to feel. And yet Ethan was showing her in this kiss that he still cherished her just the same, and she knew without doubt that opening up this way, letting her more sexual side take over, was indeed bringing them closer, was delivering them to a new intimacy, even just half an hour into this weekend of ménage à trois he'd planned for her, for *them*.

Only when the kiss ended and their eyes met once more, his filled with fresh heat, did she think again about Rogan behind her. It wasn't that she'd forgotten him—only that her focus had narrowed so tightly on Ethan for a moment. But

Lord, Rogan's hand remained between her legs and had been there—even if unmoving—the entire time she'd shared that sweet, sexy kiss with the man she loved. The very realization kicked up her heartbeat anew.

That's when Ethan stood upright and, without warning, walked away, across the room.

And Rogan thrust his demanding fingers back into her, jolting her slightly and making her cry out.

She began to pant as he fucked her with them—because she couldn't *not*. She got lost in it again, her body taking over as he brought his other hand up to her mouth to touch her lips—then he pushed two fingers inside her there, as well.

She didn't think, just responded, sucking on his fingers almost as if they were a cock—and she realized she *ached* for that now—a cock, inside her, in her pussy, where it belonged.

She stayed vaguely aware of Ethan in the distance, saw him heading back in their direction now, carrying a thick couch cushion in hand. He dropped it to the floor before her and she had no idea why—until he knelt atop it and she realized the added height put his erection at exactly the right level to fuck her.

She sucked in her breath at knowing she was about to be filled, finally, and it was suddenly all she wanted in the world. Rogan's fingers left her mouth, and her pussy, as well, both hands moving to her breasts. He used his fingertips to rub the moisture from both areas onto her nipples, forcing a breath of fresh arousal from her lungs as she sat before Ethan, legs still spread.

"Aw God, I love you," he murmured deeply as he placed his hands on her thighs, leaning in, positioning himself.

And something about those words, now, took her breath away. They seemed at once so out of place and yet so . . . incredibly perfect. Like that kiss, they reminded her. *No matter what I do, he loves me.*

"I love you, too, E," she told him.

Now please, please, put it inside me before I die.

She watched, and so did he, as the head of his cock pushed inward, and then he glided deeply, smoothly, to the hilt. All three of them let out soft moans and she realized Rogan was watching over her shoulder just as closely as she and Ethan were.

Ethan stayed like that, buried within her slickness, for a long moment while they all simply took in the sight, at once obscene and profoundly personal. "Please, more," she heard herself whimper without quite planning it.

Her boyfriend flashed a slightly incredulous grin. "That's all I got, honey. Are you saying it's not enough?"

"No, I'm saying . . ." She shook her head, feeling a little frustrated, then whispered, "Fuck me. Please." Saying that to Rogan had once been easy. And to Ethan she'd said it plenty of times, too. But something about saying it now, asking for it, in front of them both, had come a little more difficult.

Yet she reaped her reward when he replied, "Oh, I'm gonna fuck you all right," just before he eased the thick shaft halfway out and then thrust it back in.

"Oh!" she cried out in pleasure. *Yes, thank God!* Because all of this foreplay had been hotter than hot—the most exciting experience she'd ever had—but now she was ready for the main event.

At first, Ethan repeated what he'd just done—pulling back in a slow, wet glide, then plunging deep and making her cry out each time. Rogan alternated between caressing her breasts fully and then just teasing or pinching at the hard nipples, adding to her lust. And all three of them seemed fixated on watching the way Ethan moved in and out of her pussy.

"Watch that pretty cunt take that big cock," Rogan said, low, squeezing her breasts. *Cunt.* Rogan had always used that word interchangeably with *pussy,* and though she knew it offended some people, she'd always taken it in the way he'd intended, as just one more name for "my favorite place on your hot body," as he used to tell her. Now, as ever it seemed, his dirty talk upped her desire as the opening between her legs swallowed Ethan's erection again and again.

And soon he stopped going slow—his strokes became more pistonlike, driving, driving, each filling her with nearly overwhelming pleasure that echoed from the crux of her thighs outward. Without planning it, she drove back, meeting his movements, soaking in the sensation, basking in the wonder of this naughty ecstasy she'd never imagined experiencing.

And then, as Ethan continued fucking her—hard, hard—Rogan began to thrust against her from behind. He and his colossal hard-on had been admirably still through *all* this, but clearly he could resist no longer, and Mira's ecstasy from a moment earlier increased. She wanted him to fuck her, too. She wanted them *both*, fully, equally.

Ethan's passionate plunges increased, his eyes falling shut, and soon Mira let hers close, as well, leaning her head back, taking it all in. She'd never felt so desired, so sexual, in her life, and in a moment of total hedonistic abandon felt *elated* that she'd told Ethan her fantasy that night last summer. God, to think life could have passed by without her having experienced this. It was . . . astounding to be wanted—and pleasured—by the two men she'd loved most, both at the same time.

"God, God, I'm gonna come," Ethan muttered—and then he was thrusting hard, plunging deep, letting out one low groan as he emptied into her, and she found herself moaning along with him as she witnessed the release on his face, absorbing the passion he was pouring into her.

Her breath came heavy, overriding the music that now seemed lower in volume than before—she knew it wasn't really, but the sex taking place seemed to almost blot it out, push it far into the background of what was happening.

Ethan slumped slightly into her, bringing his forehead to rest against hers for a moment that, again, made her feel so very close to him now.

"I love you," she whispered while he was right there, his face touching hers.

He opened his eyes, drew back just far enough to look at her, and even spent, she could see that same affection still lingering in his gaze. "Love you, too, my perfect girl," he told her.

But then he eased back even farther, going upright on his knees again, and his expression shifted back into one filled more with lust than love. And she didn't mind at all since she knew the two could coincide very happily together. "Ready for more?" Ethan asked.

Was she?

Lord. In one sense, she was mentally and physically exhausted. She felt she'd already shared so much with them both, been so open in ways. And yet . . . Rogan's erection still jutted demandingly against her ass. And just thinking about that made her pussy swell with a brand-new arousal she couldn't deny.

So she nodded. That was all—no words. Maybe she'd begun feeling a little shy again. It had been one thing for Ethan to fuck her while Rogan held her, watched. But for Rogan to be inside her while Ethan observed . . . well, somehow that seemed as if it would raise the stakes. For them all.

But maybe you're overthinking this, overworrying it. Just be . . . the way they *are. Like this is simple. Like it's easy. Like sex is just sex.* She still couldn't believe that was ever true, for anyone—you opened yourself up in unique ways during sex; it mattered. But for now, since she was with two men she cared about who wanted this for her and were acting as if a threesome was a perfectly normal thing to be taking place on a summer Friday night, she would try. Not to think too much. Not to worry. And mostly, she'd been doing pretty good at it. *So just keep going.*

Ethan replied only by shoving aside the couch cushion and getting to his feet, his cock still shiny and slick from sex, his nakedness somehow feeling more obvious to her now than . . . well, perhaps ever in their entire relationship. *Because there isn't usually a third person in the room to see it.*

But stop thinking and get back to feeling.

That's when Rogan's voice came in her ear. "Stand up." And even just that one small command made her pussy shiver.

It was almost challenging to unloop her legs from over his knees—she'd gotten stiff from being in the same position for so long—but finally she pushed to her feet, very aware of her own nakedness, too. Finally standing, she stripped her tank top over her head and tossed it aside, simply because it made no sense to have it on anymore. And she was reaching behind her to undo her bra—when Rogan stood, as well, quickly, stepping in close, cupping her boobs in his hands from behind again, somehow firm yet tender. He brushed his thumbs across the ever-sensitive nipples, once, twice, each touch making her sigh with the small but potent rush of pleasure, and she instinctively looked over her shoulder at him.

Their gazes met, held. And he turned her in his arms to face him. Then let his eyes drop to her breasts for a few potent seconds before he bent to rake his tongue across one stiffened pink peak.

She trembled in response—oh Lord, it had been over four years. And suddenly he was touching her again, kissing her again. About to be fucking her again. She drew in her breath, just letting the realization wash over her anew.

And then it was he who reached behind her to smoothly unhook her bra, drawing it down her arms and casting it onto the table where playing cards and drink glasses still resided. After which he simply said, "Go to the bed."

Where was Ethan now? She didn't know. And almost didn't even care.

But she was supposed to be sharing this with him—all of it, right? So she *had* to care. And he'd just brought her so much pleasure and made her feel so cherished, worshipped, and he was such a good, kind, hot, and sexy man. Practically her fiancé, even. Other than the neglect she'd suffered due to his law practice, they were perfect together. And he'd made all this happen.

And yet Rogan was so . . . commanding. Back when they'd been a couple, she'd hated that at first—but had secretly learned to love it in the bedroom. He always knew what he wanted and didn't hesitate to take it. There was something she admired about that boldness, something in it that even made her want to submit to him. And now, without thought, she simply obeyed him and went to the bed.

She sat down on the edge of the calico comforter sprinkled with a summer garden's worth of blooming flowers—yellow, red, purple, orange—and waited as Rogan followed. A second later, he stood directly before her on the hardwood floor, which put the bulge in his jeans around eye level. That bulge she'd been feeling all night. That bulge she'd once known so well.

"Unzip me," he said.

Again she suffered the urge to look around, to locate Ethan—yet Rogan's very tone commanded all her attention and left her almost afraid to look away. He'd been unerringly patient and now almost seemed *im*patient, ready to have his way with her.

So she didn't hesitate to reach up, unbutton his jeans, slide the zipper down over that tremendous bulge. As the denim parted, she could clearly make out the cylindrical shape of his cock behind the black boxer briefs he'd always worn. And mmm, just seeing it, even still covered, sent a bolt of need through her chest. And it made her unthinkingly reach out, run the flat of her palm up the thick ridge concealed beneath the fabric. He sucked in his breath and she liked it. He could act all tough, but even tough guys had their moments of weakness.

His passed quickly, though, and he met her eyes again to say, "Tell me what you want, babe."

Don't think too much. Don't worry about anything. Just keep it simple. Tell him what you really, really desire right now. Listen to the overpowering longing vibrating through your body.

"Please just put it in me," she said.

Chapter 5

At this, Rogan just peered down at her, then lifted her face in both his hands to say, "Aw, babe."

And though she sort of hated to spoil the hot mood by bringing this up, she said softly, "Do you have, you know, a condom?"

"Of course," he said. "But I haven't been with anybody without one since you."

"Really?" She swallowed back her surprise, remembering full well Rogan's view on condoms. He was careful about using them—until he was with someone he felt serious about and, of course, fully trusted. Then he didn't want anything between them, not even one thin layer of rubber.

"Really. And I don't want to use one now, not with you."

Lord, he was looking at her . . . the way he *used* to look at her, like she was amazing, like he'd never been so into any other woman in his life. *But that's his charm, remember. He knew how to do that, how to make you feel so, so special. And then it turned out you weren't quite as special as you'd thought or he wouldn't have let you go so easily.*

But none of that really had any bearing on this—she had to remember that. That was the past. And this was not about her and Rogan; this was about her fantasy of being with two men.

Still, she swallowed again and said, "Okay." Because she knew he'd never lie about something like that. And she was on the pill—had been for years. And the truth was, if she was doing this, she liked the idea of having no barriers, either, of it being just his flesh and hers.

He let out a low, pleasured sigh at her response, as if it mattered to him that much, and the soft sound ran all through her. She simply hadn't expected him to do anything here that would make her feel like this was . . . more than sex.

But then, maybe she was reading too much into it. Maybe it was just a matter of not really needing a condom. Maybe the way he was looking at her right now was about nothing more than lust. And the truth was, even the *lust* between them had always been good, fiery hot. Had Ethan realized that—considered it—when he'd invited Rogan to join them?

Just then, the mattress shifted and she looked over to see Ethan lying down on the bed next to her. And even though she was glad to finally know where he was, somehow, now, it almost alarmed her a little to see him. Their eyes locked and his held nothing but the same heat as they had so far. Did he see everything she was feeling, all her questions about Rogan? Was he that confident—did he trust in their love that much? Or was he just so caught up in the naughty passion of this night that he didn't observe anything happening between her and Rogan other than sexual response?

And even if so, it still shook her a bit that he was totally okay with that—she'd had so little time to adjust to that stark change in thinking.

"I want to watch," he told her then. "I want to watch him fuck you."

And she let out a breath. Why was the idea of that suddenly daunting? She'd been doing so well, after all, being so brave and open.

But maybe it was because up until now it had been Ethan fucking her, and Rogan had been only a secondary character in this drama. Having sex with Rogan—while Ethan simply lay there observing it all, no less, in effect making her feel all the more on display—seemed to up the ante. At least in her own mind.

But she had no time to examine the idea further before Rogan instructed, "Roll onto your side, babe." And she looked up to find that during her moment with Ethan just now, Rogan had shed his jeans and underwear and stood before her as naked as she and Ethan were, and just as beautiful that way as she remembered.

Like Ethan, he clearly still worked out, sporting a washboard stomach and the firm muscles she saw on the softball field but that were more noticeable here. His barbed wire tattoo served as a warning that he could be dangerous if you got too close to him. His cock stood as long and hard and majestic as a spear between his legs.

The sight of him like this after so long stunned her in a way she hadn't expected—in fact, it made her freeze in place. So when she didn't do as he'd told her, he simply put a hand on her hip and turned her that way—until she faced Ethan.

Again their eyes met and as Rogan joined them on the bed, which they lay across sideways, she instinctively reached out to lift her fingertips to Ethan's chest. She didn't know why and didn't even wonder—she simply touched him. *I'm still yours. No matter what.* Maybe *that* was why. Maybe it was her small, silent way of reminding him of that. Or of reminding herself.

She thought Rogan would simply ram his cock into her now, but somehow the tempo had slowed and instead he returned his hand to her bare hip and ran it gently up her side, over the curve of her waist, and then onto her breast. He nestled his erection against her ass again, letting them both feel it there, letting her again want more of it. She looked at Ethan the whole time, taking in the utterly surreal quality of the moment, and she kept her hand on his chest—as Rogan touched *her, she* touched Ethan.

Now Rogan kissed the back of her shoulder, her neck. He could go from demanding to tender in a heartbeat, always. And she still kept her gaze locked on Ethan's the whole time. Somehow that connection made it feel . . . less like being with another man and more like . . . just being with *him* but in a different way. A *very* different way.

And then Rogan's fingers were slipping down behind her, coming in between her legs, stroking her there, and she parted her thighs instinctively, aware that the move drew Ethan's gaze there and that it added to her arousal.

And then—oh Lord—she desperately wanted Rogan to fuck her, same as she'd wanted a few minutes ago before Ethan lay down beside her. But she couldn't ask, wouldn't ask—she was already turning herself inside out for these two men, and in this situation she found it challenging to be aggressive. It all came easier if *they* were the aggressive ones, if they did it all *to* her. Maybe she wanted to believe she was an innocent bystander in all this. Maybe that idea made it all more palatable somehow.

But that didn't stop her from biting her lip as Rogan raked his fingers through her wetness from front to back. It didn't stop her light gasp as he slid them into her opening. It didn't stop Ethan from eliciting a small, guttural moan at her response. He even tenderly stroked her arm, the one she held out to touch him, and then bent to kiss her hand, now curled into a loose fist against his chest.

Rogan didn't say anything more; he simply—finally— positioned his cock at her pussy and pushed it deep inside her. The gasp she emitted this time was louder, and her eyes fell shut. *Oh God, he's in me.* She'd never expected to share this experience with him again. And how strange it was to be filled so enormously full with a man's erection and yet be staring into Ethan's eyes and know it didn't belong to him.

Behind her, Rogan moaned, as well. "You feel so fucking good, babe," he murmured. "So hot and wet."

Back when they were a couple, she would have replied that he felt good, too, that he felt *huge* inside her—but now, in- stead, she only let out a whimper of pleasure.

"Feel good, baby?" Ethan asked. Maybe he'd noticed her lack of response.

But this meant it was okay to say it. "Yes. So good." She was still learning the rules here.

And then Rogan began to move in her.

And she began to respond, meeting his thrusts.

And she could smell him again, his musky scent filling her senses, and it made her even hotter, wilder.

And as he began to fuck her hard, harder, making her grit her teeth with the rough pleasure it sent pounding through her, she realized she'd actually braced herself against Ethan's chest and that he held on to her elbow now. "Oh God, oh God." She felt blessed to be reminded that both of her men knew how to use their cocks so, so well. She'd had a boyfriend or two who *hadn't* been especially skilled with that, so she knew the difference and knew to be damn thankful for it.

"Look at me, honey," Ethan said, and she realized her eyes had fallen shut amid the harsh pleasure Rogan delivered, and so she forced herself to do that, though for the first few seconds, it was challenging all over again. *I'm used to sharing this kind of raw intimacy with one man at a time, not two.*

Yet the longer their gazes met, the more she understood with further clarity that *such* raw intimacy was making her feel closer to him, closer each moment. He was watching another man fuck her; he was watching how she responded to every hard stroke. He was listening to her cries of pleasure, the ones she couldn't hold in. And she was letting him. And looking into his eyes. And she was pretty sure she'd never felt more vulnerable—and therefore more truly, deeply open— with another human being, ever.

Soon she found herself actually clutching at him with her fist, trying to hold on to him somehow—and so *he* held on to *her*, gripping her arm tighter while Rogan moved in her, saying, "That's so good, baby, you're so hot. It's so hot to watch him fuck you, so hot to watch you take it," and his words struck her as both dark and unerringly arousing.

She didn't quite understand the pleasure he derived from this, but if they were both enjoying it, who cared? And maybe there was a dark part of *her* that liked finding out that even all-around good guy Ethan possessed a shadowy, mysterious sexual side, a kinky side she couldn't completely grasp or take control of.

It surprised the hell out of her, though, when Rogan went still, then pulled out of her.

She even gasped her shock and turned to look over her shoulder.

"Sorry, babe," he said, panting softly. "Didn't want to come. Not yet. Too fucking excited."

Yeah, she guessed she could understand that. He'd endured a lot before finally getting in on the act. "It's okay," she said. But her pussy instantly missed him.

And—oh Lord—he must have known that because he didn't waste another second before standing up, rolling her onto her back, spreading her legs, and bending over to lick her.

"Ohhhh," she moaned as the sudden pleasure rushed up through her like a fountain someone had just turned on. It came with the light scratch of his stubble on her soft, recently shaved flesh, and though she normally found such a scratching sensation painful, right now, at this moment, it was one more unrefined sensation adding to her lust. She responded on pure instinct by clutching at her own breasts as she leaned back her head to soak up his ministrations.

And then Ethan was there, hovering over her, kissing her, kissing her slow and deep and passionate, pressing his tongue into her mouth as Rogan feasted on her below. Her arms came around his shoulders and his hand caressed her breast and she tasted remnants of herself in his kiss—and she slowly sank deeper and deeper into what it was to be pleasured by two men.

"Oh!" she cried out when Rogan suddenly thrust his big cock back into her without warning—and it ended the kissing since both she and Ethan looked up with a start. Rogan stood between her thighs, hands clamped to her hips, plunging into her with deep, hard strokes that shook her body and made them both let out little groans at each impact.

Ethan sat up now, watching—watching her face, at other moments watching where Rogan's shaft entered her so powerfully. At some point, her legs curled around Rogan's hips and his hands rose to frame her tits as he rammed into her.

And then Ethan's cock was in his hand, hard again, and the sight turned her on further, especially when he moved in close to her, near her shoulder, and leaned over to rub his stiff length across her nipple. "Ohhh," she heard herself moan as the dirty little added delight swept through her. She almost wanted to reach out, grab on to his dick, and pull it to her mouth, but she was still a little too shy here to be the one making moves—and she was already completely well-pleasured with the moves being made on *her*.

She watched, sighed, began to pant as he stimulated her beaded nipple with his cock, sliding it back and forth over the pink tip—and then finally began smacking the shaft against the soft flesh of her breast, over and over, almost as if spanking it. And—oh Lord—why did that feel so good?

Ethan let out low groans as he continued slapping her tit with his rock-hard erection while Rogan still fucked her, and she relished looking up to see both their faces contorted by lust, relished knowing she pleasured them both by doing nothing but lying there, making her body available to them.

"Shit, aw shit," Ethan murmured—and then he was working his cock in his fist again, even as he thrust it against her breast, and finally the come spurted from it, the first shot creating a thick white puddle where he thrust at the side of her tit, the next two arcing across both mounds of soft flesh.

She gasped, watching, feeling the wet splatter. The truth was, she'd never liked having a man come on her—but this time she did. Because she was still being fucked, still absorbing more pleasure, and as Ethan used both hands to thoroughly massage his semen into her plump breasts, it was just one more hot stimulation. Given that Rogan continued to plunge slickly into her pussy below, she'd never felt more sexually wet, more . . . *bathed in sex* in her life.

Though after Ethan finished rubbing his sticky come into her, he fell to his back, on the bed beside her, clearly exhausted. Which made her shift her full focus on to the man between her legs.

Their eyes met—for the first time in a while. And maybe it was the only time since Rogan's arrival that she'd unthinkingly allowed herself to *really* look at those eyes, really connect with them on a level that drew her back in time to what they'd once shared.

Before a few minutes ago, despite all the dirty things happening, he hadn't been inside her; their bodies hadn't been intimately joined. And for her, that took things to another level. His dark brown gaze shone with a brazen heat that ran bone deep, and it was as if he spoke to her through them without ever saying a word. *I'm fucking you again. I'm making you feel me—again, again, again. And it's still every bit as hot between us as ever.*

Her face flushed with new warmth. It was like . . . embarrassment. Or . . . maybe an admission. Of guilt.

Oh. That's what it is. It's that Ethan's eyes are shut now and it feels almost like Rogan and I are alone. Fucking.

So it's not about Ethan at all right now. It's only about Rogan.

Their gazes never broke the whole time. And she knew hers spoke to him, too, telling him the obvious. *I still want you this way.* She hadn't known that before today. Though they hadn't broken up because either of them had no longer desired the other—their problems had been about his level of commitment, dependability.

So had she ever really stopped wanting him? Did *anyone* ever really stop just because of a breakup? Time had healed the wound; she'd found Ethan and fallen in love with him—but did those things kill the chemistry, the lust, the want with someone else? Of course not.

Now Rogan slid his hands beneath her ass and eased her farther back on the bed as he climbed on with her, his cock leaving her for only a few seconds before gliding smoothly back in. And then he was bending down over her, bringing them face-to-face, eye to eye. His strokes had slowed to a rhythm more sensual and potent than hot and hard. She heard herself breathing heavily as each warm drive permeated her core. Her arms automatically rose to circle his neck as he dipped to kiss her.

The missionary position hadn't been his usual way—hardly ever—and yet here she was, peering up at him as she wrapped her legs instinctively back around him, digging her heels into his firm ass. *Damn it, you're supposed to be thinking of Ethan, feeling tighter with Ethan.* But it was so difficult right now; she felt too strangely close to this man she'd only made small talk with for the past four years.

Next to her, Ethan appeared to have fallen into postsex

sleep while all she knew was Rogan—inside her, all around her, filling her senses. "Wanna be deep, deep, deep inside you. Deep inside that sweet pussy," he murmured over her, and she felt the words echo through her chest as well as below, where he moved in her.

"You are," she whispered. "You are."

She thought about the fact that his bare chest touched hers where Ethan's semen had left her sticky, and that it felt almost like a metaphor for how intermingled the three of them were becoming, in old ways and new. And then, rather than think so deeply about it, she began to wonder if Rogan *remembered* the come being rubbed into her there, if he was aware of it, if it bothered him in any way, or if it... aroused him at all. But mostly, she felt that renewed connection with a man she'd never expected to be this close to again. Felt it, soaked it up, in both the soft ways, when he kissed her and moved in her slowly, and in the harder ways when he drew back slightly to drive more roughly between her legs.

Even then, their eyes stayed locked and Mira began to cry out again at each deliciously mind-numbing stroke—until finally Rogan said, "Aw, babe. I'm gonna come in you now. I'm gonna come in you so fucking hard." And he did.

He let out only one long, low groan, tipping his head back, his eyes falling shut, and she watched him even as she took her own pleasure in those last hot, pounding thrusts.

And she experienced the same sense of connection she'd been feeling with him all along, only more now.

And then she let her head drop to the right—to discover Ethan's eyes on her. He wasn't asleep anymore. "Hey," he said, voice tired but blue eyes sparkling.

"Hey," she softly replied.

Rogan splashed some cold water on his face, cupped a little more from the faucet in his hand to drink, then looked at himself in the bathroom mirror.

He was getting older. Next year he'd turn thirty-five. He wasn't sure why he was thinking about his age, but maybe it had to do with Mira. With the fact that he figured she and Ethan would probably get married one of these days soon. Not that *he* wanted to be married, but . . . well, something about the thought made his gut pinch up, just a little.

She once wanted to marry you. *That's the kind of girl she is, always has been—the settling down, marrying kind. The kind who wants some security, wants to know what tomorrow holds.* And he just wasn't that kind of guy. Or he hadn't been back then anyway. He hadn't even turned thirty yet when they'd broken up, and that had felt young to him. Young in a good way. Young in a not-ready-to-get-tied-down way.

Walking quietly back out into the cabin's main room in blue jeans, no shirt, he found Ethan and Mira lying snuggled in bed, still naked but now under the covers and with their heads on the pillows instead of lying crosswise like before. They looked like they were asleep. Another twinge pulled at him inside.

He'd made mistakes with her back then, for sure. When he'd sensed her getting too serious, becoming too attached, he'd pulled back emotionally, gotten a little distant—his gut reaction. And when he'd felt she was making too many demands on his time, he'd started showing up late for dates, breaking plans—his way of letting her know he needed his freedom. He'd loved her, but he just hadn't been ready for what that meant, the kind of expectations it brought.

Heading across the room, he turned off the boom box, bringing a quiet solitude over the tiny cabin. Then he went to the fridge for a bottle of water, chugging half of it down, still thirsty.

He'd known after his relationship with Mira was over that he'd screwed up, but by the time he'd been smart enough to realize it, she'd been dating Ethan. In fact, maybe that had been what had opened his eyes—seeing his girl with another guy, and a guy he was longtime friends with, no less. Not that he and Ethan had ever been close, even during their police academy days—but he'd never had a problem with Ethan, and the guys on the Hostage Ops Team had a kind of unspoken code, that they'd always be there for each other. He'd just never imagined he'd end up being there for Ethan . . . like this.

Even after realizing he'd fucked up by letting Mira go, though, he hadn't sweated it much. He'd just . . . turned off the feelings. Because that was what he did, the kind of guy he was. If you couldn't have something, why stress over it? He'd moved on. To other women, other ways to occupy his time. He'd considered Mira a regret, but it was in the past and she seemed happy with Ethan. In fact, Ethan seemed more like her type. Clean cut. Dependable. Ethan would always be good to her; he'd never let her down. So maybe he'd let himself think things had worked out the way they were supposed to for Mira.

Except now . . . hell, he didn't know *what* to think. He'd been shocked enough when Ethan had invited him to this naughty birthday party for his old girlfriend. But at the moment, he was even *more* dumbfounded. By the emotions bubbling up inside him. He found himself standing there peering over at the bed, somehow unsettled by what he saw. It made no sense.

It wasn't his first time doing something kinky and wild—just last Labor Day he'd found himself as part of a very hot and nasty foursome on a boat trip on Lake Michigan. But what shocked him tonight was . . . how different this felt. How much seeing Mira like this had excited him. It was a side of her he'd never imagined, and he knew her well enough to know this didn't come easy to her, so he loved that she was being bold enough to step beyond her usual boundaries, and he felt lucky to be there to witness it, be a part of it.

But still, there was more to his emotions than just that.

There was that strange tug in his gut when they'd looked into each other's eyes. He'd fucked plenty of women, but being with Mira was just . . . different. Still, now. He couldn't quite explain it to himself. Hell, he didn't even know if he was happy or sad at the moment. He'd gotten to be with her again, gotten another taste of how gorgeous and sexy and amazing she was. But he couldn't keep it. It was only temporary. Which meant it didn't count for much. And shit, since when was he a guy who wanted sex to count for much?

Yeah, he felt lucky to be a part of this with her and he enjoyed bringing her pleasure more than he could understand, but in the end, would this weekend arrangement be, for him, more about ecstasy . . . or torture?

"Shit," he whispered then, and rolled his eyes at his own thoughts. *You're being fucking ridiculous. Since when do you look into a girl's eyes—any girl's—and get sappy about it? Your life is fine the way it is*—damn *fine.* Sure, Charlevoix was a little quiet for his taste—at times he even found himself wishing for more crime, more action, the kind that got his blood pumping— but he liked his work, he *still* liked his freedom, and he liked not having to be accountable to anybody. Well, other than his fellow police officers, but that was part of the job.

As for what he'd just experienced with Mira and how it had stretched beyond his groin all the way up into his gut . . . well, that was about old times, nothing more. Old feelings.

But that didn't mean he really still felt them. He'd come here to give her a happy birthday for old times' sake, and because, hell, being invited to a threesome had just plain turned him on. He loved sex, after all. And he'd seen the fact that Mira was involved as just a perk that would make it even more fun.

So that's why you're here, what you're getting out of this weekend: sex. That's all.

And that's enough.

Chapter 6

Mira opened her eyes as the first pale pink hints of dawn sifted their way through the cabin windows. Then she remembered where she was—and why. Today was her birthday. And Ethan had given her . . . well, a birthday party unlike any other.

That was when she realized he was no longer in bed with her. In fact, neither guy was. The idea almost made her laugh—*I'm sharing a cabin, not to mention sex, with two hot guys—but I'm in bed by myself?*

A glance revealed Rogan sprawled on the couch across the room—he hadn't bothered to pull out the sofa bed. And she suddenly wondered about the sleeping situation here. Had Rogan chosen the couch because he hadn't felt welcome in the bed with them? Had Ethan at some point asked him not to share their bed after the sex was done? And was it weird that she felt a little bad that, after what they'd shared last night, he was sleeping alone?

And as for Ethan, he must just be in the bathroom or something.

Now, remembering exactly what had taken place the previous evening, she rolled to her back, peering up at the wide-beamed ceiling above. God, she'd been so wild with them at moments. And despite herself, that surprised her. But maybe it shouldn't—after all, she knew them both so well sexually. Yep, Ethan had definitely nailed *that* aspect of this most elaborate gift.

She wondered now, though, did this change what Rogan thought of her as a woman, as a person? And should she care?

Well, it didn't matter if she *should* care; she *did* care. That was just who she was.

And that took her back to all the nuances of everything that had happened last night. She hadn't had much time to prepare for the ménage à trois, but one thing she hadn't anticipated was how close she'd feel to Rogan again, that fast. And how her emotions would flip-flop so much, alternating between the deep new bond of intimacy she now shared with Ethan and the old feelings that had bubbled up for her ex.

Most girls probably wouldn't do this—wouldn't pick it all apart so much. Most girls would probably just be smart enough to simply enjoy it. It was a once-in-a-lifetime opportunity, after all. And during the parts when she'd been able to let herself go and stop thinking so damn much...well, *those* moments had been what this weekend was supposed to be about. Or at least she *thought* that was what Ethan had wanted for them. Good sex. With the *focus* on good sex. Not anything else.

And speaking of Ethan, where on earth was he? Growing impatient when she realized she didn't hear any sound coming from the bathroom, she eased out of bed and moved quietly to her weekend bag, quickly putting on a pair of white cotton panties and a fitted white eyelet camisole that buttoned up the front. Then, looking for the jeans she'd worn last night, she caught sight of someone in the hammock on the front porch. Ethan.

Forgetting about the jeans altogether, she padded to the cabin's screen door and stepped outside to find him lounging there in his white boxer briefs. "Hey," she said softly.

Their eyes met. "Hey, you," he murmured sweetly. "Happy birthday."

"Whatcha doin' out here?"

"Thought it'd be nice to watch the sunrise and didn't want to wake you. But it's starting to look like rain."

Mira moved on bare feet to the edge of the wood cabin's covered porch, then peeked up at the sky through the trees surrounding the place. Indeed what had glowed a pearly pink a few minutes ago was now more blank and gray.

"Climb in here with me," he requested then, so she cast

him a soft smile and accepted the invitation. Unlike the hammock in the yard, this one of course wasn't suspended between trees—it was stretched so that four corners of netting connected to a metal stand beneath.

"This is nice," she told him, curling into his embrace. And it was. Last night had been . . . utterly exciting, but nothing quite beat crawling into the arms of a man who loved you.

"You doin' okay? About last night?"

She lifted her head from where it rested on his shoulder and found him peering down at her. "Yeah. I mean, I think. I mean . . ." Oh hell. The truth was, she didn't quite know what to feel yet. Dirty? Alive? Ashamed? Liberated? And did she have a choice on what to feel? Or was she at the mercy of her inner being, her soul, whatever lay at the very core of her? "Was it all okay with you?" she finally asked Ethan. Since surely his feelings here mattered as much as hers—at least in some ways. "Was it what you envisioned?"

The tilt of his head and the expression on his face told her he could read her uncertainty. "Honey, I wouldn't have put this into motion if I didn't want you to enjoy it. I don't want you to be worried—about anything. I want you to just do what feels good, without any hesitation, all right? That's part of the gift."

She let out a breath she hadn't quite realized she was holding. *Okay. He still loves me. And he's even encouraging me to let it continue.*

Though she pointed out, "You didn't answer the other part. Was it what you wanted, what you expected it to be like?"

She watched then as he leaned his head back into the white netting, appearing to weigh the question. And she liked that he was taking it seriously, not just tossing out the simplest answer. She'd always loved his analytical mind and considered it one of the things that made them compatible. "Sort of, sort of not," he said after a moment. "I feel like we . . . took turns with you more than shared you, if that makes any sense."

She bit her lip, peered down at him. "I'm not sure what you mean."

He met her gaze, his warm and penetrating. Beyond the protection of the covered porch a soft drizzle began to patter against leaves in the trees that kept the cabin feeling so isolated and shaded. "I thought you might like us to . . . do things to you at the same time," he said. "That's all. That was more how I saw it."

"Oh," she said, a little taken aback—but she wasn't certain why. After all, there had been *some* moments like that— like when Ethan had rubbed his hard length over her breast while Rogan had fucked her. So why did she find his suggestion a little . . . shocking? Maybe because, now that she thought about it, he was right—in ways, the two men had taken turns pleasuring her; her focus had, at most times, clearly been on one of them or the other. And during the period when they *had* both enjoyed her at the same time, the sensation had felt different—there'd been a heightened sense of pleasure and abandon. And she'd experienced that when they'd both been touching her, too. Maybe that stunning sense of abandon—loss of control—frightened her just a little.

"There were *some* times when . . . you both were . . . you know." Damn, she couldn't quite get the words out, even with Ethan. She hated that, how shy and Victorian this situation was turning her. She wasn't that prim. But new boundaries—big ones—were being breached here. It had been one thing when Rogan had taught her to appreciate dirty talk. Having them *both* teach her to appreciate being with two men at once was a big leap.

"I know," he said softly. The air smelled like rain now, cool and sweet. "But I thought you might want to take that further."

Just be honest. This is Ethan. If you're seriously considering marrying this man, you should be able to say anything to him. "I . . . I felt shy about it a lot of the time. I know I'm not normally shy in bed, but I guess this situation . . . intimidated me. It's strange to . . . to show desire for someone else in front of you."

The light of understanding dawned in his eyes then. "Oh. I guess I can get that. It's like . . . you don't want to hurt my feelings or something?"

She nodded gently. "Sort of. And . . . and I guess there's a part of me that's afraid of looking really slutty or something. Afraid that if I act like I want this, that even though you think it's okay with you, maybe it really *won't* be. And so . . . it was just easier to wait for you two to make all the moves and let it happen."

He kept his warm gaze on her, reached to caress her cheek. "I promise, baby, this weekend it really is okay. It's really what I want. You don't need to be shy. Whatever your body wants, I want you to have it. *That's* the *gift*," he said as if to drive the point home. Again.

"And it's a little weird with Rogan," she went on, thinking aloud now, getting more comfortable with the topic. "I mean, I know he and I are long in the past, but once upon a time I cared about him, and I have to wonder what he thinks about me doing this."

At this, however, Ethan raised his eyebrows. "Rogan? Seriously? I'd think you'd know Rogan well enough by now to realize that he's, uh, not a judgmental kinda guy. In fact, when I invited him, he told me this wouldn't be his first time doing something like this."

Mira blinked, utterly surprised. "Really? I didn't know that."

"I think it happened after you. But anyway, he's all about having sex and having fun—and he even said he liked the idea of you opening up that much, being that free. He always felt you held back a little."

Hmm. Rogan *would* think that. But it bothered her. Because she *had* been fully open with him. Or at least she'd thought so. Though maybe he'd yearned for a true wild woman; maybe that was the way to Rogan Wolfe's heart.

She decided not to dwell on her past with Rogan at the moment, though. This weekend wasn't about their past, after all—it was about right now. And in a way, it was also about the future. So she changed the subject to something else still lingering on her mind.

"I . . . never quite realized it was only you and Rogan who were involved in that hostage situation."

"Well, there were the other local cops."

"I know. I just meant I didn't realize you were the only two from your team. And I guess it just surprises me a little that you could go through something like that with someone and not, you know, feel a little closer to them than you and Rogan do. Or . . . am I thinking like a girl here?" she asked with a grin.

But Ethan just shrugged. "You know Rogan and me just don't have much in common—other than softball, the badge, and you. And I gave up the badge. And he . . ." Then his face clouded.

"Gave up me," she finished for him. "That's okay, you can

say it. It's true. And I got over it a long time ago." Or . . . well, she'd always *thought* she'd gotten over it. But last night . . . for her anyway, it was just hard to have sex with a guy and not have it mingle with emotions. Hard to impossible. Not that Ethan needed to know that, at least not right now.

"So . . ." Ethan said with a soft grin, "back to us. Are we good?"

"I'm good if you're good," she said with a small smile.

His grin widened. "Well, I'm good if you're enjoying this to the fullest."

She gave him another nod. "I will. I mean, I'll try anyway."

"Just . . . make it whatever you want it to be, honey. Okay?" he said with a wink. "It's really okay for you to . . . cut loose, follow every urge you want to follow. I promise."

And she leaned down and kissed him. Her way of saying *thank you*. And *I love you*. And *I will*. Because she was beginning, slowly but surely, to understand this. To understand that she needed a new attitude here.

This was a once-in-a-lifetime opportunity, one most women would never get. And yeah, she was an analyzer, and she'd been raised with certain mores, certain ideas of what was right and wrong and normal. But maybe she was simply overworrying this. Maybe this was the one weekend of her life where she was meant to throw that all out the window— all that history, all that moral training. Maybe now was the time to truly embrace this gift from Ethan and enjoy it the way he wanted her to. Maybe, beginning now, she would follow her physical whims, answer her body's calls, and start doing . . . whatever she felt like.

One kiss with Ethan turned into another, and another—slow, deep, lingering kisses that reached down inside her, leaving a warmth that radiated from her core outward. And whether from what they'd experienced together last night or the conversation they'd had just now, she felt closer to him than ever before—and maybe just a little bold, too.

Looping one leg over him as they traded sensual tongue kisses, she eased her hand downward, squarely between his legs. He moaned when she found his hardening cock, closing a gentle but firm fist around it through his underwear to knead and caress.

Working on pure instinct now, she sat up and straddled him in the hammock, same as she had yesterday afternoon down by the lake. But already this time, things were hotter than yesterday just by virtue of the new bond she shared with him. As they looked into each other's eyes, she sensed that bond solidifying. And at the same time she truly *felt* what she'd merely just *decided* a minute ago—she'd been too sensitive last night, evaluated it all too much. She needed to simply enjoy this, let herself go, be as dirty as she wanted to be, as sexual as she wanted to be, even aggressive if that's what she chose.

With that inspiration in mind, she reached between her breasts and yanked sharply at the thin cotton fabric that kept them bound until the top buttons came undone. She then used both hands to pull the white eyelet open, freeing her aching tits. Ethan released a small growl that fueled her, making her pussy hum as she rubbed it against the stiff length in his boxer briefs.

As she began a slow, rhythmic grind, he spoke in a deep rasp. "Be my dirty birthday girl and fuck me."

She bit her lip, turned on. That was more like something Rogan would say—*would have said* to her, years ago—than Ethan, but she understood. He was pushing her a little, letting her know it really *was* okay. For her. For him. And she couldn't help but respond. *Whatever your body wants, I want you to have it.*

She followed the pure animal instinct to reach up, pinch her taut nipples, pulling, tugging, the sensation shooting straight to her crotch, and amplified by the glaze of lust now shimmering in Ethan's eyes. She undulated harder on that beautifully stiffened shaft of his, drinking in the sensations now as easily as she inhaled the scent of summer rain. Was Rogan hearing them, listening, watching? She didn't care. Did the look on her face tell Ethan that she really did feel dirty right now, in the good way, the liberating way, the letting-go way? She didn't care much about that either, yet at the same time she hoped he was enjoying this as much as she suddenly was.

Without further ado, she leaned back slightly, reached into the opening of his underwear, and extracted his erection, which she thought looked particularly hot and hard this morning. She let out a "Mmm" as the very sight of it trickled through her like a warm drink of alcohol, and she worked the shaft in her hand easily for a moment before rising on her knees, using her free hand to pull aside the strip of cotton between her legs, then smoothly impaling herself.

They both moaned as their bodies came together during her descent, and unexpected images filled her brain. The way Rogan had felt inside her last night. Ethan putting this same cock in her mouth, then using it on her breast. And at the same time, she absorbed how it felt *now*—perfect and big and strong inside her.

As she began to ride him, he murmured, "Let me suck those pretty titties." And she leaned over, playfully letting them both hover just above his mouth before finally lowering one hard, pink nipple into the moisture there. He sucked and she purred—again, the feeling shot like a pinball straight to her pussy. He knew her well, knew that sucking her tits would make her come faster, harder.

And as the hot orgasm rushed through her just a minute later, she reveled in it even as she reaffirmed her new way of thinking about this little birthday party. Last night had been ... the breaking-in period, the orientation. Whatever happened today would be easier for her. Would be still more freeing for her. Would be whatever her body wanted it to be in the moment.

She *wanted* this now, all of it.

She wanted it in a way she simply hadn't been able to process that quickly last night. But now Ethan had helped her make sense of it, helped her accept it and begin to embrace it.

Everything from this point forward would be more than just a gift Ethan was giving her—it would also be a gift she was giving herself.

The day was working out nicely. So far anyway. Turned out Ethan hadn't minded the morning rain at all—it had made him feel intimately cocooned with his girl while they'd had some damn good sex on the front porch. But he'd been glad to see the skies brightening beyond the windows as he and Mira cooked up some bacon and eggs together in the small kitchen area, him in his underwear, her in her white panties and cute little button-up cami. She'd started to grab her jeans when they'd stepped back inside, but he'd touched her arm and quietly suggested, "Leave 'em off. It's just us." *The three of us,* he'd meant. Because he'd also meant every word he said to her—he wanted her to be comfortable with this.

And he'd been happy when she'd considered it for a second, then dropped the jeans back on the floor, saying, "Okay," as merrily as if it had been just the two of them.

About the time the aroma of bacon had started filling the cabin, Rogan awoke, ambling over in blue jeans and mussed hair to say, "Damn, smells good."

"Figures you show up when the work's done," Ethan said to him on a laugh. That was sort of how he really saw Rogan, but he'd meant it good-naturedly—he didn't believe you could really change people at their core, so he accepted them as they were.

Rogan just laughed, running a hand back through his hair to say, "Sometimes my timing's better than others." Then he'd leaned in to kiss Mira on the cheek. "Morning, babe."

"Morning."

Ethan hadn't really seen that coming, the kiss, but under the circumstances he supposed it made sense. Just like prodding her to cook breakfast in her panties, it encouraged her to relax into this situation.

And since then, he thought she really *had* seemed more at ease. And though he didn't think you could change people, he thought you *could* find sides they kept hidden for whatever reason, and he'd known there was a more sensuous person lurking beneath Mira's soft skin than he'd seen before. Not that she wasn't sensual—hell, she was sexy as sin—but Mira was a class act, and she cared what people thought of her in a way that went deep and was more about habit than decision. And even though he liked and respected both those traits, he also didn't want her to miss out on life, living, because of it. Ever since the night she'd told him her fantasy about two men, he'd known there was a wilder aspect to her sexuality than even *she* really understood—and he was determined to bring it out this weekend. And so far, so good. At least after their talk in the hammock this morning.

Now he'd driven his SUV—Rogan going along for the ride while Mira stayed behind to get the picnic basket ready—out to the highway and down the Lake Superior coast to a small marina where he'd reserved a speedboat for the day. Nothing fancy or superfast—just a way to get out on the water, especially since the weather was so unaccountably warm this weekend.

As he drove the bright yellow boat up the lake's shore across calm water, he remembered seeing its name painted on the back: *Fun in the Sun*. And that's exactly what he planned for them to have. If the brief rain shower this morning had turned into more ... well, they could have certainly found plenty to do indoors together, that was for sure. But as it was, the bright sun had transformed this into a beautiful day, and he was now viewing the boat outing as a sort of transitional activity between the new state of mind Mira had developed this morning and the sex to come later. This evening they'd grill up steaks for her birthday dinner, open a bottle of wine, and let the night lead them on their next hot adventure.

"So," Rogan asked loud enough to be heard over the sound of the motor, "you still cool with this arrangement?"

Ethan tossed him a glance from behind his Ray-Bans. "Sure. Why?"

His H.O.T. comrade gave his head an easy shake. "No reason. Just checking, I guess. Figured it was always possible you'd change your mind after the first night, that's all."

Ethan understood what he was asking then, and hell, it was a reasonable question. Considerate even, coming from Rogan. "No, I didn't suddenly get jealous when it actually happened. I'm good with it all."

"Is she?"

It reminded Ethan how well Rogan knew her. "I think so. A little skittish this morning—but I talked her down. I think I got through to her, too. I told her I really want her to enjoy this, to do whatever she feels like doing with us. And she seemed a lot more relaxed about it afterward."

Rogan nodded. "I thought so, too. Was afraid she might be stiff or jumpy or something this morning, but was just the opposite."

The whole truth was that maybe Ethan *had* experienced a little jealousy at moments last night, but that was natural. So he didn't see any reason to tell Mira or Rogan about it.

And it hadn't been caused by anything in particular that either of them had done—it was only that maybe when he'd planned all this, he'd forgotten who Rogan really was to her. He supposed it was a catch-22 or something: To make this work, he'd had to come up with someone she'd be comfortable having sex with, but to come up with someone she'd be comfortable having sex with meant it also needed to be someone she'd once cared about.

Still, it had all excited him, even if the occasional thread of jealousy ran through the heat and lust. And if having to feel a little jealous was the worst thing to come out of this, he saw it as a small price to pay for everything they'd be getting in return.

Just then, they rounded a clump of land sprouting with tall cedar trees, and just past it, the small dock down the hill from the cabin came in to sight. Even though Ethan hadn't seen the fairly nondescript dock from this view before, it was easy to recognize because Mira stood on it wearing a bikini, short sarong, and flip-flops, with a straw beach bag hanging from her shoulder.

"Damn, I forgot how good she looks in a bathing suit," Rogan said.

Ethan tossed him a look. "It must be new. I haven't seen it." Then, for some reason, he took a little silent pride in the knowledge that she'd had no idea Rogan would be joining him when she packed, that she'd brought that new bikini up here just to share with *him*.

As he slowed the boat and steered in toward the dock, he noticed the smile on his girl's face and the color in her cheeks. She really did seem happier and more at ease. Good.

Easing the speedboat up alongside the dock, he gave a playful whistle and called, "Hey, good lookin'. Wanna go for a ride?"

She gave her head a saucy tilt. "With two big, strong, handsome men like you? You wouldn't try to take advantage of me, would you?"

All things considered, it made him laugh. Okay, she was *definitely* at ease now.

After stepping up onto the boat's bow, hollowed out with a cushioned area for sunbathing, Rogan grabbed on to the dock with both hands so the boat would be close enough for her climb in. "Damn straight we would, babe," he told her. "Now get that pretty little ass in here."

Ethan watched as his girlfriend picked up the picnic basket next to her on the dock and passed it—followed by a cooler—to Rogan. Then she took Rogan's hand as he helped her climb in. Yeah, that new bikini was damn cute—the small coral-and-white-flowered print was at once playful and sexy, like Mira herself. And as Rogan had already noticed, her body rocked the triangle top and small bottoms, which, he could see through the sheer coral-colored sarong, tied at each hip.

"Cute suit," Ethan told her with a wink as she took a seat in front of him in the bow.

She put down her beach bag and got comfortable, flashing a smile. "Glad you like."

"Think he *really* likes what's in it," Rogan pointed out, a familiar hint of mischief in his eyes. And when she looked over at him, he added, "So do I."

And that's when Ethan's groin began to tighten—not just from seeing Mira's curves, but from the new mood warming up the boat along with the sun overhead. When the idea for taking a boat out on the lake had come up, it was before Mira had known there would be anyone joining them, and Ethan hadn't necessarily planned this part of the weekend to be . . . sexual. But with Mira's fresh, saucy attitude and Rogan already flirting . . . hmm, he suddenly had a feeling this might turn into a more interesting day than he'd expected.

Chapter 7

Mira leaned back, stretching her legs out across the cushioned bow of the speedboat, soaking up the warmth of the sun on her face. They didn't get too many days like this in upper Michigan—especially having driven a few hours farther north from home—so even while having two sexy men at her disposal, she couldn't think of a way she'd rather spend the day than soaking up some rays.

Now Rogan manned the steering wheel as the boat cruised slowly across the vast blue waters, and when she sensed him eyeing her body appreciatively, she didn't mind. Her attitude adjustment had been real and remained in place. Somehow something had just clicked inside her this morning—or maybe it had simply taken being totally honest with

Ethan. Whatever the case, she felt so much less shy, so much more ready to embrace this experience.

"Babe, you'd better be careful not to burn," Rogan said to her through the small half windshield that separated them. "We want that skin touchable, don't we, E?"

Never timid, her Rogan, and not even now, in this . . . unusual situation. But since *she* was no longer shy, either, it didn't faze her, this reference to being shared by them. She only laughed and said, "You're right. But I just got comfy."

Just then, Ethan appeared from the back of the boat, where he'd been investigating some skiing equipment stored in bins. "Never fear, birthday girl, I'm here. You don't have to move."

"My hero," she teased, more than happy to let him put on her sunscreen.

It wouldn't be the first time he'd helped her out this way, and he wasted no time digging into her beach bag and extracting a bottle. Taking a seat near her feet, wearing the red swim trunks they'd picked out together last summer, he sprayed coconut-scented liquid into his hand, then proceeded to apply it, starting at her ankles and slowly working his way upward, massaging it thoroughly into her skin to leave it looking slick and shiny when he was done.

She found herself tenderly biting her lip as she watched— his hands felt good as he took turns rubbing the sunscreen into each calf, going all the way around her leg, not missing a spot. And then she realized she felt his touch in her breasts, too, and between her legs. Wow, she was getting excited. Just from sunscreen.

Was it because they weren't alone, because Rogan was there? Or because she always found something about the sun on her skin sensual in and of itself? It truly felt like the sun was touching her, and maybe Ethan's *added* touch was just enough to elicit such reactions. Or was it simply one more response to everything happening this weekend, one more awareness? Maybe *any* sort of touch would turn her on right now.

Whatever the case, she heard her own sexy sigh waft upward as his hands slid over her knees. Somehow he'd scooted between her legs now, which meant she'd parted them without even thinking.

And it was in that moment when, beyond Ethan, she caught sight of Rogan. The man in the driver's seat watched the sunscreen application with rapt interest, his dark eyes becoming shaded with lust, that fast. She sucked in her breath in response. But she no longer felt nervous about any of this—she'd truly shed that emotion, truly stepped beyond it now. All she felt was a curious anticipation to see where this would lead.

The scent of coconut smelled more exotic than usual when Ethan sprayed more into his palm, then began smoothing it over one thigh. She spread her legs still farther, without thought, naturally. And when a small "Mmm" escaped her, his eyes rose to hers and her pussy flared with even more arousal. Neither said anything, but it was clear they both experienced the same gathering desire.

When Rogan cut the boat's engine, leaving only silence while the boat teetered on the water, she looked around and drank in the wonderful isolation. Occasionally another boat passed by, but only in the distance, and it made her thankful for the vastness of the great lake—even out in the open, they were alone here.

She was only vaguely aware of Rogan getting up, moving to the back of the boat, dropping the anchor off the stern to keep them from drifting too far—because Ethan remained busy massaging sunscreen high onto her legs. Now he worked at both inner thighs and she instinctively spread them open wide. She glanced down, saw what he saw, and felt naughty— but in the good way, the way she wanted to feel it from now on. She could hear herself breathing.

And when he eased his fingertips right up the edge of her bikini bottoms but not beyond, she sucked in her breath— and wanted more.

"You should, uh, take off your sarong," he told her softly. "It's in my way."

Without saying a word, she untied the loose knot at one hip and let the sheer fabric drop to her sides, then leaned back on her elbows, patient, waiting.

From there, Ethan began applying the sunscreen onto her stomach, setting the bottle aside again to use both hands. He smoothed it upward, under her breasts, then worked his way back down, again being sure to rub it in right up against the bikini bottoms that began several inches below her navel. She liked watching him work, taking in his every move, seeing his hands, fingers, on her skin.

She noticed in her peripheral vision when Rogan took the captain's seat again—he was watching, and now drinking a beer, the same way she thought he might observe a stripper on a stage. But her change in mindset was so complete that nothing about it turned her off—in fact, it turned her *on*. To be what she wanted to be this weekend, to have what she wanted to have with these two men, she had to welcome a little objectification. She had to take pleasure in seeing herself as a tool for *their* pleasure. And as long as that brought *her* pleasure, she didn't see any harm.

Continuing his ascension up her body, Ethan sprayed a burst of sunscreen directly on her chest, between the triangles that covered her. He used both hands, mostly fingers now, to spread and knead it to the edges of her top. And at the very second her breasts longed for even more of his touch, he boldly slipped his fingertips inside both flowered triangles and slid his palms fully over her tits, the move pushing the bits of fabric completely aside. She sucked in her breath, and as he began a slow massage over her sunscreen-slickened flesh, a moan wafted from her throat. She felt his firm, deep caresses squarely in her bikini bottoms, and though she liked watching the way he touched her, molding her breasts, she let her eyes fall shut for a moment just to soak in the delicious sensations.

"Feel good, baby?" he murmured.

At first all she could do was sigh her response. But then she managed, "Best time I've had putting on sunscreen—ever."

He flashed a lascivious grin in reply, and the sound of Rogan's deep chuckle a few feet away somehow only deepened the hunger she suffered between her thighs.

But she didn't want to rush this, or even direct it. Yes, Ethan had encouraged her to be aggressive if she wanted—but right now she was enjoying this just as it was, letting it progress on its own. Only whereas last night that feeling had frequently been laced with nervousness, uncertainty, today it came with a growing confidence, a true acceptance of where she was, what she was experiencing, and how much she was starting to let herself bask in it.

"Damn, I want you," Ethan murmured—and then, still sitting between her legs, he ran his thumb up the center of her crotch, making her gasp as the tingling heat of it fluttered all through her.

Reaching down to both her hips, he found the strings tying her bikini bottoms and simultaneously pulled until they fell away, leaving her exposed before him—and before Rogan, too. Ethan let out a low growl at the sight, and she heard herself whisper, "Please."

"Please what, honey?"

"Please fuck me," she said, softly, but with full self-assurance.

"Mmm, couldn't stop me if you tried," he said. And then he was undoing the front of his swim trunks, and his hard cock burst free, and Mira realized how badly she wanted him—*it*—right now. It was as if last night had somehow primed her, readied her—and yet because she hadn't succeeded in fully letting herself go then, she hadn't gotten enough, not even close, and now she wanted more. Unashamedly.

Kneeling on the boat's cushioned bow, Ethan gripped her outer thighs and lifted her legs across his, bringing the key parts of their bodies into proximity. Then he used one hand to position his sturdy erection—until he was easing it inside her.

"Ohhhh," she moaned as it smoothly filled the place that had suddenly seemed so vacant. Nothing in the world could have felt better in that moment, or more satisfying. She leaned her head back and shut her eyes as the sensation washed over her, rushing through her like a brisk ocean wave. "God, yes," she murmured.

Ethan said nothing in return, but his eyes shone glassy

with dark arousal as he began to slide in and out of her pussy with firm, even strokes. She felt each at her very core, as if the shaft reached much farther into her body than was actually possible.

"Damn, I'm getting jealous back here."

Ethan's rhythm didn't change when Rogan spoke, but Mira's gaze drifted from the spot where Ethan entered her to land on their companion. She met his dark eyes as Ethan's cock pistoned into her moisture, again, again. And then she did the thing that truly proved to herself, if any doubt at all had remained, that all her good-girl concerns were a thing of the past—she said exactly what came to mind without even weighing it. "No need for jealousy." Then she held up her hand and curled one finger toward her, summoning him.

A few seconds later, Rogan stood at her side in the walkway that cut between the cushioned seating—then he was dropping to his knees and leaning over to draw one nipple into his mouth.

"The sunscreen," she warned.

But he only paused to say, "I don't give a damn," then resumed raking his tongue over the pointed peak as he smoothed one palm across her belly.

And there it was again, that extraordinary sensation she'd briefly allowed herself to get lost in last night: two men's hands on her at once, two men working to pleasure her at the same time.

She watched Rogan kissing and suckling her tit, drinking in the delights he delivered, then raised her gaze beyond him to Ethan, whose face now flushed with excitement. She peered directly into his eyes and didn't attempt to disguise in any way how good it all felt. She bit her lip, so well-pleasured that it was almost agonizing.

"Wanna make you feel *so* good," Ethan murmured to her.

"You are," she whispered, her breath gone slightly ragged. "You both are." That was what he'd wanted, after all, right? For her to enjoy being with them both at the same time. And oh God, she was—she really was.

As she met Ethan's strokes, she also found herself raising her chest slightly, just enough to press the tip of her breast a little deeper into Rogan's mouth. Part of the time, she let her eyes fall closed and simply luxuriated in the hot sensations being showered upon her beneath the warmth of the midday sun. But at other moments, she enjoyed keeping her eyes wide open, watching the naughty sex she was taking part in. She felt like a woman in a porn movie, and though she'd always sensed, heard, read that those girls weren't really having a good time, right now she had to wonder if that was always true.

When Rogan, whose long-lashed lids had been shut as he feasted on her breast, suddenly opened his eyes to find her watching him, the feeling moved through her physically, affecting her as deeply as any touch or kiss. Because his face was so close to hers. While he was kissing her nipple. While Ethan was fucking her. She'd just . . . never expected to find herself caught up in such strange intimacy. With Rogan Wolfe, no less.

Like when he'd been inside her last night, she experienced that unsettling sense of connection to him, connection she shouldn't be feeling—since this was all about lust and sex and pleasure. And if anyone was supposed to be growing closer here, she reminded herself once again, it was her and Ethan. And yes, that was happening, undeniably. But right now, again, as she let Rogan and Ethan witness this wild and erotic new side of her, as she let herself open up to physical delights in a more extreme way than she ever had before . . . God, it was impossible not to feel shockingly close to Rogan, too. In a different way maybe. They'd spent more than four years apart. But perhaps that made it even more powerful in a sense. God knew it was more *startling*—at least for her.

After a while, Rogan released her breast from his mouth and quietly pushed to his feet, opening his black trunks to extract his large erection. Larger than Ethan's. Just by a little. So little that it barely mattered—it wasn't something she could feel; it was simply something she saw. Now he positioned himself next to her to hold that big cock down, rubbing it back and forth across the same nipple still left moistened from his mouth.

Ethan continued to slide in and out of her and she

couldn't help admiring his amazing staying power. Steady in so many ways, Ethan—steady in even *this* way.

And as she continued basking in the hot, nasty joys they brought her, it hit her that now the two guys had reversed positions from last night when they'd been on the bed together, and she realized why that had been the most exciting part: not only because they were both working on her but because she was experiencing both cocks at the same time, both rigid shafts pleasuring her at once, just in different fashions.

And when Ethan began to rub his thumb expertly over her clit—oh Lord, she craved *more* of that sensation of having two cocks.

Working on pure, guttural instinct, she reached for Rogan's dick, wrapping her hand fully and boldly around it—oh God, it was like stone in her grip—and murmured, "Want it in my mouth."

"Aw, babe," he rasped—then he let her pull his erection toward her face as she turned her head slightly, parting her lips, hungering for it in a way she never had before. She simply knew the yearning to have it inside her in some way—if she had two at her disposal, she suddenly wanted to experience them at once, together, fully and intensely. Her mouth physically ached for the stimulation of taking it in.

Still, she didn't want to end up overwhelmed, so as she drew the penis near, she simply licked at the head—and mmm, loved the feel of it on her tongue, the taste of the pre-come. Part of her wanted to look at Ethan, to let him know she was thinking about him, but the urge to keep her eyes on Rogan's dick overrode that. She licked it again, this time running her tongue sensually around the entire engorged tip, and thought of the playful ministrations—almost like teasing herself with what she wasn't quite yet having.

Rogan's hot sighs wafted down over her as Ethan said, "Aw, honey, you look so hot right now, so amazing." And with her tongue still touching Rogan's shaft, she glanced up at her boyfriend and felt the full measure of the shared lust filling the boat.

It pushed her onward, compelling her to slide her lips over the cockhead, taking it inside. A peek up at Rogan, then Ethan, made her envision how she looked just now—how daringly obscene. But she *liked* looking that way for them—that was part of this, part of opening herself up to such extreme intimacies. Both men let out deep sighs, sounds of approval, spurring her on, and she let them—she took more of Rogan's cock into the depths of her mouth, inch by hard, filling inch.

Ethan's stimulation of her clit had slowed, even stilled at points, but now it increased again. She whimpered around Rogan's cock, which seemed to excite them both further even as she began to thrust her cunt against Ethan's plunges inside her. Soon Rogan began to gently fuck her mouth—and though she knew the instant urge to maintain a sense of control in such a position, at the same time it only increased her arousal.

Lord, had anything ever felt so raw and satisfying as having two men inside her at once? Had anything ever felt so freeing even as she relinquished a big part of her control? It was as if they both literally pumped pleasure into her body, as if pleasure were a tangible thing.

She gave herself over to it completely, simply following her physical cravings. The silence that had filled the air when Rogan turned off the engine had now been replaced by a chorus of hot sighs and moans. *This* was what Ethan had been talking about this morning—she completely understood that now. Last night had truly been like a breaking-in period, a time of letting her adjust to being touched by both of them at once, of being watched by them both, as well. But *this, this* went far beyond that.

As Ethan's deft touches to her clit vibrated through her whole being, her pleasure rose higher and higher, finally reaching that pivotal moment when she knew orgasm was on the horizon. Feeling almost like some feral animal now, she moaned frantically around Rogan's thick length, rocking her pelvis madly against Ethan's thumb and cock. When finally the climax broke, she released the phallus from her mouth in order to cry out as the waves of ecstasy tumbled through her body over and over and over.

"Aw God—me, too," Ethan growled, then grabbed her hips and pounded into her relentlessly hard as he came.

She heard herself muttering, "Oh God," too, again and again, as he rammed into her most sensitive flesh, the timing of his orgasm almost extending her own—she felt his pummeling more than usual. Or maybe he was doing it harder than usual. Who knew? Who cared?

When it was done, both were left panting from exhaustion. She realized her hands were on her own breasts. They looked at each other. "You're fucking perfect," he told her, low, deep, between rough breaths.

And then Rogan said, "Now it's my turn in that hot little cunt."

She only sighed in response, but inside found herself happily thinking, *Yes, yes, yes, yes, yes.* Because she wanted still more. Wanted all she could get. All they could give her.

When Ethan pulled out of her, she instantly missed being filled up that way, but she kept her legs spread wide, ready for Rogan to replace him. She *was* a feral animal now. Transition complete.

He wasted no time stepping between her legs, clamping on to her ass, and thrusting inside her. "This isn't gonna take long," he warned her. And that almost disappointed her, but then she forgot all about it as the sensation of being filled up again took over.

She cried out at each stroke he drove into her, her body

still eager for more. He plunged into her so hard that she found herself gripping the edge of the cushion beneath her on one side and the boat's railing on the other.

And then Ethan was kneeling next to her, simply caressing her stomach, adding his touch to the mix. And she shifted her eyes to his, and even as Rogan fucked her hard, hard, hard, her gaze locked on Ethan's, and—oh, God, yes—she again experienced that almost startling intimacy with him. That was part of what he'd wanted, she remembered, part of what he'd promised her this would bring. And though it all got mightily confusing in the moments she allowed herself to examine it, right now the bond between them felt deep and pure and indisputable. He was gazing into her eyes as another man fucked her, his face all heat and tenderness, lust and love, and what could be more profoundly intimate than that?

"Jesus, *now*," Rogan rasped above her, then rammed into her harder still, both of them calling out as he came in her.

And then there was stillness. More silence, except for Rogan's labored breath as he tipped back his head, clearly spent—then he pulled out of her to lean back on his ass, resting against the driver's side windshield.

She looked back at Ethan and whispered, "I love you."

He bent down to lower one gentle kiss to her belly. "I love you, too. You're gorgeous. And incredible." Then he delivered another to the tip of her breast. "Thank you for trusting me on this. Opening yourself to this." Clearly she wasn't the only one who felt the difference in her approach today.

"Kiss me," she said in reply, and so he did.

Until Rogan said, "Um, hello. I'm here, too."

Which broke their kiss and made them all laugh. "And who are you again?" Ethan said on a chuckle.

And Rogan answered, "I'm the guy who just helped you give her what she really wanted. Two cocks at once."

Okay, that made *three* of them who knew today was different. And leave it to Rogan to be so blunt and just put it out there like that. She didn't mind, but at the same time, on the heels of such intensity, now that she was coming back to herself, feeling a little bit normal again, it made her blush—the heat of the sun might be brightening her skin, too, but she felt her cheeks flush in a way that came from inside.

Seeing her reaction, Rogan simply nudged her leg with his foot and cast one of his typical bad boy grins. "Come on, babe—don't go back into that shell *now*. Just say it. Say you wanted two cocks."

She found herself glancing back and forth between them, smiling even amid the slight return of a little embarrassment. He was right. If she was going to do this, if she was going to be this woman this weekend, there was no reason not be honest about it. "I wanted two cocks," she said.

And to her utter shock, just saying it, just being as

forthright as Rogan had been, made her feel . . . wow, even a little freer.

Free enough, in fact, to go on. "And I loved it," she told them. "And I'm going to want two cocks again tonight, and probably tomorrow, too. So all I can say is . . . you two better rest up."

Chapter 8

She loved having stunned them. And clearly, from their expressions, that's exactly what she'd done. It even made her laugh out loud. "You guys look surprised," she taunted.

Of course, from the expression on Ethan's face, it had an additional—but entirely favorable—effect on him, too. "Damn, honey, besides shocking the hell out of me, I think you just gave me another hard-on."

She let out a soft laugh. "Well, mister, I'm afraid that'll have to wait, because no matter *what* I loved, I need a break. Maybe some lunch. Need to get my strength back. You two wore me out."

Rogan's eyes twinkled beneath the sun. "Bet you never had a better time getting worn out, though, did ya?"

She met his mischievous grin, returning a playful look of

her own. "Probably not. Now somebody get me some tissues or napkins or something," she said, giggling a bit more—because no matter how hot it had been, there were practical matters to deal with before she could get her bikini back in place.

A few minutes later she'd tidied up, tied her bikini bottoms back on, and reapplied sunscreen where needed, adding some to her face, which Ethan had never reached the first time around. She was busy readjusting her triangle top when Rogan, who had risen to get beers and the soda she'd requested, suggested, "Why not just take the top *off*?"

She raised her eyebrows, meeting his gaze across the space that separated them. "Um, because someone might see me? We're in public, you know."

He just shrugged. "The lake is big. You noticed any other boats close enough to see what you're wearing?"

Sitting near the back of the vessel, pulling sandwiches and a large bag of chips from the picnic basket, Ethan laughed. "Yeah, maybe *all* the girls boating around the lake have their tops off today and we just don't know it. And besides, if someone were to see, they'd just think you're gorgeous and that we're lucky, that's all."

Now her questioning look was for *him*. "You wouldn't care if someone saw me topless? I mean, Rogan is one thing, under these particular circumstances. But you wouldn't care if somebody else came along?"

And now, to her surprise, *he* was the one shrugging. "Well, I wouldn't want my grandpa to see. Or a bunch of little kids or anything. But let's just say . . . I'm feeling kind of easygoing and generous about that right now. It just . . . wouldn't bug me the way it normally might, I guess." Then he tilted his head, gave her a wink. "Your call—whatever you like. Just seems like a weekend for . . . being carefree."

"You mean naughty," she corrected him with a smile.

"They're only boobs, honey," he said, his grin teasing her. "Damn pretty ones, but still only boobs. I, for one, would enjoy the view if you want to take your top off. But like I said, no pressure—whatever you want."

"I, on the other hand," Rogan added, "am applying pressure. Take your top off. I want to see 'em all damn day, every time I look at you." He ended with a wink of his own, which she felt squarely between her legs.

So Mira thought about it for a minute. Any other time in her life, she just wasn't the sort of woman who would be comfortable with this idea. And yet they both made good arguments. This weekend was about rule breaking, wasn't it? About stepping outside her comfort zone? And as she reached behind her neck to untie the top, she realized even just this, being bold enough to sit topless on a boat in broad daylight, would bring still more of that new feeling of freedom Ethan and Rogan were inspiring in her.

Of course, if any other boats did come near, she would be

scurrying to get the triangles back in place before anyone could see. But for now, she took a private, forbidden bit of pleasure in tossing the bikini top aside.

It surprised Mira to discover an even deeper sense of freedom merely by doing what they'd suggested. To lounge on the boat, talking and eating lunch while wearing only her bikini bottoms made her feel...confident, above worry, like a woman without inhibitions. And afterward, when she lay on her back, knees bent, on a padded platform at the boat's rear, quietly sunbathing, she felt almost...exotic, cosmopolitan— like some sexy, sophisticated woman who hadn't a care about what anyone thought.

She also spent that time basking in the memories of what had just taken place. It had been the most exhilarating thing she'd ever experienced. She'd always been a woman who needed to care about the man she was with in order to enjoy sex, but today she was discovering that...sometimes, when you cared for and trusted who you were with, the sex didn't always have to be *about* the caring. Sometimes the sex could just be about the sex. She still didn't think she could fuck a man she didn't know well and feel comfortable with, but the abandon she'd experienced with Ethan and Rogan together went beyond any other sexual encounter of her life. She'd had plenty of good sex before, and even *great* sex, but this had skyrocketed beyond measure. There'd been times when she'd forgotten to think, forgotten who she was, forgotten everything but how her body felt in that moment.

Will I still be this free, exotic, confident person after this weekend is over? Or will that part be as temporary as this liaison itself? And now that I've had this . . . what will my sex life with Ethan be like afterward? It would be good, yes, she knew that, but . . . would she always yearn for two cocks now? Would she yearn for more of this freedom? Would Ethan ever suggest doing this again? With Rogan? With someone else? Would *she* be bold enough to suggest it if she wanted it? Or would she return to being the classy, respectable woman with boundaries she'd always been up until now, the person who, like it or not, did care a little—or maybe even a lot—what people thought of her.

Is it possible to be both ways? Can a woman be both respectable and free? Classy and wild at once?

She wasn't sure. But she decided to stop thinking about it. After all, wasn't that her goal for the rest of her time here at the cabin, and wasn't that what had allowed her to lose herself in the pleasure of this? *So stop analyzing. Even this part of it. Just let yourself be carefree now, like Ethan said.*

"I'm about ready to try some skiing, dude," Rogan announced then.

And she turned her head to flash an incredulous look just as Ethan said, "You're crazy, man." Yes, they'd discovered skiing equipment on the boat, but taking a dip in chilly Lake

Superior wasn't for the faint of heart. Granted, Michigan's upper peninsula coast would be among the warmer spots on the great lake, but even with unseasonably warm temperatures in the eighties this past week, the water would still be frigid.

"Maybe, but life is short," he said.

Ethan just shrugged, laughed. "Whatever, bud. If that's what you really want to do, then we'll do it."

A few minutes later, Ethan had hooked up the ski rope and Rogan had pulled out a set of skis and donned a bright yellow life jacket. Dropping off the side, he bobbed in the water, shaking the wetness from his hair with a "Holy fuck, that's cold."

Ethan chuckled and Mira smiled over the side to say, "You can always get back on the boat. Nice and warm up here, you know."

He grinned in return. "Nah, babe, not my style," he said even as he battled a shiver. "You should know that. If I say I'm gonna do something, I do it."

"Even when you shouldn't," she pointed out.

"Damn, your tits look nice in the sun," he said in return.

And she just rolled her eyes and let out a laugh. "What brought that on?"

"They're a good distraction from this fucking cold water," he told her as Ethan dropped first one, then the second ski onto the lake's surface near Rogan. "And you be sure to

131

keep putting extra sunscreen on those babies, too. We don't need those, of all things, getting burned."

It was after Ethan eased the boat forward a bit, enough that Rogan was positioned behind it as he put on the skis, that Mira saw her man giving her a look she couldn't quite read. Taking the seat across the narrow aisle from him, opposite the captain's chair, she tilted her head and said, "What?"

"Just . . . impressed as hell with you, that's all."

She smiled. "Oh?"

"You know what I mean. Letting yourself go like that earlier. And now, sitting here in only your bottoms like it's nothing. You couldn't have done that . . . even yesterday. Even earlier this morning."

She appreciated his pride, but tilted her head the other way now. "Was I so prim before? Because I never saw myself that way."

It relieved her when he shook his head. "No. You were . . . normal, I guess. Like most women. And the only reason I planned this whole thing was because I wanted you to live out your two-guy fantasy—it had nothing to do with . . . coming out of your shell or anything, like Rogan called it earlier. But guess I hadn't thought about the fact that you'd kinda *have* to do that to really enjoy this. And turns out I like seeing that. A lot."

"Yeah?"

"*Oh* yeah. Kinda even turns me on, you being this confident, in-control woman." His grin aroused her a bit, made her aware of her exposed breasts tingling beneath the sun.

"Well, thank you. For . . . making it happen. For making me feel so comfortable, and for giving me so much freedom."

"You're very welcome, baby," he murmured, then leaned over to deliver a long, slow, heated kiss, his hand rising to the side of her breast, his thumb brushing across the peak—and as usual, such attention to her nipple shot straight to her pussy.

"Hey! Yeah, you two, on the boat! I'm freezing my ass off back here and ready to ski. How about it?"

Ethan sat behind the wheel, steering the boat easily up the lake, not far from the shoreline. After skiing—having stuck it out for an admirable half hour, no less—Rogan was back on the speedboat with him and Mira. Sometimes he thought Rogan was crazy, like now, but the guy was usually interesting to have around.

When he thought of the H.O.T. program they'd gone through together, it sometimes surprised him that guys so different in ways both possessed the skills and mindset that made them particularly adept at dealing with hostage situations. During their years of hanging out together with the guys in the H.O.T. program from police academy, he'd learned that Rogan was the kind of person who might sit quietly drinking all evening one night, then the next be completely outgoing and sometimes even outrageous. He could be unpredictable, for sure, and moody, too, but one thing you could count on from Rogan was that he did what he damn well pleased at about any given moment. There was no holding back with him—he followed whims, went after the things he wanted, and lived his life exactly as he chose most of the time.

In ways, Ethan admired that. Hell, you didn't see Rogan come close to losing the woman he loved because he'd gotten so caught up in his passion for his work. And if Rogan ever did do that, he'd realize it; it would be a conscious decision. But on the other hand, Ethan wasn't sure how much Rogan really cared about . . . anything. He seemed to take life in stride—easy come, easy go. He liked being a cop and took pride in catching bad guys—Ethan could say that much about him—but beyond that, he wasn't entirely sure what made the guy tick.

He thought back to that morning they'd been called in to rescue the little girl in Traverse City. It had felt a little awkward in a way at first, them not being the best of friends and yet having to deal with this together unexpectedly. It had been challenging to figure out who was in charge. And the truth was, the whole time they'd trained together, he'd never seen Rogan display any particular sensitivity or finesse and he'd wondered why the guy had even been selected for the program.

Once they'd reached the house where the girl was being held, though, they'd both automatically started using what they'd learned. And Ethan had seen that what Rogan lacked in finesse he made up for with brute frankness. They'd both talked to the father, a guy named Frank, on the phone, and without even discussing it, they'd fallen into a good cop/bad cop routine, Ethan being the nice guy trying to reason with him and Rogan laying down the law and making it clear there was no way out. And to his dismay at the time, before it was over, Rogan *had* assumed charge of the situation—but by and large, they'd worked well together that day.

Funny, despite serving on the same police force and playing on the same ball team, they'd never really had occasion to work that closely again . . . until now. Although it was hard to call this work.

Now Rogan sat sprawled in the seat next to his while Mira lay stretched out in front of them on the bow, looking gorgeous and a little wild without her top on. The change he'd seen in her today still astounded and pleased him. It wasn't that he wanted her to become some reckless woman who would share her body with just anyone—it was that he liked uncovering this exciting new side of her, this *confident* new side. Sex was something to be enjoyed, and he was glad his little weekend party was going so well for her now.

"See that rock?" Rogan pointed to what was actually a large outcropping of sandstone that created a cliff, leading down about twenty feet to the lake. A small, sandy beach lay at one side of its base, while atop it sprouted cedar trees.

"Yep," Ethan said.

"Looks like a good place to jump in and go for a swim."

Like earlier, Ethan just gave him a look. "Dude, you can't be serious."

"Um, didn't you get enough of the freezing-cold water a little while ago?" Mira asked from the bow.

"Won't be as cold there," he said. "It's in a cove."

When Mira looked to Ethan for confirmation, he could only shrug. "It's true." He knew for a fact because he'd spent a lot of summer weekends camping along this shore as a kid. And more than one of the H.O.T. reunions over the years had taken place in this area—most of the guys enjoyed the whole hunting, hiking, fishing thing, even if sometimes it really turned into more of just an eating, drinking, bullshitting thing. "Coves are more shallow, so the water there warms up faster in summer. But that doesn't mean it's actually *warm*— it just means it's not *as* cold."

"You two should come with me," Rogan suggested.

At which Mira just laughed, as Ethan said, "And why the hell would we do that?"

He grinned. "Get your blood pumping."

"Mine's pumping fine, thanks," Ethan told him with a quick nod.

But not easily thwarted, Rogan looked to Mira. "Come on, babe, how about it? Go jump in with me. It'll be fun."

And, predictably, she just looked at him like he must think she was crazy.

"Be one more brave thing you can do this weekend," he said then, though—and as she gave her pretty brunette head a tilt, Ethan realized the last part might actually have her starting to consider it.

"Is it . . . even safe?" she asked. "I mean, how shallow is it? And how do you know?"

Ethan had driven the speedboat slowly closer to the shore just since this conversation had started and now took a closer look at the area. "Water's plenty deep for jumping," he observed, "and the ledge juts out enough that you wouldn't be in danger of hitting the wall or anything." Then he raised his eyebrows at her, smiling. "But you're not seriously gonna let him talk you into that, are you?"

Now Mira was studying the sandstone cliff carefully—Ethan saw her eyes travel from the top of it down to the water, as if imagining the descent. And instead of answering his question, she simply said, "I've never done anything like that, never jumped into water off anything higher than a diving board."

"Well, now's your chance," Rogan prodded.

And she gave him a suspicious smile. "How cold will it *really* be?"

He held out his hands. "Do I look like a Magic 8 Ball, babe? I don't know for sure. Just less cold than when I was skiing, and that's less cold enough for me."

"You just have to be ready for it," Ethan warned her. If she was really contemplating this, she needed to be prepared. "It'll shock your body when you go in—you just have to ignore that and get back to the top. And then get the hell back out if you know what's good for you," he finished with a laugh.

"Hmm..." she said, still examining the small clifflike structure, clearly trapped by indecision.

"Tell you what," Rogan said. "We can even jump together if you want. I'll hold your hand if it'll make you feel better."

Now she bit her lip, gazing thoughtfully at Rogan for a moment—before she looked back to Ethan. "I...think I want to do this."

He just lowered his chin, cast her a grin. "Really?"

She answered with a nod.

"I think you're a little crazy—both of you. But far be it from me to try to talk you out of it."

From there, he drove them closer to the shore until they neared a thin ribbon of sand to one side of the rock wall. Rogan hopped out into the shallow water without a care as

Ethan let the boat idle and then stood to help Mira over the side into Rogan's arms.

Damn, it should probably feel weird to be delivering my nearly naked girlfriend into another guy's embrace. But it didn't. Not this weekend. This weekend, everything was different.

The boat continued idling in the water as Ethan watched them make their way onto the narrow beach area, and again he took in just how lovely she was, the tips of her long hair wet and curling now as it spilled down her bare back.

Neither had taken shoes, so it looked like slow going as they picked their way up the incline that led to the ledge at the top. Though soon enough Rogan called down to where Ethan sat waiting in the boat, "There's a small trail. We're not the first ones to get this idea."

When the two reached the top, they stood talking for a minute—Ethan couldn't hear them, but he guessed Rogan was playing cheerleader and probably also giving her instructions. Even from that distance, he couldn't help but sense a true . . . newness in her. In fact, he found it downright exhilarating just to watch her. There was something starkly beautiful about seeing her in only those bikini bottoms out in the wild.

He watched as Rogan took her hand, holding on to it as they stood getting ready to jump. At moments, he did wonder if he'd been taking some kind of chance by bringing her old boyfriend here—it would be impossible *not* to wonder.

But every time the thought occurred to him, he remembered that he trusted their love enough not to have those kinds of fears.

That's when Rogan and Mira stepped up near the sandstone edge and a few short seconds later took off with a running start and jumped.

There was something just magnificent and astounding about her suddenly being bold enough to leap from a cliff, and with her top off, no less. He watched, both excited and anxious as she plunged into the blue water, thinking how cold it must be and that she might be enduring a second or two of fear right now—but he knew she could handle it.

Still, he breathed a sigh of relief, even letting out a small laugh when her head popped back up through the water's surface, Rogan's followed a second later, a few feet away. She appeared a little breathless—but then she smiled. "Did you see me?" she called happily to Ethan.

"Yep, I saw. You're completely amazing me right now, by the way!" he yelled back. Then watched as she began to swim in the direction of the small beach.

"But Rogan lied—this water is freezing!" she yelled over her shoulder, clearly rushing toward the sand.

A moment later, she rose up out of the lake, the water sluicing from her skin as she got to her feet, and she soon stood on the beach looking cold and soaking wet and gorgeous.

And as Rogan followed after her, quickly reaching the sand, as well, Ethan heard him say, "Damn, babe, you're a tougher chick than I thought."

Yeah, she was.

And as she leaned her head back then to soak up the sun, a big smile still brightening her face, Ethan thought her no less than breathtaking. And he suffered the urge to be with her right now on that little stretch of sand. He wanted to give her a hug; he wanted to kiss those wet, berry-colored lips.

And he couldn't help wondering, as Rogan approached her, if he felt the same way, if he was as spontaneously drawn to her right now as Ethan was.

That's when he noticed her hobbling a little, though, and then sitting down in the sand. "What's up, honey? What's wrong?" he shouted.

"Not sure. Foot hurts," she called back.

Damn. He cupped a hand to his mouth. "Stay where you are. I'm coming over." And as he drove the speedboat closer to shore, nosing the bow up onto the sand, he saw Rogan sitting down with her, lifting her ankle in his palm and beginning to examine the bottom of her foot.

"See anything?" Ethan yelled to Rogan as he anchored the boat.

With his eyes still on the sole of her foot, Rogan said, "Yep—looks like she's got herself a good-size splinter." Then he lifted his gaze toward Ethan. "Bring the first aid kit. But might not be able to do anything for it right here—gonna need a set of tweezers."

Ethan grabbed the little first aid box the boat had come equipped with, then hopped over the side into knee-deep water—shit, it was cold!—and made his way up on to the sand. "How bad does it hurt, baby?" he asked, kneeling next to her.

"Bad when I put weight on it. It's fine when I'm sitting down, though." Only then she shot Rogan a look. "Except for when he keeps poking and prodding at it."

He still held her foot. "Had to get a look at it," he told her defensively.

Meanwhile, Ethan opened the first aid kit and began rifling through. "Damn, no tweezers."

"Didn't figure there would be," Rogan said, but then, inspecting the contents himself, he confidently plucked up a small pair of scissors intended for cutting gauze bandages or tape.

"Uh, what do you think you're doing with *those*, mister?" Mira asked doubtfully.

"Relax, babe," he said, low, calm—and maybe Ethan would have been more worried, but over the years he'd observed that Rogan was good with first aid. And then he remembered another reason why Rogan had probably been placed on the Hostage Ops Team, and also why Ethan actually thought he made a good cop—it took a lot to ruffle him; he stayed calm and levelheaded when other people might not.

Now he held the scissors' blades flat against the ball of her foot where Ethan could see a dark sliver of something embedded, probably a bit of wood or bark she'd stepped on while ascending the sandstone. Keeping his eyes on his work, Rogan spoke slowly, clearly concentrating on what he was doing. "I'm just gonna try to use the tips of the scissors like tweezers and grab the little black tip sticking out. Might not work, but . . ."

He went silent then, focusing closely on the scissors—and Mira let out a "Yow" just before Rogan said, "Got it," and held it up for them to see.

"My hero," Mira said, all smiles again, that quickly.

And Ethan ignored another small pinch of jealousy as he said to her, "Feel better now?" After all, *he'd* been her hero just a few hours ago, and what Rogan had just done actually seemed a lot more heroic than Ethan's double-edged offer to apply her sunscreen.

She nodded. "I think so anyway. Just hurt when he was pulling it out."

"We might want to cover that with a bandage, at least until we get back to the cabin, while you're walking around barefoot," Rogan suggested. "If we can get one to stay on the bottom of your foot and keep it halfway dry, that is."

A few minutes later, they'd bandaged her up, and after

she'd gotten to her feet, she announced that it was a little sore but mostly fine.

"Be good as new in a couple of hours," Rogan replied easily.

And Mira smiled up at him. "I didn't know you were such a splinter expert."

He just laughed. "Got a lot as a kid, and I usually took care of 'em myself."

The answer was just enough to remind Ethan that Rogan had had a pretty bad childhood, and it occurred to him that, though they'd never discussed it, Mira probably knew more about that than he did.

Ethan was just about to suggest they all get back on the boat when Mira, clearly in a good mood now that the splinter was gone, looked playfully up at Rogan to ask, "What can I ever do to repay you, kind sir?"

Rogan just took on a slightly lascivious look and said, "I'm sure I could think of a few things." Then his gaze dropped to the front of his shorts.

Ethan guessed Mira noticed the same thing he did, at about the same time, since she bit her lip and flashed Rogan an amused expression. "You got a hard-on removing a splinter from my foot?"

Rogan simply laughed, shrugged. "Doesn't take much for me. Especially when it comes to *you*. Never did. But you probably remember that."

It surprised Ethan when *that*, of all things, made her lower her eyes, her cheeks blooming with a soft blush beneath the sun she'd picked up today. Maybe because Rogan had referenced their old relationship in front of him.

"And besides, you have great tits and you being topless this whole time has kinda kept me turned on."

The words made Ethan think once more about this bold new Mira. And Rogan was right: She did have great tits— medium-size, soft but perky, with mauve-colored nipples that were almost always erect. He'd almost forgotten about her being topless when the splinter had put her in pain—he'd been more concerned with taking care of her and hoping it didn't hurt too much. But now that Rogan had drawn her near nudity back to his attention, now that she stood before him in the sand, wet brown hair flipped back over her head and beginning to dry in the sun, wearing nothing but those little bikini bottoms—hell, he was starting to get excited all over again, too.

When Mira looked at Ethan, he could see the beginnings of fresh lust sparkling in her eyes, as well, so he reminded her, "It's *your* birthday, *your* weekend, hon. Do whatever you want."

And she responded by taking on a mischievous look the likes of which Ethan had never seen on her face before. "Then I think the only appropriate thing for me to do is thank Rogan properly."

After which she gave her lower lip a provocative little bite, stepped forward to deftly pulled the tie on Rogan's trunks, then shoved them down until they fell around his ankles, revealing his completely erect dick.

Then, dropping to her knees before him, she took it into her mouth.

Chapter 9

Rogan's head dropped back as his groan echoed skyward. And Ethan's own erection lengthened, hardened, as he watched his girl pleasure his old friend with her mouth. She worked with her eyes shut, one fist wrapped around the base of Rogan's cock, moving her lips vigorously up and down the large shaft.

He wasn't sure he'd ever seen her be this sexually aggressive, and he discovered he found it wildly arousing even as he suffered a little more jealousy. Damn, what was that part about? Because at the moment, he couldn't deny the piercing sting of it, and that it went beyond any previous such emotion he'd experienced last night or today. Why was he feeling that? He'd *invited* Rogan here, after all. He'd *invited* all of this to take place. It had been his idea; he'd wanted it.

Maybe he just hadn't ever envisioned her going down on

Rogan *first,* and so damn enthusiastically, too. Maybe on some level he'd sort of seen Rogan as being . . . on the periphery of it all, just a third body, a second penis, when needed. If so, that had been stupidly naive and shortsighted of him, and he had to just accept the reality now that Rogan was a full and equal partner in their sex this weekend. But had he ever seen Mira go down on *him* that energetically? The sensation of being excited and envious at the same time was strange as hell.

Okay, so clearly he'd thought *he'd* be more in control of the sex they shared with Rogan. *But you told her to do what she wanted, that this was all about her. How on earth did you think you'd control the sex if you encouraged her to control it, too?* Yep, he definitely hadn't thought through that part very well. Had he been foolish to put all this in motion? Would he end up regretting it somehow?

But just then, she released Rogan from her mouth and turned, still kneeling, to look up at *him.*

Yeah, that's more like it, honey. Her gaze swam with hungry lust and he knew without either of them saying a word that it was his turn now. About damn time.

He stepped near her, peered down on her—and he thought about undoing his trunks but decided to leave that for her. She'd gone after Rogan's cock; she could go after his, too. He wasn't angry at her—hell, how could he be?—but he felt the urge to *make* her be aggressive now, make her work for it a little.

She clearly didn't mind that, either, since she immediately untied his shorts in front, then tugged them down until she was face-to-face with his dick. And the way she looked on it so longingly . . . well, hell—plain and simple, it killed that jealousy of his in a heartbeat. It wasn't Rogan she'd wanted— it was *cock*. It was as Rogan—and she—had said on the boat earlier: She wanted two cocks. And that was what he'd wanted her to have, what had started this whole thing—he'd wanted to give her an experience he couldn't provide by himself.

So he followed the urge to reach down and take her face between his hands, to run one thumb across her pretty, now slightly swollen lips as they looked into each other's eyes. He'd wanted to kiss those lips a few minutes ago. But now his desire for them was much more feral.

Even as he cupped her cheeks in his palms, she leaned in and delivered a long, thorough lick from his balls to the tip of his dick. "Shit," he whispered, the pleasure echoing outward from his groin.

Her eyes told him she liked his reaction—and then she did it again, pressing her tongue flat so that it covered far more of his flesh than if she'd just used the tip. After which her hand curled around his length and pulled it down until she could maneuver her mouth over it and begin giving him the same energetic blow job she'd given Rogan.

"Aw, babe, yeah—suck that dick," Rogan murmured.

When Ethan raised his glance briefly to his friend, he thought Rogan appeared to be enjoying watching almost as much as when he had been the recipient of her ministrations. "You suck it so good."

Or maybe Rogan had just wanted to remind her he was there—because after he spoke, she reached over to take his cock in her hand, working it even as she worked on Ethan with her mouth.

Damn, the sight increased the animal impulses echoing through him, made his groin tighten all the more, made him pump his erection lightly between her gorgeous lips. "So hot, honey. So hot," he heard himself breathe unplanned, spurring her on.

After a few more minutes of pleasuring them that way beneath the warm afternoon sun, she lifted her mouth off Ethan and switched again, her knees shifting in the sand to face Rogan once more. And as she lowered her mouth over his hard length, now she wrapped a fist around Ethan's superstiff shaft.

As it went on, Ethan slowly got more and more caught up in the passion until he stopped pondering any worries or regrets he might be developing and instead focused simply on feeling, and watching. Watching *her*.

She'd become like . . . a porn star, something in a dirty fantasy. Relentlessly hungry and taking all she could get. It excited the hell out of him.

And yet, remember, she's still your Mira. She's still the girl who helps your nieces and nephews hunt for Easter eggs, still the woman who sets the table for your mother on holidays. She loves books and puts her heart into making the perfect gift basket with every single order she receives. She makes you homemade chicken soup when you're sick. She watches legal dramas just to try to learn more about what you do and why it means so much to you. She snuggles up to you in bed just to be close to you when you sleep.

And somehow, to his surprise, remembering all that . . . made it all even *hotter*. That she could be all those things and also be this aggressively wild, erotic, sex-craving woman before him now. He'd thought he knew her so well, yet suddenly here he was, discovering this beautifully dirty new part of her.

And isn't that what you really *wanted? To come here and discover something new with her? To somehow feel closer to her through having shared this?* Yeah, that was exactly what he'd hoped for, envisioned, but right now he was finding it even more profound than he'd imagined. Especially when she shifted her gaze over to him, her mouth still filled with Rogan's cock, and their eyes met, and he felt them sharing . . . everything. The rawness of it. The stark honesty. The stark *intimacy*. His breath grew shallow and for a second he feared he'd come in her hand just from the profound thrill he was taking in watching her.

"Jesus God, baby, I need to lick your sweet little pussy," he told her suddenly. The powerful desire had come over him without warning—he *needed* to give to her what she was giving to both of them. And so he dropped to his knees, same as she had a little while ago, at the same time reaching to turn her body toward his.

The move shook Rogan's dick from her mouth to send it plopping wetly against his belly as she rolled onto her ass in the sand. Ethan wasted no time yanking at the little bows she'd tied at each hip, then tossing the damn scrap of fabric away. Before she could even spread her legs, he did it for her, prying her thighs roughly apart, seeing the shock and delight mingle in her gaze. He wasn't usually this forceful—but he was doing what he'd told *her* to do this weekend: He was letting go of every inhibition, letting his lust drive him. And apparently it turned *her* on, too.

Mira watched as Ethan sank his tongue greedily into the pink flesh between her legs, then let out a yowl as the pleasure shot through her. Oh God, she hadn't realized how much she needed some attention there, but she could scarcely remember anything ever feeling more welcome than this did now.

She moaned and whimpered her delight as she watched him, looking downright ravenous as he licked and mouthed her. Leaning back on her elbows, she murmured, "So good. So good." And oh, what a difference a day made. Less than a day, actually. And even in the few hours since both guys had fucked her on the boat, she felt she'd let herself come alive even more, let herself go after what she wanted. It was as if jumping off the sandstone ledge behind her right now had given her some amazing new power. To take what she wanted. To trust her instincts. To be braver than ever before.

Just then, Rogan dropped to his knees beside her, his large hands coming to cover her breasts. He molded and massaged them, adding still more sensation to everything that was happening. But her mouth felt empty. That simple. Before this weekend, she often experienced the urge to give her lover a blow job, but she'd never quite . . . recognized it, indulged it, welcomed and accepted it in the way she did now. So as Ethan licked between her parted legs, then thrust his fingers into her pussy, making her release another low sound of pleasure, she found herself peering needfully, hungrily up at Rogan, then reaching a hand to curl around his still rock hard erection.

He read her look immediately—she saw the dark delight enter his gaze. "Aw yeah, open up, babe, and I'll give you a sweet treat," he told her, rising, leaning, until his thick length hovered just over her mouth.

"Oh God, I want it," she whispered without forethought. Then grabbed on to the shaft and pulled it between her lips, loving the feeling of her mouth being filled almost as much as she loved having her pussy filled. Like a wanton. Like a sex-crazed slut.

Then she had a revelation. *Maybe it's okay to be those things. Sometimes anyway. Under the right circumstances. With the right people.*

"Mmm, suck my cock," Rogan told her, sliding it a little

deeper into the recesses of her mouth. "Suck it good for me." And as she lay all the way back, resting her head in the sand, he began to move it in and out between her already stretched lips.

She looked up at him the whole time. There was something indescribably personal about meeting a man's gaze when you were going down on him. More personal than when fucking him. Like on the boat earlier, it struck her how vulnerable she was, under him that way—that she really had no choice in sucking him now, that he held the position of power. And oddly, she liked it. And even more oddly, it actually made her feel . . . strong. To let herself be so vulnerable, so at his mercy. It somehow only added to the new sense of freedom she was experiencing with Rogan and Ethan today.

Below, she undulated against Ethan's mouth, and though her position no longer allowed her to see him, she could feel his eyes still on her. *Watch me, E. Watch me.* That's suddenly what she wanted, what being with two men gave her. Turned out it was about more than the dense pleasure of having two cocks—it was also, in some ways, about sex becoming a spectator sport. With two guys at once, there were moments where one of them did nothing but observe, and it almost shocked her to discover how much being watched aroused her. Last night she'd felt that part, felt it nudging at her, trying to break down her walls—but now that those walls had collapsed, she experienced the full force of it.

When Rogan leaned his head back, breaking their gaze, she looked skyward. She took in a few wisps of white clouds dotting the blue, then the ledge she'd jumped from came jaggedly into view. The sun on her skin was indeed like one more touch, one more sensation adding to it all.

Meanwhile, Ethan's ministrations now focused on her clit, which she thought must be swollen to the size of a marble. Although she'd let out a few mewling cries around Rogan's cock from the pleasure Ethan delivered, now she began to moan around it in earnest. Orgasm was nearing and she knew already that it would come hard.

She pumped at Ethan's mouth now with abandon, with the unabashed need to reach that hot peak. And she knew both of them noticed the change in her, in her movements and amplified reactions. Rogan's eyes were on hers again, his sparkling lecherously as he cast a dirty little grin and whispered, "Aw babe, is that naughty little pussy gonna come for us? Is that hot little cunt gonna come in Ethan's mouth?"

Her answer? Another moan around Rogan's thick length. And then her hands instinctively went to her breasts. They were sensitive, always, and they wanted stimulation now.

"Mmm, let me help," Rogan said, pressing his palms over her hands, making her own palms knead and mold them more firmly.

And then she found herself giving a brisk shake of her

head, letting him know she wanted his cock out of her mouth, and he got the message, extracting it.

Then, through lips that felt swollen, sore, she whispered, "Fuck them."

And Rogan didn't hesitate—he knew exactly what she meant. Lifting one leg across her body to straddle her midsection, he let his wet cock drop between her breasts. He used both hands to press the flesh up around his length, then thrust in short, firm strokes through the soft valley created there.

She could barely understand why it felt so good, that hard column moving between the two mounds, but it made her bite her lip as fresh pleasure washed over and through her. Her moans began to slow yet become more intense. And though she couldn't see Ethan at all anymore, God knew she could *feel* him as she fucked his mouth.

Rogan's dark gaze was on her again, and something about this weekend, the intensity of it all—including this current position beneath him—transformed the present connection between their eyes into something more powerful than it had ever been before. He'd always been a man who liked to lock gazes during certain phases of fucking, and she'd always thought it powerful, lush, intimate. But looking at him through the sex they were indulging in this weekend surpassed that. And when he then began to pinch her nipples, squeezing, pulling—oh Lord, that was it. She toppled over the edge she'd been so precariously balanced on for the last few minutes.

The orgasm blasted through her in dirty, sweet waves of the hottest release she'd ever experienced. She let out high-pitched cries as each of those waves pushed its way outward through her body, over and over, until finally they stilled . . . and she stilled.

She shut her eyes, her body going limp in the sand—and then she heard herself let out a small, sated laugh.

"Good?" Rogan asked her.

As she came back to herself, she grew aware that he was climbing off her, leaving her torso a bit wet with perspiration from where their bodies had met. "*Crazy* good," she replied.

That's when she felt a small kiss to one inner thigh and managed to lift her head and peer into the handsome face of the man who'd done all the work. "Crazy good, huh?" he asked with a wicked little grin.

"Mmm," she purred. Then managed to add, "Amazing."

"That's what I like to hear," Ethan said with a playful wink. And now it was *him* her gaze locked on, and his eyes slowly turned less lighthearted as he asked, "How tired is your mouth?"

The truth was, at this point, it was pretty tired. But sometimes sex was about reciprocation, and it wasn't *that* tired. "You jealous?" she teased him then. She wasn't sure why—it had just come out.

Yet it only led a leisurely half smile to unfurl on his face, and he spoke with a slow, sure confidence that turned her on a little even after having just come a few seconds before. "I just want to feel your lips wrapped around my dick."

She touched her tongue gently to the roof of her mouth, aroused by everything about him right now, everything about this moment. "I want to feel that, too."

He gave his head a tilt, his grin softening. "That's my girl."

He'd risen up on his knees now, though, between her spread legs, and she pointed to his erection, still hard but now also sprinkled with sand. "All I ask is that you wash it off first. Cock, good. Sand, yuck."

He glanced down, too, and said, "Fair enough, baby." Then pushed to his feet and walked the few yards to the water's edge, kneeling down to splash a little of Lake Superior onto it, letting out a shiver along with a laugh. "Damn, I forgot it was gonna be so cold. That's not gonna be helpful here."

She just giggled in response, rolling onto her side to watch him and thinking how beautiful he looked. Now that they were all naked, out in the middle of nature, alone, it gave her the wild sensation of being alive in . . . ancient times or something, of being early humans who just lived by their primal instincts, fucking freely as they wished. And she knew, of course, that they wouldn't have looked the same—she thought to herself that no cavewoman would have ever been so lucky to have two such hot male companions—but she liked the idea anyway.

Just then, she felt Rogan behind her in the sand, leaning near, almost spooning her. His palm curled over her hip, then drifted down over her ass, to the center of it. One finger drew a tingling line from her pussy upward to slowly cross her anus, making her shiver. And then he was whispering in her ear. "Does he ever fuck you in the ass?"

The question shouldn't have stunned her, coming from Rogan, but it did. She looked over her shoulder. And she had the strange urge to tell him it was none of his business, but somehow, right now, that would have sounded silly. So she just whispered, "No."

"Ever want him to?"

"No," she said again, but the answer was more complicated than that. And Rogan must have known that, because he just let out a light chuckle.

The fact was, back when they'd been a couple, Rogan had wanted to fuck her that way many times, but she'd refused. Truthfully, she'd never even thought about it until he'd brought it up, and it had sounded a little barbarian to her at the time, or at least on the painful, kinky side. And toward the end of their relationship he'd pressed her harder on it— he'd played with that part of her using his finger, sometimes even his mouth—and to her shock she'd discovered such attention did bring her a strange, yearning sort of pleasure she wouldn't have predicted.

But they'd been growing apart by then, so she'd still said no, partly afraid it would hurt and partly from a sense of self-preservation, maybe wanting to keep some piece of herself from him since she'd begun to suspect they would break up soon anyway.

Since getting together with Ethan, though, that form of sex had never come up. And maybe there had been times when she'd almost wanted it to. Times when she'd felt curious, remembering that Rogan had awakened her interest in it. But she'd just been . . . too much *herself* to ever introduce the idea.

Now, as Rogan reminded her of her body's stirrings in that area, she decided this weekend was no time to explore them. Even as aggressive and carefree as she felt and as Ethan had encouraged her to be, it seemed like it would be . . . a delicate operation, not something she wanted to rush into. Still, maybe she'd be bolder now with Ethan when they returned home and it was just the two of them again. Maybe now she'd suggest it sometime, ask him if he'd ever thought about trying that.

As Ethan returned from the water, massaging his penis in his hand, he wore a quirky smile. "Trying to warm it back up," he told her. "Damn—remind me not to get sand on it again."

And God, she loved this man. She was reminded of it over and over. And moments like this—when he was just honest, open, playful, and still sexy as hell—those were the times when she thought she loved him the most.

So now she bit her lip, cast her best come-hither look as he lowered to his knees before her, and said, "I think I can help you."

And his expression edged from playful back toward heated. "I like your attitude."

"Fuck my mouth," she whispered.

A low groan left him and she could have sworn she saw his erection stiffen further in his grip. And then his demeanor became more like what she'd witnessed from him last night, more commanding. "Get on your hands and knees."

She didn't hesitate. She instantly wanted to please him. Within a few seconds, her hands and knees were planted in the sand and she faced him. Now that she'd found this brazen part of herself, she felt eager to continue exploring it—with him. *For* him.

As he positioned himself, bringing his cock to the right height, she peered up at him and felt . . . pleasantly subservient. She hadn't known that concept could please her, but she was learning all *sorts* of things about her sexual self on this, her thirty-second birthday. And it struck her that it was high time she had.

Taking the shaft back in hand, he brought it to her

waiting mouth, then eased the head inside. A hot sigh left him as she closed her lips over it lovingly.

And as he took her face between both palms, sliding his cock deeper, toward her throat, he looked into her eyes and said, "Do you want Rogan to fuck your pussy while I fuck your mouth?"

She could only give a slight nod, but even the mere suggestion set her whole body ablaze. *Yes, yes, yes.* Two cocks again. Filling her. She could think of nothing she wanted more.

Of course, Rogan didn't wait for direction—she couldn't see him any longer, but his hands gripped her hips almost immediately. And there was a tiny part of her that had been almost irritated at him for his question about Ethan and her ass—it had felt almost like he was implying there was something wrong with them for not having done that, even though she'd never done it with him, either—but right now, she was ready to forget about that and focus on pleasure.

And then—oh Lord, the tip of his cock pressed into her moisture. And slid smoothly, deeply into the depths of her cunt.

She moaned around Ethan's cock as the thick pleasure encased her. This . . . this was even better than on the boat. *Must be the position.* After all, it was one of her personal favorites—she always felt Ethan's cock more this way, always

Party of Three

felt a little wild and untamed this way, like an animal, as the very position implied.

She arched her back, soaking in the hot delight filling her from two opposing angles, letting her eyes fall shut as it nearly overwhelmed her.

"Feel good, baby?" Ethan asked from above.

Another nod, a soft sound around the hard column that stuffed her mouth. Nothing had ever felt better.

And then she began to rock her body just slightly, a signal to them both that she wanted more—she truly wanted to be fucked.

Rogan began slamming into her—hard, hard, hard— making her cry out even as Ethan thrust forward between her lips in small but potent drives. Very soon, she ceased thinking. There was simply no *room* for thought. Her body, even her brain, was too full with sensation. And if she'd found the ecstasy overwhelming when they'd first entered her, it was nothing compared to this. In her mind, she became nothing more than a machine, a machine made for fucking. It was as if her sole purpose on the earth was this, this profound, enveloping pleasure that seemed to swallow her whole.

She never wanted it to end. Even as her lips again grew stretched and weary, even as her legs threatened to give out beneath her, she wanted it go on and on forever.

She was a thinking woman, always had been—smart and

on the verge of being an academic type in college, a lover of books and movies who enjoyed analyzing the world at large. And she couldn't have imagined ever taking such mindless joy in having her thoughts simply disappear, vanish, turn to dust in the face of pleasure—but right now she welcomed it. She wanted nothing more than the physical, nothing more than the strong cock pummeling her hungry pussy as another fucked her mouth. Everything else was simply . . . gone.

But then she raised her gaze to Ethan—and one thing came back. The bond she felt with him. It was something like that starkly intimate sensation she'd experienced with Rogan a little while ago—but with Ethan . . . oh God, with Ethan it ran deeper because it was about so much more. Somehow the look they exchanged spanned their whole history together and every aspect of their lives. It said, *Look how dirty we can be together and still have sane, productive, sensible lives to return to.* It reminded her that he gave her *everything*—everything from love and security to the hottest, nastiest sex she could never have imagined.

"I want to come in your mouth," he murmured down to her.

Oh Lord. He'd never done that before. It was kind of like her ass with Rogan—something he'd always wanted but she'd feared a little. Yet without even weighing it, she kept her eyes on his and gave one more nod, that easily. She was that excited, that pleasured, that eager to please him. She wanted that liquid part of him inside her, shooting down her throat, spreading all through her body in a whole new way. She wanted to feel that powerful explosion of ejaculation in a whole new place.

"Aw baby," he rasped at her acquiescence, clearly as surprised by it as she was. "I love you."

And oh, she loved him, too. And she wished she could tell him. But she would just have to say it in a different way now, even if it was still by means of her mouth.

Behind her, Rogan persisted in plunging incredibly deep and hard with each thrust—and though her thighs pretty much *had* given out on her now, he held her up, anchoring one arm around her waist, and he also braced her knees with his. And as Ethan pistoned with smooth precision in and out between her welcoming lips, she remembered the advice of a girlfriend back in college—a group of them had sat in a tiny dorm room as Deena Fightmaster had instructed them in the art of swallowing. She'd said to do exactly that, to try to loosen the throat muscles and keep swallowing, swallowing, swallowing to avoid being overwhelmed.

And that's when Ethan said, "Aw baby, honey, now, now—I'm gonna fill your perfect mouth with my come." And even as Rogan rammed into her from the back, she concentrated on opening her throat, and then the warmth filled her mouth and so she swallowed briskly, again, again, over and over with

Ethan groaning his pleasure above her until she knew his climax had ended.

And as he drew his cock out of her now-unbelievably-exhausted lips, she knew the sense of yet another new bond with him—she'd taken him inside her in yet another hot new way and it came with a surprisingly warm sense of satisfaction that flowed through her body the same as she imagined his semen doing right now.

"You okay?" he whispered tenderly, lifting her chin with one bent finger.

Even without her mouth filled, though, she still couldn't speak. Not yet. So she simply offered another nod and hoped he somehow understood how much she meant it, that he could see it in her eyes—and he just answered with a replete sigh that told her all she needed to know.

"Jesus Christ," Rogan said behind her then. "Fuck, I'm gonna come, too. I'm gonna come so fucking hard in this tight little cunt."

And then he did, ramming into her even more forcefully, pleasure warring with utter fatigue inside her as her arms gave out, leaving only her ass raised in the air as he delivered those last ferocious drives, groaning deeply with each.

All she knew after that was the need to rest. Although it came with total satiation.

She heard Rogan's voice. "Aw, babe, you are so fucking phenomenal, so fucking amazing."

And Ethan's, coming softer. "I love you, Mira. You're perfect." And then his kiss, tender on her swollen lips, and then another on her breast as she found herself rolling to her back in the sand.

The sun was like a balm, caressing, comforting, and over the course of a few minutes the warm rays began to feel almost healing to her, like some reenergizing treatment that was restoring her, bringing her back to life.

She was aware that Ethan lay on her left, Rogan on her right, all of them recovering from what they'd just shared. Her body had never felt so well-used—so thoroughly well-pleasured—in her life, and as a small, slightly naughty-feeling smile stretched her sore lips, she summoned the strength to say, eyes still skyward, "Ethan?"

"Mmm-hmm?"

"Thank you for my birthday present."

Chapter 10

Mira stood before the mirror in the small bathroom, naked and refreshed, having just left the shower. She ran a blow-dryer over her long brown locks for a minute, to take away some of the dampness, but she'd leave the rest to dry on its own, knowing it would curl prettily by the time she sat down to her birthday dinner with her two lovers.

As she turned off the dryer and set it on the sink, she went still, peering at herself in the glass—at her face, her eyes. Because she'd never felt more . . . empowered. And she wondered if that was the sort of thing that showed on a person.

Mainly, however, she noticed only her sun-kissed skin, like a blush on her face, though blessedly more tan everywhere else. Even her breasts, never exposed to the sun before, had fared well because her companions had so diligently, repeatedly kept them covered with sunscreen.

So she didn't look any different. Not in the sense she was expecting anyway.

Or did she? Maybe around the eyes?

Maybe if someone looked closely now they'd be able to see that she had secrets. Hot, naughty ones. Maybe they'd see that she was a braver, more daring woman now who had faced her darkest desires.

Or maybe it was all in her head. But it didn't matter. She found herself smiling anyway, since whether or not it was visible, *she* knew the truth and always would.

After dressing in a pair of cute khaki drawstring shorts and a flowered tank that hugged her shape, she exited the bathroom to find the cabin quiet and still. As Rogan had promised, the spot where the splinter had been on the sole of her foot felt fine now and was only a pinprick dot she could barely see when she sat down on the sofa to check it out. Still, even if she'd have preferred her flip-flops, she immediately grabbed a pair of ankle socks from her weekend bag, along with a pair of canvas tennis shoes to keep it protected. After putting them on, she ventured outside.

Descending the cabin's porch where she and Ethan had had sex just this morning, she took in the lush, green surroundings.

So much had happened so fast since they'd arrived here that she'd barely had a chance to notice how much she liked this place.

The cabin lay nestled in a sea of tall, old trees that felt rooted in time, with wildflowers blooming all around, giving her the sense that nature really owned this place and they were just visitors. Bunches of tiger lilies peeked from the tall grasses at the yard's edges, and delicate pink lady slippers blossomed at the bases of a few of the trees. Daisies and black-eyed Susans bloomed in small flower beds below the porch and around the cabin's walls.

A glance off to the left revealed still more trees, some of their trunks covered with ivy or moss, and nearly hidden in the greenery she noticed a thin trail making a winding path toward a more thickly wooded area. And though normally she'd feel more wary than lured by such a trail leading off into the unknown, for some reason she suffered the urge to follow it. *Hmm, maybe I really* am *braver now. In lots of ways.*

Still, she decided this probably wasn't the time to just go wandering off—especially when she spotted Ethan down on the dock, a large cooler and a couple of shopping bags resting nearby.

And when she realized he was covering the picnic table there with a lavender tablecloth, and that a few lavender and white balloons were tied to one end of the table, her focus shifted completely from the wooded path to the man in the distance. She couldn't help smiling as her heart warmed. Lavender was her favorite color. And he'd clearly gone to some trouble to make her birthday dinner more than just another meal.

God, he was a good man. And though this whole trip had begun to restore her faith in their relationship, she was really beginning to *feel* that now, bone deep.

Funny—giving her a hot ménage à trois had seemed like the ultimate gift, yet it was *this*, watching him set a special table for her birthday, that tightened her chest and reminded her how perfect they really were for each another.

By the time she descended the stone steps that led to the lake, Ethan stood at the nearby grill, tongs in hand, the cooler she'd spotted before by his side.

"Hey, you," she said sweetly.

He looked up with a smile. "There's my pretty birthday girl."

She met his gaze, feeling more simply, deeply good inside than she had in a very long time. This was indeed the guy she'd fallen in love with. "The table looks wonderful, Mr. Thoughtful."

He just shrugged, a hint of a smile playing about his lips. "Well, I wanted to make it special."

"You did. You are. In every way."

He looked pleased, comfortably confident, maybe as if he could feel what she felt, too—her coming back to him, in a *real, true* way. It wasn't that she'd ever left, but any distance that had grown between them was now diminishing.

She could smell the grill as Ethan began extracting the steaks from a sealed package he'd pulled from the cooler.

And then she looked around, remembering to wonder, "Where's Rogan?"

"Hell if I know," he said easily. "Haven't seen him since he went into the shower after me. He's not in the cabin?"

She shook her head.

"Well, I'm sure he'll turn up. Especially when he smells the steaks grilling."

"Do you need any help?" she asked.

He gave her another sexy grin. "Nope, birthday girl, this one's all on me. You just relax and enjoy."

And she couldn't keep a fresh smile from unfurling on her face.

"What?" he asked her, clearly curious what had brought it on.

"I don't know," she told him, shaking her head. "I'm tired, but at the same time I'm just not really in a . . . relaxing sort of mood. I still feel . . . energized."

He slanted her a teasing, sexy look. "Today was good, wasn't it?"

She nodded in reply, then spoke honestly. "I never knew I could be that way, feel those things, without cowering in shame."

"You were beautiful and amazing. You know that, right?"

She gave yet one more comfortable, confident nod. She did know that. She *felt* beautiful and amazing. "I love that you can still love me after that. I love that you . . . gave me all this. I never knew I wanted it—I mean *really* wanted it—as more than just a fantasy, which is so much more . . . simple. Not real. But to experience it, with you, and to know it's okay . . .that's just"—she stopped, shook her head—"beyond my wildest dreams."

He leaned forward, placed his hand on the back of her head, and lowered a kiss to her forehead. "Of course I love you— always. And I didn't know it was possible, Mira, but I think maybe I even love you more now than I did just yesterday."

She gave her lip a bashful, almost flirtatious nibble, look- ing up into his blue eyes as she grabbed his hand and squeezed. And they stood like that, just soaking up the moment, and the newness that had suddenly blossomed around their relation- ship, until he finally said, "Well, I better get these steaks on if we're ever gonna have this birthday dinner."

She smiled. Then, for some reason, thought of the little trail up by the cabin. "Do you mind if I take a walk for a few minutes?"

"No, but where to?"

She pointed up into the treed area. "I saw a path and I guess I'm wondering what it leads to. Probably nothing—it'll probably just fade away. But thought I'd check it out."

He looked to where she indicated and said, "Just be careful. Could be snakes around."

And she nodded, figuring that was a good piece of advice. "I'll watch where I'm going. And I'll only be a few minutes."

"Sounds good." He turned toward the grill and picked up the package of steaks once more. "Let Rogan know we're eating soon if you see him. Don't want him messing up your birthday dinner," he added with a wink.

"Got it," she said, still smiling at him and enjoying the simple fact that Ethan was a planner, and that it was one more thing they had in common—they both liked things to turn out the way they envisioned and expected.

Of course, this weekend was *nothing* like she'd envisioned, and she'd managed to roll with that—eventually. But as she took the twisting stone steps back up the hill, she still found herself looking forward to the simplicity of the dinner, too—maybe because, even as well as she was handling this party of three *now*, change didn't come easy, and their steak dinner would feel familiar, like one part of the trip that would come off mostly as she'd anticipated. Even if there was a third person present.

And she was looking forward to later, too, to more fucking. To her astonishment, it didn't seem to matter that her entire body nearly ached with fatigue—she still just kept wanting more and more. Her skin felt hypersensitive to every touch, every stimulation—even the shower had felt sensual.

And now a light breeze sifting through the trees wafted over her flesh to leave her slightly aroused.

Maybe it was because they'd had so much sex already in the last twenty-four hours—maybe it was a snowballing sensation; the more she got, the more she desired. Or maybe in the back of her mind she was growing aware that this weekend wouldn't last forever. When it was over, it was over—and though she and Ethan hadn't discussed it and she *had* wondered about it, she just had a feeling this was a once-in-a-lifetime experience that would never come back to her. And now that she was fully enjoying it, she knew she had to get all she wanted, all she could take, before they all headed back to their real lives tomorrow afternoon.

As she found the little path she'd seen a few minutes earlier and started down it into the trees, she began to realize the area was even more densely wooded than she'd expected. As she put one foot in front of the other on the thin trail, she was careful to watch her footing and, as Ethan had advised, keep an eye out for snakes or anything else worrisome in the thick, low-lying brush and ivy between the trees.

She quickly found herself surrounded by greenery—it even formed a tall canopy above her where the evening sun shot through only in spots here and there. The very lushness of it seemed to wrap around her, and the deeper she ventured into the woods, the more immersed in the forest she became; she could even smell the leaves. Stopping to look around, she began to study the nearest tree, one of its branches jutting out over the path, and she reached out to touch one broad leaf to see what it felt like between her fingers.

And then, looking ahead, she gasped. The trail *didn't* fade away—and now she saw exactly what it led to. A stone well. The perfect little wishing well, hidden here in the woods.

The small, gabled wooden roof that covered it had certainly seen better days—it was dilapidated and leaning to one side. And she knew that once upon a time it must have served a very practical purpose before their cabin had become a vacation home, when someone had really lived there, apparently in a time before running water. So maybe it wasn't truly *perfect*, but it was still idyllic. And what could feel more magical than discovering her own personal wishing well tucked away down the path that had beckoned her?

And what did you do at a wishing well? You made a wish, of course, and tossed in a coin. But she didn't have a coin with her—she was on a rustic getaway and hadn't exactly seen a need to tote her purse through the woods. Even so, though, she began to think about what she would wish for right now if she could.

Rogan thought back over the day, and damn, it had been a full one already—with more still to go. Mira's birthday. It occurred to him that it was odd to suddenly be celebrating it with her again, as he had once before. Although this was one hell of a different kind of celebration.

He'd heard them fucking this morning, her and Ethan. On the porch, outside the window above the couch. It had woken him, in fact. He'd peeked out to see her riding Ethan, her back arched in some cute little white piece of fabric he'd sort of wanted to rip off her so he could see the muscles there, her shoulder blades, the curve of her waist.

But then he'd let the curtain fall back into place and lay down again, closing his eyes and feeling, weirdly, a little glum. He'd had no idea why. He'd already seen Ethan and Mira fucking last night, after all.

Yet maybe it was different watching the two of them when they thought they were alone, when he wasn't involved in the sex. Maybe it had reminded him a little more that he was just a temporary addition to their relationship—that she really belonged to Ethan in a deep-down way.

And she'd been on top this morning. He'd always liked her that way, on top. For a guy who liked to be in control, he'd always taken a surprising amount of pleasure lying beneath her, watching the way her body moved on his, the sway of her breasts, the way she grinded that hot cunt on him. Probably he'd liked that a woman on top had to be the aggressor, at least a little.

And this morning he'd seen the same liquid rhythm she always took on in that position, the circular movement of her hips, and she'd looked fucking beautiful like that—but maybe, even if he wanted her to let loose and be aggressive . . . well, maybe it wasn't quite as fun to observe when he wasn't involved. He liked watching—the visual aspect of sex was big for him—but somehow, studying her out the window while she rode Ethan to orgasm had just made him feel like some twisted peeping Tom or something. So he'd even pretended to be asleep when they finally finished and came inside.

On the boat had been better. And then on the beach— hell, even better than that. Something had happened to that girl overnight, something inside her had truly opened her up to her darker, dirtier side—and whatever it was, he liked it. A lot.

Now he stood on the trail, watching her. Because he'd followed her. Not in a creepy way, but he'd just been coming around the corner of the cabin, ready to head down to the dock, when he'd spotted her hiking back into the woods. He'd wondered where the hell she was going and if it was even safe. Soon he'd realized she was simply meandering, exploring, and he'd thought about calling out to her, but somehow he hadn't wanted to disturb her. Only he hadn't wanted to turn back, either. He'd wanted to keep going.

She got more beautiful to him every moment. Nope, he wasn't sure what had happened, but finally, *finally*, the animal inside Mira had been set free.

He'd known it was there all along; back when they'd been

together, he'd coaxed it from its tight little cage, at least in ways. But now . . . this was the Mira he'd longed to see, to experience. Hell, if he'd known a threesome would be the thing to turn her nastier side loose, maybe he'd have even considered that back then.

But that didn't matter. What mattered was the realization coursing through his veins. It had been coming on throughout the day, and now it was hitting him in the face, hard, leaving him drawn inextricably like a moth to a flame as he followed her deeper into the forest. Damn.

He wanted Mira.

In a big way. For keeps.

She was his perfect woman.

She'd just *become* his perfect woman—she'd just become everything he could possibly want.

Which pretty much sucked at this point.

Fucking timing. Timing was everything in life.

Five years ago, he'd loved her without fully appreciating her. And she'd been a little timid for his taste, too. He'd loved bringing out her naughtier side in bed, but at the same time, maybe he hadn't liked having to work so hard for it. Maybe he'd wondered, *If I have to work so hard to bring it out of her, is it real? Is it right?*

He'd worried that maybe she just didn't love sex the way he did. For him, being down and dirty with a woman he cared for was about as good as it got; when a woman he loved let herself go completely with him, it not only turned him on but also made him fall in love with her a little bit deeper. Since sex was such a big part of who he was as a person, that was—for him—the ultimate connection.

And so to find out now that Mira could *be* that, could let herself go that much—shit, it just amped up his emotions that much more.

Goddamn it, dude, this isn't right. This isn't what was supposed to happen here. She's with Ethan. They're happy. The guy invited you here trusting you, as a friend. And even if he and Ethan had never been especially close, they *had* gone through that first hostage situation together, and to betray one of his H.O.T. brothers—because that's how he thought of them, as brothers—was fucking unthinkable.

Except that's exactly what you're doing. At least in your head.

And the truth was, he didn't *want* to just keep it in his head anymore.

But you have to. No other choice, dude.

Still watching her as she stood over that old well, everything about her beckoning to him, he ran his hand back through his hair. As wrong as it was to want to wrest her away from Ethan right now, he knew it was equally as wrong to be spying on her like this. Despite himself, maybe he *was* following her in a creepy way now. Shit.

But in another way, he felt . . . powerful. Because of the chemistry that still existed between them, because he could feel it when they fucked. Because she wanted him, too, even if on her part it was still only sex. His groin tightened just remembering today, and just thinking about . . . well, about what he wished could be.

But she belongs to someone else. And standing there so silent, so still, he began to feel a little like a hunter, like she was prey. But he didn't want her to be prey. Not really. He only wanted her to be . . . his. Just his.

And hell, he didn't want to be a stalker; not letting her know he was there was pretty damn ridiculous. So without quite weighing the move or having a plan, he walked forward on the path. He even purposely brushed up against a tree branch sticking out over the trail to make a little noise.

She swung around abruptly, spotting him—but then appeared relieved. "Oh, hey. You startled me a little."

He tried for a smile, but wasn't sure it worked. "Sorry, babe."

"What are you doing out here?" she asked, tilting her head to one side, smiling even as she looked perplexed. He supposed it seemed a little too coincidental.

So he just avoided the question, saying, "Could ask you the same thing."

"I saw the trail and wondered where it led. And look, a well." She motioned to the old stone structure topped with a slanting roof. "Like a wishing well. But I don't have any coins."

He liked that about her, her childlike fascination with

things. It never would have occurred to him to do something so silly as to make a wish—but he liked that she made him think about things like that: wishes, dreams. In response, he dug his hand into the front pocket of his jeans and found a quarter. "Here," he said. "Make your wish."

She smiled as she took the coin, leaving him glad he'd had one. Then he watched as she peered down into the well's darkness, seeming to concentrate very hard, then tossed the coin in. He never heard it hit bottom.

"So what'd you wish?"

She flashed him a look like he must be crazy. "If I tell you the wish, it won't come true, silly." Then she pushed her long hair—still a little damp and getting curly—over her shoulder, giving him an alluring glimpse of her long, slender neck. He wanted to kiss it. "Are you going to make one?"

He tried to look sad as he said, "You took my only coin."

She punched him in the arm, laughing.

"I don't really believe in stuff like that anyway," he told her. "I believe you make your own fate, ya know?"

She shrugged. "I guess. Maybe."

"You impressed the hell out of me today, Mira," he said boldly then. He just needed her to know. And the longer he stood there next to her, the more difficult it became to ignore his newly revived feelings for her. If she looked down to where that quarter had come from, she'd see the bulge behind his zipper starting to grow.

She met his gaze and said, "What do you mean?"

But she knew good and well what he meant. It showed in the slight blush coloring her cheeks even pinker than the sun had. It showed in the eyes that stayed more confident and sure of herself than they would have if he'd said the same thing just yesterday.

Still, he tried to think how to answer, tried to distill all the thoughts and feelings swirling through his brain down to what was most important. And he kept his gaze on her as he spoke, his voice low. "You've always turned me on. Always. In bed and out. But today ... damn, babe." His dick grew harder still. "Today you turned me on more than I knew was possible. You turned me on more than any woman ever has."

And shit—that *wasn't* the most important part. It just *felt* like the most important part at this moment, with his prick aching in his blue jeans, with the woods closing around them dark and shady and lush. And it was the part he could tell her. He was allowed to lust for her this weekend, after all. But saying he wanted her again, in a real, lasting way, that he wanted her *back*—*that* he just couldn't do.

Yet maybe he didn't have to say it—maybe she could read it in his eyes. She'd certainly read *something* there—because that's when her expression turned serious, her mouth gone slack, her eyes glassy, and she looked like a woman who was as ready to be fucked as he was ready to fuck her. They froze that way, like statues in the forest, the only sound that of a bird emitting one lone tweet somewhere in the distance.

His heart beat harder as his chest tightened; his dick pulsed with need. His fingers itched with the urge to touch her.

And that's when she pointed vaguely back in the direction from which they'd come and said, "Ethan's grilling the steaks. We should probably get back." Then she turned to start on her way up the path.

He never made the decision to reach out and grab her wrist, to stop her—he just did it.

She looked up at him, then down at where he touched her. And he knew she felt it, too, just from that. Electricity. Heat. Whatever other problems they'd had, that had never been one of them.

When she peered up at him again, he stepped closer to her, lifted his other hand to skim his knuckles across her cheek, then curl his palm around her neck.

He could hear her breathing; he felt it in his cock.

"Rogan, we can't do this." Her voice was a mere whisper.

"Why not?"

"Because . . . because Ethan's not here. And . . . and . . . I just don't think . . ."

Yeah, he knew that. He'd been invited here to have sex with *them*, not just with her. But he wanted to break the rules so damn bad in that moment that it was easier to pretend there weren't any, that nothing about this was wrong. "That's a good idea," he replied. "Don't think. Just stop thinking." He could hear the low lust in his own voice, his words coming slower than usual. "You always did think too much, Mira. You never just let yourself go and let things happen."

She blinked up at him. "Didn't I? Don't I?"

He nodded. Kept it simple. His mouth was no more than an inch from hers now. "Let this happen. Let me fuck you. Let me bend you over this well and fuck your pretty little brains out."

She never said yes. She never said yes as he circled one arm around her waist and pulled her to him, the crux of her thighs molding to his erection through his jeans. She never said yes before he kissed her, pressing his tongue into her mouth. She never said yes when his free hand rose to cup her breast fully, kneading, caressing, his thumb playing over the taut nipple he could feel even through her top and bra.

But she never said no, either.

Chapter 11

Mira wanted to pull away. She wanted to go running up the path back to Ethan. Because this was . . . this was like cheating on him in a way. Wasn't it? Even if he'd brought Rogan here to have sex with her, he hadn't meant for it to be like *this*, just the two of them, off by themselves in the woods. So yes, this was definitely like cheating. And she couldn't quite believe she was letting it happen. *Who am I? What's happening to me? I have to put a stop to this right now.*

And yet Rogan's kisses threatened to consume her. So did his touch. And—oh Lord—she truly ached for that incredibly hard column of flesh she felt trapped behind his zipper.

With each seductive kiss, she was reminded more and more of what they'd shared, how strong it had been once upon a time. There had been a period during which they couldn't even look at each other without wanting to fall into bed—or do it wherever they happened to be. They didn't always, because sometimes they were in public or maybe they were supposed to be somewhere, but on the occasions they'd fought off the urges, the decision had always been hers. And right now . . . right now, despite herself, despite how much she knew she loved Ethan, despite the utter wrongness of it, she just wasn't sure she had the strength to stop.

And . . . Lord, he'd brought Rogan here. He'd . . . dangled her old love in front of her, telling her she could have him, that he *wanted* her to have him. And she knew he hadn't meant like this, but still . . . it suddenly seemed all too confusing, and what had felt extremely black and white just yesterday had now become a dark and intense shade of gray.

Rogan said nothing more, so she stayed quiet, too.

Because somehow . . . somehow that made surrender easier.

Since, no matter how horrible it was, that's what she felt herself doing—giving in.

But again—oh God, what about Ethan? He's making your birthday dinner right now! How can you possibly . . .

Yet that's when Rogan's hands closed over her ass, firm, and began to knead. And each stretch of his fingers seemed to vibrate all through her. She felt it in her pussy. And she felt it in the tiny orifice up above, in her ass. Where he'd always wanted to fuck her but she'd never let him.

And mmm, God, she couldn't believe how good it felt

right now—the sensation expanded like a rubber band being pulled in all directions, and she felt weak, like the clichéd putty in his hands. All rational thought left her then. All she knew was that her body wanted more, a deeper connection. And that he could give it to her. He could give her everything she wanted right now.

After he nipped at her neck, then ran his teeth down one earlobe, making her shiver, he murmured in her ear. "Goddamn, babe, I need that sweet little pussy wrapped around my hard cock before I lose my fucking mind."

And still she said nothing, nothing at all. *You can still stop this. And you know deep down that you should.* But she'd begun to feel drunk on him, like the world was swirling a little and like the only thing that could save her was being pleasured, fucked, by the man who held her. She'd been brought here for sex, she'd been totally immersed in sex, and now here was *more* sex put before her, pulling her in to its pleasures, and her body remained crazily hungry for it in a way that defied her senses, her ability to reason.

But she knew it wasn't just sex itself luring her. It was Rogan. Rogan had always turned her on, *always*. And maybe he didn't know this if he thought she'd held back in bed—or who knew, maybe he did—but he'd possessed the power to seduce her almost from the moment they'd met. And he still seemed to possess that power now.

When he reached beneath the hem of her top for the

drawstring on her shorts, she looked down, knew still that she should say no. But instead she simply found herself observing, taking it in, like watching a movie where you have no control over what happens on the screen in front of you. *Except you do have control. You can change this. It's just that you want it. You want it to happen now. You need it to happen as badly as you need to breathe.*

She banished that thought, though, as quickly as it came. And she focused on the way her body felt and the things she saw around her—anything to keep from thinking about what was right . . . or about what was wrong. She studied the tattoo on Rogan's arm, which seemed to dance a little as the muscles beneath it shifted. His dark T-shirt stretching across his broad chest, his hands at the waistband of her shorts. Greenery and old leaves on the ground around their shoes. A bruise she'd picked up on her thigh.

And then *her* hands, working at *his* waistband. Undoing the button, pulling down the zipper. Her palm, pressing over the hard ridge just barely contained in another pair of black boxer briefs.

Rogan's low groan bit through the air. She felt it in her gut as it mingled with the sound of her own slow, labored breathing. Her entire body hummed, as if being touched by some sort of electrical prod—until she was reaching out, forcing her fingers inside the front opening on his underwear, wrapping her hand firm and rough around his cock. Oh God, so big in her hand. Like holding on to some kind of power . . . like holding a lightning bolt.

He used one bent finger to lift her chin, make her look at him. "Tell me you want it," he rasped.

She nodded. She could hardly deny it, after all.

But that wasn't good enough. "Tell me," he insisted.

It struck her as cruel in a way—she was trying so hard not to speak, so that maybe later she could talk herself into believing his seductive charms were so great that she hadn't really had a choice, that it had happened before she could stop it. And yet he was forcing her to verbally submit. "I want it," she whispered, her voice barely audible.

His answer was little more than a low growl. *But good. At least he isn't asking any more of me.*

No, instead of asking, he simply maneuvered her shorts down to her thighs.

Then he turned her around to face away from him and said, "Brace yourself on the well."

As she pressed her palms into the old stone, she smelled moss and cool brown earth. She waited as he tugged her shorts farther, until they dropped around her ankles, then she instinctively lifted one foot out so she could part her legs a little.

And she was sure he'd plunge his thick cock into her then—she was dying for it, in fact—but that's when a feather-soft touch came, starting high on the center of her ass and grazing downward—Rogan's fingertip. She sucked in her breath, trying to withstand the almost tickling pleasure.

Only, when he reached her asshole, he lingered. Just like earlier on the little beach. She was forced to bite her lip.

He seemed to be drawing circles around it with that finger, making her crazy, filling her whole body with a frustration she couldn't even quite understand. And then the warmth of his chest curved over her and he whispered in her ear, "Want me to fuck you in the ass, Mira?"

"No," she said quickly, almost harshly. Finally, the right word, the one she should have been saying all along. Only she wasn't saying it for the right reasons.

"It would be . . . mine," he said, his voice deep and smooth as dark velvet. "The one spot on your body that only I would know. I want that, babe. For one little piece of you to belong to *me*. Me alone."

God. It sounded like a dirty little secret. But almost like a *hot, exciting* dirty little secret. She bit her lip once more. Fought off the sensations, the temptation. "No, damn it."

The tip of his finger still flirted with that tiny fissure. "Let me," he said. "Let me show you how good it can feel."

She shut her eyes. Stood her ground. "Not here. Not like this." Okay, she wasn't positive that sounded exactly like *not ever*, which was what she'd *meant* to imply, but at least it was still a refusal.

"Are you sure?" he practically purred, not sounding defeated just yet. And at the same time—oh!—he pushed the tip of his finger into her anus.

She cried out, gritting her teeth, wanting to claw at something to help stave off the strange yet frustrating pleasure. "God," she whimpered. "Yes, damn it, I'm sure."

Behind her he let out a sigh she could feel on her shoulder. "You're just denying us both, babe," he told her.

She turned to look at him, feeling a little desperate, wild, almost angry. "Please stop. You're making me crazy. If you want to fuck me, then fuck me. *Now.*"

Their eyes met and she couldn't quite read his. All she knew for sure was that they were both tangled up in mutual lust at the moment. And the next thing she felt was the head of his cock nudging against her cunt. *Oh God, yes. At last!*

And as he slid it in deep, firm, solid, making her moan, he withdrew his finger from her asshole—but just a second later he pushed another back in! She thought it was his thumb, and the combined sensations had her instantly whimpering and trembling and begging. "Please fuck me, Rogan. Please fuck me. Hard."

And that's exactly what he did. He kept his thumb in place in her ass the whole time, the fingers from the same hand splayed across her ass, his other hand at her hip to keep her balanced. And then he pounded his cock into her over and over, each rough stroke echoing through her like thunder as she bit her lip, trying to keep from crying out in case it echoed through the woods and down to the lake. The pleasure was sublime and complete, stretching from her head to her toes. It required effort to keep standing, especially given how tired her leg muscles already were from earlier exploits—but she managed, withstanding every hot plunge, letting it reverberate all through her, giving herself over to the overwhelming sensation.

He never stopped, never rested, just kept driving and driving and driving that magnificent shaft into her welcoming pussy. Eventually each thrust came with a low grunt, by which time her eyes had fallen shut, her whole being taken over by sex. She could smell that now, too—the ripe aroma of sex now overpowered any scent nature had to offer.

"Aw fuck. I'm gonna come," he muttered—and for a brief burst of time he rammed into her wetness even harder, almost violently, and it was all she could do to absorb what he delivered, the tender skin on her palms being pressed more roughly into the stone she held on to. He growled his orgasm behind her—his final thrusts jolting her again, again, again—and when it was done, together they sank to their knees in the dirt next to the wishing well.

They stayed that way a long moment, Mira leaning forward to rest her head against the cool stone. He was still inside her, although he'd removed his thumb from her ass—she'd felt it leave and missed it when it was gone.

"I didn't make you come," he finally breathed against her shoulder.

"I don't care." She meant it. Not because she wasn't still suffering frustration—mainly from the anal play—but because now that it was over, she was *thinking* again, and she had much bigger things on her mind.

She'd gotten this magical new gift of freedom—but was it too much? Had it just led her down a dark, dangerous road? This sense of sexual liberation had seemed good, healthy, earlier today—yet maybe it wasn't. Maybe a little restraint was a healthy thing, a smart thing. Ethan had *given* her this glorious freedom from a place of generosity and wanting to bring them closer, yet now it had made her do something that would wound him if he knew.

"How can you not care?" Rogan finally asked, clearly still stuck on the idea of orgasm.

She began to separate their bodies, his cock leaving her as he placed his hands on his hips to help her rise upright onto her knees. As she maneuvered her shorts back on, still facing away from him, she said, "I can't believe we did this." Her own voice sounded hollow to her.

"It's not that big of a deal," he argued. And that sounded like a typical thing Rogan might say, yet . . . she heard something in his voice just then, a tiny little catch when he'd spoken, that made her almost . . . not quite believe him.

She turned around, lowered her butt to the ground. He

was sitting now, too, though his pants remained undone. "It *is* a big deal," she said.

He tilted his head, eyes half-shut, the set of his mouth grim. "What does it matter? Who did it hurt? It was just . . . a fuck. Just old animal attraction that didn't mean anything."

But she watched his eyes as he spoke, and she knew for sure now that she saw something more in his gaze, more than his words or voice relayed. "You're lying," she said. She was that confident about it.

"What?" he asked, dark brows knitting

"It's . . . more than that, more than old animal attraction. That was more than just a fuck, Rogan, and you know it."

They just looked at each other for a long, quiet moment in the shade of the green canopy overhead, the air around them growing darker as time passed and the night grew nearer.

"Say something," she finally demanded.

And he let out a sigh. "Okay," he said, sounding irritated. "Maybe you're right. Maybe I'm having some old feelings for you. Only they feel . . . new. Happy now?"

A big whooshing breath left her. As if she hadn't felt weak *enough* a minute ago. "No, I'm not happy at all. Rogan, you can't . . . have those kinds of feelings for me! You have to stop it. And you certainly have to stop acting on it. Right now."

Facing her, he gave a nod, appearing sure, like a man in full agreement. "I know."

For God's sake, how had this happened? Rogan had feelings for her again? And . . . and had she ever *really* given up all her feelings for *him*? She'd thought she had. He'd been the one to break things off, after all. She'd wanted more than he could give her. And she knew Ethan was the right man for her now, of course—she knew that to the marrow of her bones. But . . . just to hear Rogan say that, that he was having feelings for her—it shook her inside. To the core. She wasn't ready for this.

"We need to go," she said. "I'm sure dinner is ready by now. We've been gone too long." And Lord, remembering that was enough to panic her even without the news Rogan had just shared. They had to go eat dinner with Ethan. They had to pretend they hadn't just had rough, animalistic sex in the woods. She had to act like Ethan was the only man alive who truly moved her.

Though as she pushed abruptly to her feet and began to brush off the back of her shorts, praying she didn't look too disheveled, her guilt almost mingled with a sense of anger at Ethan. This was all his fault, after all. If he'd never brought Rogan here, the last half hour wouldn't have happened. Everything would be fine. But suddenly nothing felt fine at all.

"I know," Rogan said again. Just that.

Then he stood, too—but she was tired of waiting, tired of feeling like they'd suddenly become some sort of couple again, so she simply said, "Come on," and started to march away, back up the path that had led to this.

And just like the last time she'd tried to do that, he reached out and grabbed her arm.

Shit, what now?

She stopped, darted her gaze up to his. "What is it? We have to go."

"You're happy with him, right?" he asked.

Damn it. For some reason, the question nearly stole her breath. "Yes." She'd thought they were done discussing this. She'd *wanted* to be done. Desperately. She didn't want to go down this road.

And that's when he said, slowly, and more softly than she'd remembered he could speak, "I'm glad you're happy, Mira."

Oh Lord, when was the last time she'd heard Rogan sound so earnest, so . . . almost gentle?

"But . . . if you weren't . . ."

She held her breath. "Yeah?"

Then saw him swallow visibly before he replied. "Look, I know I bailed on you before, back when we broke up. But if we ever got together again, babe, I think I could make you happy. Really happy. The way you wanted back then."

It felt as if her heart dropped to her stomach. She'd never been so taken aback by anything Rogan had ever said to her. He wasn't . . . this guy. He just wasn't. She'd wanted him to be. But she'd finally figured out that you couldn't change someone.

So . . . how the hell was it possible that he was saying this? She tried not to let the depth of her reaction show on her face. And besides, she was still pissed about what had just happened between them. "What? You're suddenly Mr. Settle Down and Commit?"

He met her gaze and looked . . . like he didn't quite know himself, didn't quite know who he was in this moment. "I'm suddenly . . . Mr. I Realized I Was a Fool to Ever Let You Go."

"Oh," she heard herself say, even more shell-shocked now. And she wasn't sure there was any hiding it at this point. Then she whispered, "Seriously?"

"Seriously."

She stayed silent, her head rushing with thoughts. She'd once loved him so much. Their chemistry had been electric and it still was. He'd been the uncatchable guy, the bad boy every girl wants and can't quite have. Oh, it had been good for a while—it had been amazing—but she still remembered with clarity the night they'd fought in his car outside her apartment. She'd seen him flirting with another girl and called him on it. And things had been heading south for weeks by that time anyway. She'd just hoped against hope that he would see her point of view, feel bad, apologize, love her the way she loved him.

Instead, he'd just kept staring at the steering wheel, not saying anything, and she'd felt him slipping away, bit by bit, long before he'd finally said, "Maybe this thing between us has run its course."

"What?" she'd asked, feeling as if he'd just stabbed her in the heart. Yes, she'd known it was coming, but hearing it was something else entirely.

"Look, you just want this to be a more serious thing than I do. I don't want to feel tied to you every second."

God, that had stung. Because for a while, it *had* been a serious thing; for a while they'd been glued at the hip and he hadn't been able to get enough of her, and suddenly he was acting like that had never happened, like she'd never been that big a deal to him at all.

They'd talked a little more, but he hadn't really said much else. And finally, just to clarify, she'd said, "So you're breaking up with me. We're done. Am I hearing that right?"

"I guess," he'd said.

And she'd stormed at him, "You guess? It's a yes-or-no question, Rogan. Are we done?"

And he'd simply said, "Yeah."

And now—now, after all that and so much time had passed—he was saying she could have him?

On a gut level, she couldn't deny that it felt exciting and magical, like the impossible dream come true, the happy ending of a movie.

But . . . what was she thinking? She loved Ethan. Ethan loved her.

And he was solid and predictable and dependable. And damn sexy, too.

And he'd just cooked her a birthday dinner and blown up lavender balloons and he never even looked at other women and he wanted nothing more than to make her happy. Yes, they'd had their problems, but that seemed to be in the past. It would be . . . beyond foolish to even *think* about giving up what she had with him.

And as for Rogan . . . how dependable was he? Could she trust what he was saying here even if she wanted to? He'd once had no qualms about hurting her, after all. And though she'd eventually forgiven him and moved on, he hadn't done it very gently, either.

"I'm sorry, Rogan," she simply said now, stalwart. And then she started away again, up the path.

She wanted to run—she wanted to run away from this whole situation—but she made herself keep a steady pace. Even if he knew she'd been affected by this, she still didn't have to let him know how much.

"Mira," he said.

And one more time, she looked back. But more distance lay between them than the last two times he'd stopped her, thank goodness. She was finally starting to get away from him, finally starting to head back where she belonged.

"I'm sorry I said anything, okay? Forget I did. I don't want to ruin anything for you here, and this . . ." He stopped, shook his head. "This was all spur of the moment and doesn't mean anything. Just old feelings, like I said. But I'll get over it. So . . . don't feel like you have to worry about this now, all right?"

She bit her lip. "I'm . . . not worried," she lied.

"So you're not gonna rush back and tell Ethan? Because . . . we might not be the *best* of friends, but he *is* my friend and I feel like shit about this."

"Nothing to be concerned about—I'll keep it between me and you."

"And you're not gonna declare the party over, tell me I have to leave?"

Hmm, that was a good question. "I probably should."

"But you won't." Now he sounded like the old Rogan again. In the blink of an eye.

"You sound so sure."

He tilted his head, and even in the dim, shady light, his eyes sparkled. "You're liking this, having both of us. You're not ready for it to be over yet."

And at that, she just turned and walked away.

Chapter 12

She tried to act cool, not too rushed, as she made her way down to the dock. But the fact was, she remained shaken. To her core. Not the least of which was because hearing Rogan tell her that what he'd just said, what they'd just done, didn't mean anything...somehow told her the opposite. Maybe it was the look in his eyes when he'd said it. Maybe it was the tone of his voice. But whereas a minute before she'd been questioning his sincerity, his dependability, now she knew with her whole heart that he'd really been serious; he really wanted her back.

And now, with that mind-numbing news fresh on her brain, she had to face Ethan after what she'd just done. Oh God.

"Damn—about time," Ethan said, looking up.

She could smell the steaks and craned her neck to see if

they were still on the grill. She had no idea how long she'd been gone. "Sorry. I hope I didn't ruin anything."

"Nope, birthday girl, just getting ready to take them up right now. But I was getting worried."

Stepping up beside him, she felt the need to rise on her tiptoes and give him a quick kiss, a kiss of silent apology—although he appeared focused on spearing the three New York strips with a long, two-pronged fork and getting them onto a platter. "So what'd you find back on the trail? Anything?"

Oh God. Rogan. Lust. Sex. Old feelings. "A wishing well," she said.

He looked up. "Really? Cool."

She nodded. "So I guess I just . . . lost track of time looking at it."

"Did you make a wish?"

"Yeah. But don't ask me for what or it won't come true." Her voice came out sounding calm, but her heart still beat too hard in her chest.

And as Ethan gave her a grin, she thought back to that moment, that wish. *A love that will last the rest of my life.* Suddenly, though, now the wish seemed to border on absurd. To wish that and then fuck another man two minutes later—what had she been thinking?

Or . . . no. Surely fate wasn't trying to tell her *Rogan* was the man she was supposed to be making that wish about! She hadn't actually named a specific man in the wish—but she'd just assumed the kind of love she was talking about would be shared with Ethan. And she still believed that. Because that was the only thing that made sense. Wasn't it?

Just then, the sound of the cabin's screen door slamming made them both flinch and look up to see Rogan meandering down the stone steps. Mira's heart began to beat a little faster.

"Hey," he said a moment later, greeting Ethan easily as he walked onto the dock, then switched his gaze to Mira. "Happy birthday, babe," he said, then placed one hand casually at her waist as he leaned in to kiss her on the cheek. She had to hand it to him—he was good. She'd never suspect the two of them had just rutted like wild animals a few minutes ago. And, God help her, she felt his touch more than she usually would have.

"It's been my birthday all day," she pointed out, trying to act as normal as him.

"Yeah, but this is the, uh, official celebration."

"Where ya been?" Ethan asked easily.

"Took a walk," he said. "Then . . . fell asleep in the cabin for a little while. Sorry if I'm late or anything."

"Nah," Ethan replied. "Just hadn't seen you in a while. Here, take these to the table." He handed the platter of steaks to Rogan, then went about removing baked potatoes and corn on the cob from the grill, too, all of them wrapped in foil.

"Everything smells great," she told him. "Thanks for going to so much trouble."

He smiled down at her. "It wasn't that much trouble. And I just wanted to . . . you know . . . show you I care. Make it a little bit special."

"*You're* special," she told him, then stepped up close to him, looped her arms around his neck, and lifted on her toes again to give him a sexy, lingering kiss even as he held the big plate of corn and potatoes out to one side.

The only problem was—Mira wasn't sure if that kiss had been for *his* benefit, for hers, or for Rogan's.

They hadn't brought down the birthday cake or gifts from the cabin, and by the time they'd finished a leisurely dinner and a bottle of wine, the air had cooled, making them decide to head indoors for the rest of the party. It was mostly dark out anyway. Mira insisted on bringing the balloons in with them so she could keep enjoying them, though she was aware the wine might have influenced that decision.

"Presents or cake first?" Ethan asked as she tied her balloons to an old-fashioned sconce on the wall.

And though she knew it was generally cake, then presents, she decided to take advantage of the question—and her slight intoxication—and said, "Presents."

With that, Ethan reached into a shopping bag behind

him and pulled out a prettily wrapped gift complete with a lavender ribbon. She smiled upon recognizing the wrapping paper from her favorite lingerie store. Meanwhile, Rogan walked across the room, stooping down to a leather duffel bag by the couch and returning a moment later with a smaller, thinner box that she might expect to contain jewelry. Except that Rogan had *never* bought her jewelry. Ironically, she would find it more likely that Ethan would give her jewelry and that Rogan would choose lingerie. *Lord, everything is beginning to feel very mixed-up here.*

She still wished she'd resisted Rogan's seduction in the woods. She still wished he'd never said those things to her, and she certainly wished she hadn't felt them, hadn't felt that strange pull toward the past, toward those old feelings for him. Slowly but surely she was beginning to realize that his being here was a double-edged sword. So very scintillating and satisfying in some ways—yet potentially devastating in others.

But wait—what was she thinking? No, it *wasn't* devastating, because she wouldn't allow it to be. Hadn't she come skittering down to the dock eager to see Ethan, eager to put her wishing well encounter with Rogan behind her? Hadn't she realized immediately afterward that Ethan was still the man for her and that Rogan's blustery claims of wishing he'd never let her go didn't count for anything?

She supposed it was only natural that she was still trying

to get it out of her system, though, and now she resolved to concentrate only on what was happening at this very moment. This was her birthday party, after all, and she wanted to have a good time. "Can you open another bottle of wine?" she suggested to Ethan. Wine would help her focus on now more than the troubling memories from a couple of hours ago.

"Sure," he said, departing from the kitchen table where she sat with her unopened gifts before her. Grabbing a chilled bottle from the fridge and uncorking it, he poured fresh glasses for all of them while Rogan turned on the radio. After trying to find a different station than the retro one they'd listened to last night, Rogan announced it was the only one that would come in.

"That's okay," she said, recognizing a Def Leppard song. "I *like* a lot of the older stuff."

"Any other songs that make you dance on tabletops?" Rogan asked, sending a playful, friendly wink her way. It felt like . . . making peace.

So she couldn't help smiling, meeting his gaze. Maybe this thing between them would calm down now—maybe it would all be okay. "Nope, only the one," she told him, and he snapped his fingers in mock disappointment.

Once they were all settled around the table, Mira picked up Ethan's gift. The truth was, she was more curious about Rogan's, but it seemed somehow . . . important to open Ethan's first, to make him her top priority.

Untying the pretty lavender ribbon, she quietly removed the wrapping, pulled out the small box, and took off the lid. Nestled in pink pastel tissue paper, she found a gorgeous lavender bra and panty set—part intricate lace, part chiffon-looking fabric—that struck her as classy and expensive. She smiled up at her boyfriend. "Pretty," she said.

"Glad you like it," he replied, yet his expression held a bit of mischief as he added, "though you might want to take a close look, since there might be a little more to the bra and panties than you think at a glance. Or maybe I should say . . . less."

She had no idea what he meant until she picked up the undies, examining an elaborate lace butterfly at the center of the front panel—and realized they were crotchless. The butterfly's lower wings separated at the top of the opening. "Oh!" she said, taken aback.

Rogan just laughed, and Ethan said, "Hope you still like 'em. I mean, I know this makes it . . . not quite the same kind of gift."

But she just smiled. Yes, maybe crotchless panties weren't quite the classiest form of lingerie, yet the way she looked at it . . . "They're perfect for this weekend, and I'm sure we'll get plenty of use from them afterward, too."

Then she plucked up the bra and started checking it out, as well, soon realizing that the cups were so small that . . . they weren't really cups. They were more like . . . curving shelves that would hold her breasts up and frame them but leave her nipples freely exposed. "Wow," Rogan said, apparently taking in the same thing. "That's hot."

She spared him only a glance, bit her lip, and tried like hell to do what he'd said when they'd parted ways in the woods—forget he'd said anything about his feelings. That was the only way she was going to get through the rest of this weekend unscathed.

"Of course," Ethan said, half-sheepish, half-amused, "guess you could say this is more like a gift for me than a gift for you, but..."

"But I like looking sexy," she told him, which was the truth. "And feeling sexy. And these will definitely make me feel sexy."

Their gazes met warmly and he said, "Well, I'm glad you like 'em, baby." Then he leaned over to give her a soft kiss that ran all way through her like hot liquid. Thank God. That was all it took to remind her how crazy she was about him, and how much he still aroused her, that easily. "And just so you know, that's not your only present. It's just the one I didn't want to give you at your sister's tomorrow night."

"Good decision," she said on a light laugh.

Then she picked up Rogan's gift. She could see he'd wrapped it himself, and though it wasn't as tidy as the present she'd just opened, she liked the idea of that. Although it hit her then that... "You didn't have to get me anything. I mean, other than a little small talk, we haven't exactly been in close touch for a while."

"Well, after this weekend, I think it's safe to say we're back in touch."

She smiled in reply, even as a light blush warmed her cheeks. Yes, she was all free and sexually liberated now, but it was still new, and at moments the reality of it continued to surprise her.

"And besides," he added, "it's something I wanted to give you."

Hmm. Somehow that upped the stakes here. Until this moment, she'd imagined him just deciding a gift was appropriate and then having to go out and find something. She'd even, for a second, wondered from the shape of the box if it might be something totally shocking like a vibrator, because she knew from their past that Rogan liked sex toys. But now she no longer thought that was the case and felt almost uneasy as she removed the purple stick-on bow and slowly tore into the printed paper he'd used.

Removing the long box's lid a moment later, she found— whoa—a memory from her past that she'd forgotten about.

"I don't know if you remember, but it's the coral anklet you picked out in Key West."

"Yeah, I remember," she said, trying not to look too stunned.

It was the only trip she and Rogan had ever taken

together—they'd spent a couple of days in Miami visiting Colt, the H.O.T. member Rogan had mentioned last night, and then they'd driven to Key West for a weekend before flying home. She'd spotted the ankle bracelet on a street vendor's table on Duvall Street—the tiny pieces of peach and orange strung coral had struck her as delicate, sexy, and a little exotic all at the same time. It had been a bit pricy, but she could still recall Rogan winking at her as he said, "Be a good little girl and maybe Santa will leave it in your stocking." It had been October at the time, and she'd actually thought about the piece of jewelry for the rest of the trip, hoping perhaps Rogan had gone back to buy it for her. But then they'd broken up by Thanksgiving and she'd forgotten all about the anklet.

"I went back for it later, when you were taking a nap," he said. "I was gonna make it a Christmas present. But I never got to give it to you."

She drew her gaze from the ankle bracelet to glance over at him. "And you kept it all this time?"

"What was I gonna do with it?"

She tilted her head, tried to be light as she suggested, "Give it to some other girl?"

But Rogan just shrugged. "It was yours."

She said nothing, simply looked back down at the coral. "Well, thank you. It's as pretty as I remember."

When Ethan leaned over to look then, she held the box

out to show him, hoping he didn't feel overshadowed by the fact that Rogan's gift had . . . history to it, and that it was . . . well, sort of special. It touched her to finally find out he *had* gone to the trouble of going back for the anklet, and also to know he'd kept it all this time, for more than four years, when it would have been very easy to give it to someone else.

"That's nice," Ethan said of the piece, and he sounded fine about it. She *hoped* he was fine about it.

"Put it on me?" she asked. But then, was that weird? Asking her *current* boyfriend to put a piece of jewelry on her given to her by her *ex*-boyfriend? Yet when she remembered why they were all here together, she decided no, it wasn't weird at all. It even almost made a twisted sort of sense.

Ethan didn't hesitate to pick up the string of coral as she shifted her chair back from the table in order to lift her foot onto his thigh. Slipping it around her ankle, he hooked it, then slid his palm provocatively up her leg. She bit her lip as the pleasure rose higher, all the way up. Damn, apparently it took more than guilt, worry, and inappropriate sex with Rogan to quell her desires on this particularly lusty day of her life.

"Ready for cake?" he asked.

"Oh. Yeah. Cake," she replied softly. She'd pretty much forgotten all about it at this point.

And Ethan lowered his chin and cast a small grin, seeming to catch on to her mood. "We could always *skip* the cake if you want."

But she bit her lip. "No, I definitely want the cake." Both guys knew she loved cheesecake yet tried not to indulge too often, and despite everything else occupying her mind, she'd actually looked forward to it.

"All right then," Ethan said. "Cake. Then more ... presents, I guess you could say."

Rogan chuckled and replied, "This weekend has given that word new meaning."

Then he pushed to his feet and went to the fridge to get out the cheesecake, and Ethan got up, too, returning a moment later with small plates, forks, and a knife. When Rogan brought the cheesecake to the table, he'd poked two large candles in it—one in the shape of a three, the other a two. "I thought this made more sense than trying to jab thirty-two candles into a cheesecake."

"I agree," she said. "I'm not sure cheesecake is sturdy enough for that."

Meanwhile, Ethan found matches in a kitchen drawer and lit the candles.

When she leaned over the cake, ready to blow them out, he said, "Wait," then turned off the main light in the large space, leaving it lit by only a smaller one above the kitchen sink and allowing the candles to cast a soft, golden glow over the scene. "There," he said.

"Happy birthday, babe," Rogan told her.

"Yeah, happy birthday, honey. Make a wish."

Mira looked up at the two men who now stood on the opposite side of the table from where she sat. This was her second wish of the day, and the first one, at the wishing well, had ended up feeling more complicated than she'd intended—so maybe it was the wine influencing her, but she decided to keep this one simple. *I wish for more amazingly hot sex tonight. I want more of this astounding pleasure that takes away everything else, every thought, every worry.* Rogan had been right earlier—she wasn't ready to be done with this yet.

She blew out the candles, and as the room grew a little more shadowy, she couldn't help thinking what an extraordinary birthday this had turned out to be. *And it's not over yet.* Wow. In a way, that was hard to believe—yet in another, she felt as if, by accepting Ethan's birthday surprise, she had started down some very fast track on which she had no choice but to pick up more and more momentum until she reached the end of the road. It was out of her control now. And life was nothing if not an adventure. An adventure in which . . . well, in which maybe she hadn't felt very adventurous in a while. So she would just see this through, ride this out until its end, and *enjoy* the ride—every bit of it.

Mira took on cheesecake-cutting duty without being asked, knowing she had a better shot of getting three slices onto plates without demolishing the poor thing, even while a little intoxicated, than either of her two playmates. A minute later they dug in, and maybe it was just the floaty-good feeling in her head, but she couldn't help thinking that the pinot grigio and cheesecake made a fun combination. As they ate, they all discussed how good the cheesecake was, as well as a general love for the Bridge Street bakery Rogan had picked it up from.

And then the plates were empty and the lights were still low and an old band, Exile, sang a rather seductive song called "Kiss You All Over" on the radio—and Rogan changed the mood by saying, "You gonna model that for us?" He pointed to the box containing the naughty lingerie from Ethan.

She just grinned. And felt a little wicked inside. "I . . . suppose I could. If you want to see."

"That's why I gave it to ya, baby," Ethan said, just as Rogan replied, "Of course we want to see."

So after one more sip of wine, she stood up, plucked the two pieces of lace and chiffon from the tissue paper, and walked toward the bathroom.

Her limbs felt almost liquid as she stripped off her shorts and top, her undies and bra, and slipped on the crotchless panties and lavender shelf bra, hooking it in back, then putting her arms through the straps and adjusting the garment until it held up her boobs to make them look plumper, rounder, and perkier than usual. She tilted her head as she peered in the mirror, liking the tightness of the lingerie. The wide opening down the center of the thong seemed to almost circle her pussy, hold it in a way that made her *aware* of it simply by having it on. And the bra was snug, the straps taut, also somehow stimulating her by its mere presence on her body.

She'd worn plenty of pretty lingerie in her adult life. But this, with its combination of lace and missing parts, was both pretty . . . and dirty. Sweet and sinful. And she enjoyed feeling both ways at one time. In fact, she realized, everything about this weekend had, in ways, accomplished that already, so these particular bits of lingerie, again, seemed all too fitting.

Stealing one last glimpse of her sexed-up self reflected in the mirror, she took a deep breath, ready to face whatever the evening held, then opened the door and walked out, padding across the cabin's old hardwood floor until she stood before Ethan and Rogan, both still seated at the table.

It dawned on her then that she didn't really know how to model something, how to be sexy in that way, so she offered up a simple, "Ta-da," and struck what she hoped was a cute pose, pointing one toe next to her other foot as she held her hands out in the manner of a girl presenting a fabulous showcase on *The Price Is Right*.

"Jesus," Rogan murmured, voice as low as she'd ever heard it.

"Damn, honey," Ethan said. "You look . . . absolutely amazing."

She bit her lip, put on a slightly bashful air. "Glad you like," she said softly.

"By which he means 'fuckable,'" Rogan added. "You look absolutely, amazingly fuckable, babe."

She just let out a breath. Waited for something to happen—but it didn't. For some reason they were waiting for *her* to make the next move. So she said, "Then I guess you should. Fuck me, I mean."

"I guess we should," Ethan echoed gently.

And then Rogan said, as if suddenly deciding to take control, "Stand up on the chair." After which he got to his feet and motioned to the same chair beside the kitchen table where she'd been sitting before.

"Why?" she asked, casting a soft, uncertain smile.

And though he returned the smile, his was much more . . . sure. "Just trust me."

"Um, okay," she said. And she did trust him—in terms of making her feel good, she trusted them both. So she gave Rogan her hand when he offered his and let him help her step up onto the chair.

She immediately felt a bit self-conscious looking down on them, maybe partially because of what she was wearing—but at the same time she had the sense of being . . . kind of powerful. She'd experienced that feeling at other points today, too, but right now, as they both peered up at her, she thought it was because she felt like . . . the center of the universe. The center of *their* universe. At this moment anyway. And not only sexually now, but also because . . . yeah, she might be trying not to think about this, not to feel it—but because she knew they both loved her.

Of course, maybe it was too bold to call Rogan's emotions for her love.

Yet there were a lot of different *kinds* of love, different levels, that everyone experienced in their own unique way, and she believed with her whole heart that Rogan had indeed loved her once upon a time—so it didn't seem like such a fantastic stretch to think he might love her now, too. Again. Or still.

Whatever the case, the look he wore now was the same as out in the woods—it was feral, filled with a slow and intense heat but also laced with something that went deeper, something that made the animal lust . . . hold meaning, something that gave it substance.

And so as she stood on the small kitchen chair in her revealing new lingerie between her two lovers, she recognized something she hadn't before: a strange pull between them, a silent little game of tug-of-war. Each of them wanting her to experience the pleasure they could both deliver, but each also ultimately wanting her for himself.

It changed everything.

For the worse. Because now, whatever sex they shared from this point forward would be colored with the same tension Rogan had heaped on her in the forest even as he'd filled her with his hard cock. She would feel a little torn, maybe confused.

But it also changed things for the better. Because as much as she didn't want any conflict, any confusion—at the same time, what woman didn't wish to be desired? Not just sexually but for her whole self? And to be desired that way by two men she'd loved and cared for . . . well, of every idea and physical sensation she'd found overwhelming since this party had begun, this felt like the ultimate. To know the two men who would fuck her tonight also wanted her in deeper ways, wanted her for keeps.

"I want some more cheesecake," Rogan said, even as he peered up at her, his eyes dark with intent. "But I want *you* at the same time."

And with that, he reached toward the table, dipped his finger into the remaining half of the cheesecake, then turned to smudge it directly onto her nipple. She sucked in her breath at the unexpectedness of it, the creamy goo cool and moist on her sensitive skin. Then he repeated the motion, dabbing more onto her other breast.

"One for me, one for Ethan," he told her.

When Rogan flicked a quick glance in Ethan's direction, it pulled Mira's attention there, as well. Her boyfriend had stayed quiet for the past few moments, but now he appeared completely transfixed by the little game that had just begun between them.

And then it struck her: What else did you do at birthday parties besides eat cake and open presents? You played games. And it appeared that portion of tonight's party was starting in an unexpected way.

But maybe the most interesting part to Mira was the strange sensation that now, she had no idea who would win.

Chapter 13

Her pussy spasmed as both men stepped forward at the same time. Her height on the chair was just above what would have been ideal for this, but it was close enough, making it so that Ethan and Rogan had to raise their chins and look up in order to lick the cheesecake from her tits. And peering down on them—and oh God, absorbing the feel of their mouths on her, there, at the same time—was positively scintillating.

Neither rushed the act, making slow, thorough work of it that echoed through her breasts and outward, like little star-bursts exploding inside her and then slowly sparkling away. A well-pleasured sigh left her as she found herself threading her hands through both men's hair, not only to keep her balance—the sensations made her a little unsteady—but because looking down and seeing them each working over one breast again gave her a sense of power, a sense of being the center of them, and she wanted to bask in that, hold them there for a moment, let them know how much she *liked* them there.

When finally they both backed off, leaving her nipples and the surrounding flesh sticky and shiny, Rogan again reached behind him to dab new blobs of cheesecake onto each of her breasts. She drew in her breath, watching as her two men resumed carefully licking the soft, cheesy mix away, then sucking firmly, deeply, on the pink nipples—darkened and fully engorged. It struck her then that for all the wild sex she'd shared with them in the last twenty-four hours, there hadn't been many times when she'd been able to see them both side-by-side, pleasuring her together—at least not since she'd fully embraced all of this—and watching them both suck her tits turned her on all the more.

After her breasts had been very thoroughly cleaned of cheesecake a second time, Rogan placed his hands at her hips and said, "Hold on to my shoulders, babe," then smoothly lowered her to the floor. After which he instructed, "Sit down," pointing to the chair she'd just stood on.

She found herself in that moment looking to Ethan. Rogan had somehow taken control here, his voice low but brimming with authority as surely as if someone had appointed him boss, and she felt the need to make sure his commands were okay with Ethan. Especially after what had happened earlier in the woods. She had to remember Ethan was the one who'd thrown this party; he was the one she had to thank for all this phenomenal ecstasy.

But Ethan just gave her a quick, barely perceptible nod, so apparently he didn't feel threatened by Rogan taking over.

Okay, good. Because the truth was . . . she liked it. She liked the trading off of authority. Ever since last night, she'd felt almost as if they passed it around among the three of them—sometimes Ethan guided them, sometimes it was her, and at other moments Rogan took over. And she'd always found Rogan's dominant side particularly arousing, so it suited her fine right now.

The second she sat down, he said, "Spread your legs so we can see that hot little cunt."

She did, still rather enjoying the way it felt to be wearing panties but at the same time putting her pussy on blatant display. As Ethan and Rogan took in the sight, she found herself glancing down as well, and as she'd noticed before, the butterfly on the crotchless thong seemed to be spreading its wings to reveal the pink folds of her open slit. And *open* her flesh definitely was—not just from parting her legs, but because she was excited and swollen there. She thought it looked almost as if the butterfly rested on a blooming flower of female flesh.

"Damn," Ethan murmured—the first word he'd said in a while. But it heated her skin even more to know he was as turned on as Rogan.

Rogan's dark eyes settled on her pussy, as well, and having their hungry gazes on her caused that part of her body to practically weep with want. A want that Rogan wasted no time in satisfying.

Turning back to the messy cheesecake, he scooped up a whole handful, dropped to his knees between her legs, and smeared it down the center of her cunt like someone applying stucco on a wall. It felt sticky and cool for the second it was there before he leaned in to begin licking and eating it away.

A jagged sigh left her, then a small whimper, as the pleasure vibrated in waves through her body. Her breasts felt swollen, the lavender fabric that framed them growing tighter, snugger than before. She held on to the seat of the chair with both hands. "God," she whispered, her voice thready. "Oh . . . oh God."

As she watched Rogan literally eat her pussy, his hands pressed firmly to her inner thighs as if he feared she might try to close her legs at any moment, she began to sink into the pleasure still deeper, giving herself over to it. And at the same time, she grew aware of wanting more.

She'd been watching Rogan the whole time—oh Lord, he'd just sucked the cheesecake off her clit and now ran his tongue in small circles around it—but something, maybe that desire for more, made her lift her gaze to Ethan. Their eyes met darkly, but she didn't let hers linger there for long—

instead she found them descending to his khaki shorts, wondering if he was hard.

She pulled in her breath—both as a response to Rogan's ministrations and the fact that, mmm, Ethan's dick indeed made a tent, even in the loose-fitting shorts.

"E," she beckoned him, her voice perhaps silkier than she'd ever heard it, "Maybe *I* want some more cheesecake, too. Will you put some on your cock and feed it to me?"

She heard his heated exhale. His cheeks appeared lightly flushed. He said nothing in reply—just responded by ripping his T-shirt off over his head, then unzipping his shorts and letting them drop.

She grew still more excited seeing how big his erection looked in his white boxer briefs, even forcing the elastic out from his waist. Kicking off his shoes as he stepped free of the shorts, he then shoved down his underwear, as well, finally putting that hard and handsome cock on display. She heard an *mmm* waft through the room and realized it had come from *her*.

Down below, Rogan still licked her, and within her the pleasure spread and the hot tension rose higher and higher. Oh God, she might come soon.

But just then, he backed off.

And she let out a breath, her cunt feeling abandoned.

Yet that's when she realized he only wanted more cheesecake. Okay. And thank God. She still felt impatient, though, as he smeared more of the mushy dessert into her swollen folds—until finally he sank his mouth back onto her again. *Yes.*

And then—*oh God, yes, yes, yes*—there was Ethan, using *his* fingers to smudge still more of her birthday cake onto his erection, struggling a little to make it stay, but then holding the shaft down level and turning back toward her. By which time she'd never felt more ravenous in her life.

"Open wide," he said.

And she couldn't help thinking everything about him looked utterly delicious in that moment—not just his cheesecake-covered cock, but his entire body from head to toe.

Turning to face him, she found that lovely erection at the perfect height for her mouth. And peering up at him, she did exactly as he'd instructed, opening as wide as she could.

Cradling his hardened length in his palm, he leaned in, positioned the rounded tip at her parted lips, and then slowly fed it into her waiting mouth, inch by thick inch.

The taste of the creamy cheesecake filled her senses, and the combination of having two things she loved so much in her mouth at the same time felt like an explosion of pleasure on her tongue. She heard herself moaning around the shaft that moved in and out now and—oh God—for a few insanely hot and perfect minutes, her delight was so complete that she nearly forgot where she was, forgot what was happening, as she simply let all the sensations assaulting her spread through her body like hot flowing lava.

Below, Rogan's ministrations were making her wild—she fucked his mouth vigorously now even as Ethan fucked hers. She didn't think about if she was undulating against him too hard, if he liked it or didn't like it. She was consumed now by her own pleasure, and—mmm—by the mounting need to come.

And oh Lord, it was getting so, so close. She whimpered around Ethan's rock-solid erection as it filled the confines of her mouth, as he thrust gently but firmly toward her throat. She drove her hotly swollen pussy toward Rogan's face, and—yes—he sucked her clit and the surrounding flesh, pulling on it again, again.

"Oh—oh God!" she yelled, releasing Ethan's cock from her lips as the orgasm crashed through her. It came jagged and rough, jerking her body even as her hands remained clamped tight on the wooden chair below her. She cried out over and over as the hot pulses shook her, claiming control of her entire being for those few long, outrageous seconds. Oh, what a climax!

And then it was fading and she was suddenly going limp, slumping over, barely able to keep upright. Maybe it was the combined exertions of the day or maybe it was the power of that hot, hard orgasm, but whatever the reason—Lord, she felt utterly spent.

"Help me lay her back on the table," she heard Rogan say then.

And she just blinked. Jesus God—more?

Of course, a few minutes ago, she'd *wanted* more, *craved* more—but now she longed for rest.

And still she felt both men leading her to her feet, turning her around, and lifting her ass onto the table. She grew vaguely aware of Rogan pushing aside plates and what remained of their dessert—though she was *more* cognizant of Ethan locking the fingers of both his hands through hers, meeting her gaze, and pushing her to her back as Rogan had instructed. And somehow, even as exhausted as she was, the heat in her boyfriend's eyes somehow reassured her, brought her back to life inside. *Remember: This is the one and only time you get to do this. It all ends tomorrow, so grab more of it now.*

"I know you're tired, babe," Rogan murmured above her, "but you don't have to do a thing besides lie back and enjoy."

"I want it," she assured him. "Everything."

And what happened after that felt like a dream. Maybe because she was simply so wrung out from the whole crazy, lust-packed day—or maybe that was just the kind of pleasure her men began to deliver.

She heard them speaking low but didn't bother trying to make out the words, and she soon became aware of more cheesecake being smeared between her breasts. Then her body was being straddled, a hard cock landing between the two mounds of flesh. She looked up to see Rogan hovering above her, felt his strong hands close around her tits to lift them up around his length. And mmm, the cheesecake did help make for a smooth, slick glide. She heard her own sigh as pleasure began to fully override fatigue.

And then—oh!—Ethan's cock entered the picture again, too, coming over her shoulder, rubbing across her taut nipple. Finding the strength to lift her head slightly, she loved what she saw: both of those majestic cocks so close together, and there solely for her pleasure. She let out a moan at the mere sight. And then, in her still-dreamlike state, she realized Rogan was gone, pulling away, lifting off her—but she found Ethan leaning down, licking a path between her breasts to capture the cheesecake Rogan's dick had left behind.

A few minutes later, one of them—she'd lost track of who, having shut her eyes for a short time to simply bask in the pleasure—wiped a smudge of cheesecake onto her other nipple. She opened her eyes in time, however, to watch as Ethan rubbed his erection across the hardened peak, leaving it stickier with still more cheesecake—before Rogan bent to lick the sweet remnants away.

She studied Rogan as he ran his tongue around the pointed tip of her breast, and then Ethan held a bite of the creamy cake down to her mouth on one fingertip and she sucked it off, letting his finger stay in her mouth even after the sweet taste was gone.

Despite the push/pull she'd sensed between the two men before that, the languid pleasures taking place now seemed like . . . the ultimate form of sharing, Rogan and Ethan each literally eating what was left behind by the other's cock.

As they continued to move over her and around her, simply playing with her body, exploring it with hands, mouths, and penises, she experienced a fresh and intense awareness of them both, of everything about them. Rogan had shed his clothes now, too, and she loved the sight of their gorgeous bare male torsos above her, around her. She studied the thin line of hair that expanded below Ethan's navel to make a dark nest below from which his erection sprouted. She took in the unshaven stubble on Rogan's face that sometimes abraded her skin. She noticed Ethan's own normally flat nipples now sported hard little peaks, as well. And she examined the individual spikes of Rogan's barbed wire tattoo. All were parts of them with which she was very familiar, and yet right now, when placed side-by-side, something in them cumulatively felt brand new and almost shockingly beautiful.

Even so, though, inside she resumed feeling oddly torn. She found herself imagining some perfect world that was . . . well, *this* world, the world of this weekend, the world she knew in this cabin, where she could truly have them both. Not just physically—but also emotionally. A place where she didn't have to worry about that part, about which one she loved, which one she wanted more—a place where the sharing was that complete. Only ... it wouldn't last, this *real, true* sharing, this sense of wanting to love them both and wanting them both to love her.

And then Ethan was bending over her, kissing her. Which must mean it was Rogan now between her legs, his warm hands prying them apart. And ... oh, oh God, what was he doing? She thought from the sensation that he was ... she could only describe it as spanking her pussy with his cock. The shockingly stimulating little blows came in fast succession, slapping softly against her most sensitive skin, and ... God, who knew something like that could feel so ridiculously good?

She began to moan against Ethan's warm kisses, and her pleasure grew when his hand closed over her breast, kneading rhythmically.

And then—mmm, God—another hand came on her other breast, but this one was harder and she knew instinctively that it belonged to Rogan. He pinched and pulled at her nipple, making her nearly yelp into Ethan's mouth, all while he continued that ever-so-kinky little spanking, his erection landing directly on her clit over and over.

Until finally she couldn't kiss anymore. And she heard herself letting out low noises with each little smack. And Ethan's voice hovered above her saying, "Oh baby, does that feel good? You're so hot, so fucking hot," and then, before she could even fully process it, she came again.

This orgasm wasn't hard and jerky like the last one—no,

this one was just as wildly intense and pleasurable, yet it flowed smoothly through her body like a pulsing river of euphoria, lasting far longer than usual. The unexpected climax was absolute . . . *perfection*. Not only because of the way it coursed through her so sublimely, but also because of how she felt so completely and honestly shared by them just now. She knew that part wasn't real, could *never* be truly real—not on the level she'd been fantasizing about—but oh, it had been nice to imagine it for a few glorious, ecstatic minutes.

When her howls of pleasure finally quieted and she again lay spent on the table, only the sound from the retro radio station remained—Marvin Gaye sang "Sexual Healing."

After a moment, she sat up and looked around. Cheese-cake smeared the table—and the chair where she'd sat. What remained of the birthday cake was a pile of mush now on one corner of the table. All three of them studied it for a minute—until Rogan said, "That's okay, I didn't want any more anyway," making them all laugh softly. Then he switched his gaze to Mira. "But I want some more of that hot pussy I just spanked to orgasm."

She sucked in her breath. There was a part of her that honestly feared she couldn't take anymore fucking tonight.

But thankfully . . . there was a bigger part of her that knew she *could*.

So when Rogan reached for her hand and drew her up-right, she sat up willingly—even ready. For whatever came next. She was too tired to think, to concoct anything she herself wanted, but she was curious—and even happy—to see what he had in mind.

When he drew her to her feet, there was something about simply standing there with him, face-to-face, that reminded her how much bigger he was than her—it made her feel his brute masculinity all over again, and somehow in that moment, it gave her shivers. Or maybe it was the look in his eyes as he met her gaze that brought that on. *He cares for me again. He wants me in a deeper way than I realized just this morning.* That made everything happening now—and whatever was *about* to happen—mean so much more.

"Turn around," he told her, his expression still dark and commanding.

She drew in a breath. Then did as he said.

Then in one firm but smooth move, he placed one hand on her hip, cupped the other to the back of her neck, and bent her over the table until her chest pressed flat against it. It was almost forceful. But not quite. Because something in it turned her on more than she could have imagined.

The next thing she knew, both his hands gripped her ass and then—mmm, God—he was sliding the stone column of his cock into her moisture. And that initial entry, the hot intrusion, never failed to take her breath away.

"Fuck her mouth," he said to Ethan.

It made her look up at her boyfriend, still situated on the

other side of the table from Rogan. His eyes remained filled with heat. Then she dropped her gaze to the perfectly erect shaft at her eye level. Maybe her way of saying, *Yes, I want it.* Or maybe just accepting, waiting. She didn't even know anymore. And it really didn't matter, either. She felt as if she'd simply become some kind of sex machine—that her body was designed for it and was today being used for it like never before. And she didn't mind.

As Ethan once more took his cock in hand and held it down, feeding it into her mouth, she experienced that sensation all over again as if it were something new, the sensation of being filled from both ends, stuffed full. It had happened several times today already, enough that she thought she should be used to the strange, dirty joy it brought her, but she wasn't. It remained just as all-consuming as it had been the very first time. Nothing else existed. Only the cocks that packed her so tightly. Only the lusty pleasure.

As both men fucked her, she felt . . . pleasantly controlled. It was a strange reversal from the sensation she'd experienced standing in the chair looking down on them a few minutes ago—then she'd felt like she was being worshipped, but this was like being taken. And she loved both equally.

"Mmm, babe," Rogan murmured as he pounded that big shaft so firmly into her, over and over, "you're being such a bad little girl this weekend. Think I'm gonna have to give you a spanking. The regular kind this time."

The fact that her mouth was full kept her from needing to answer, but she'd already been moaning and whimpering around Ethan's dick, and now she heard herself let out an even more desperate, welcoming sound in response. Back when they'd been together, Rogan used to spank her while he was fucking her from behind. They'd never even talked about it, but now she remembered that she'd timidly liked it, liked that it felt a little kinky and naughty to her, liked the way the smacks on her ass had reverberated all through her body.

And mmm—as he landed the first slap on her bottom, she sobbed around Ethan's penis, then sucked it harder. Oh—she really *had* liked this; maybe she'd forgotten just how much.

Each stinging blow of his palm vibrated through her like hot, tiny aftershocks that echoed all the way to the tips of her fingers and toes even as he continued plunging deep, deep, deep into her wet cunt. She somehow felt it resonating even through her lips, stretched so wide and tight around Ethan's sturdy length. It intensified *everything* until, like so many other times today, she simply gave herself over to it and let herself get lost in the heady pleasure.

Caught up and consumed by all that was taking place, Ethan looked down, watching where his cock entered Mira's soft mouth. Damn, she was amazing—and he couldn't remember a time *ever* when he'd been aroused in quite this same way, with quite the same dark, ferocious intensity he'd experienced this weekend.

And when he let his gaze wander down the curve of her back and over those naughty panties he'd given her to see Rogan driving into her from behind—and spanking her, too, which she seemed to like—aw hell. He wasn't sure what was happening here.

Yeah, he'd never been more excited in his life, and yet somehow, again, Rogan had assumed control of this situation. Damn, he couldn't help thinking this was like that hostage situation all over again—Rogan just couldn't help taking charge of things. And he still wasn't sure why that disturbed him so much; this was about her pleasure, after all—nothing else. But something felt different about Rogan than it had last night.

The two of them had never talked about this part beforehand, about who would control the sex—he hadn't wanted to be that rigid, impose rules on it. Yet maybe he'd just assumed Rogan would behave more the way he had the previous evening—hanging back, following along, letting Ethan take the lead. *But shit, this is Rogan.* He should have been more prepared for that. Because—yeah, thinking back on their time together in the academy, he was remembering more and more—Rogan didn't let anyone else take the lead if *he* felt like taking it.

Ethan couldn't help thinking back to other points in the

day—those points when he'd begun to feel a little jealous.
And he'd thought he could handle that if it arose—he'd
thought through it long and hard before inviting Rogan here,
and he'd imagined various scenarios and how they might
make him feel. And so far, he thought he'd done pretty damn
well with it—a little jealousy here and there, but mostly, he'd
enjoyed sharing her, enjoyed giving her that much pleasure,
enjoyed the intense openness and intimacy this required.

Now, though . . . maybe it was just the cumulative effect
of the day or something, but warring with the brain-numbing
lust and excitement coursing through his veins was a growing
irritation that had him clenching his teeth. A disgruntlement
he could blame only on Rogan's quiet way of, ultimately, always doing whatever he damn well felt like. Maybe he should
have thought long and hard about it before including in this
little party a guy who didn't always play by the rules, written
or *un*written.

Or . . . maybe it was simpler than that. Maybe it just suddenly seemed important to Ethan that he be the one she
needed more.

And maybe it was time he made it clear—to all fucking
three of them—who was gonna control the sex here.

It wasn't his usual way to be a hard-ass about much of
anything. In the courtroom, yeah, sure, and when he'd been
a cop, he'd definitely known how to assert his authority—
but in everyday life, with Mira, his friends, his family, he was

pretty damn easygoing. Only this . . . well, this wasn't everyday life. And something about it—at least in this particular moment—had quit feeling very much like a gift to Mira and more like Rogan taking what Rogan wanted, all for Rogan, like he didn't give a shit about what anyone *else* might need.

So . . . hell. Yeah, it was time to assert some goddamn authority here and remind Rogan who'd thrown this party and exactly whose girl he was fucking.

When he withdrew his cock from Mira's mouth, she let out a small noise of distress, and as he rounded the table, he felt her surprised, confused look. But he spared her only a quick glance, because he was on a mission now.

Stepping up to Rogan, he said, "My turn."

Chapter 14

Rogan stopped driving into her, looked up at Ethan. Their eyes met.

And there was a moment when Ethan began to wonder if Rogan was going to protest—but then he silently extracted his dick and stepped back from the table.

Good.

Right now Ethan felt possessive; he needed to be in charge. *He* needed to be the center of Mira's world for a little while.

She whimpered needfully as he moved in behind her, glancing down to where Rogan's cock had just been. Her pussy had, of course, contracted, but was still visibly open, and above, her anus appeared puffy, swollen.

"You want more, baby?" he asked, his voice coming unintentionally low and deep.

"Yes," she said, still sounding beautifully desperate, hotly needy. And when he didn't push his way inside her that very second, she added, *"Please."* Something about the word sent a wave of fresh heat cascading through his entire body. And it came with something he'd never experienced with Mira before—the urge to make her beg. Just a little.

He found himself stepping up close behind her bent-over body, letting his erection nestle in the valley of her ass—and then nothing more.

Her body tensed. And then she even began to move a little, sliding her soft flesh along his length. But he stayed still. Teasing her.

In front of him, her distress grew evident, especially when she sucked in her breath and let out a another heartfelt, "Please, E. *Please.*"

Part of him felt bad for how anxious she sounded, but another part liked it, liked making her need him, liked knowing he had what she wanted so much. And it didn't matter to him at the moment whether it was him she craved or just any cock in general to fill her—but he liked being the provider either way, the filler of needs, the only man who could soothe her longings right now because he'd just deemed it that way.

Am I mad at her? Am I mad that she wants Rogan as much as she wants me? Am I mad that she obeys his every word without flinching?

And he knew the answers to each of those questions as quickly as they flashed through his head. No, no, and . . .

maybe. He'd come here knowing that sharing her meant giving her permission to want her old lover, to enjoy him, to even enjoy them equally. But maybe seeing her respond so readily to Rogan's dominance had begun to sting just a little.

Ethan had never been that way with Mira—it just wasn't part of their sex. But if she was going to be so receptive to commands from Rogan—hell, then she was going to have to start being the same way for him now, too.

So he still didn't rush. And even as he ached to fuck her brains out, it excited him further to keep holding back, playing this new little game he'd just created. Taking his hard dick between fingers and thumb, he wiggled it back and forth between her ass cheeks, making her pant a little, then he slid it slowly up the center and back, like playing two long, mournful notes on a violin.

"Ethan, please. Please fuck me. You're killing me."

"Tell me how much you want it," he demanded.

And she didn't hesitate. "I want it *so, so* bad. Please, I need your cock filling me up, fucking me hard. I can't stand it. I feel so empty now."

Mmm, God. The object of her desire had somehow just managed to stiffen a little more at her words. And though he'd anticipated all the strange, new, intimate bonds the two of them would build this weekend, he hadn't imagined this one: that maybe she wanted him to be a little rougher, more controlling, more dominant. And that maybe he could even *get into* making her submit, making her beg. Unlike Rogan, neither his nor Mira's personality fell naturally into either of those slots, so he'd never even considered the idea that such games could turn them on. But he was finding out otherwise. One more surprise at Mira's birthday party.

"Tell me you want my big, hard cock ramming into you," he heard himself say—and his dick tightened even further at his own command.

"I do," she whimpered. "I want your big, hard cock ramming into me more than anything. I have to have it, E. I'm begging you. Please, baby. *Please.*"

The rush of heat that had swept over Ethan a minute ago now settled into a comfortable warmth—he was finally ready to give her what she needed, and the fact was, he would enjoy it more for having made her beg.

Positioning the head of his dick at the moist opening still slightly parted from before, he curled his fingers slowly into her ass and whispered, "Ready, baby?"

"God, yes!"

She sounded so impatient now that it almost amused him, made him happy to at last give her what she craved. Then he drove into her—deep, rough.

The sound she emitted held both shock and pleasure. He didn't usually do that, either, enter her pussy so very forcefully—but he knew she was wet and well-primed enough at the moment to take it.

And after that, he didn't hesitate to fuck her, pounding relentlessly into that soft flesh that held him like a tight, moist glove. He loved the wild little cry she let out at each hard stroke he delivered, loved feeling how much hot pleasure he was giving her. *Him* right now, not Rogan. And he truly *was* enjoying sharing her this weekend, on many levels, but right now that felt like an important distinction—right now, it was just him and her, nobody else. Yeah, he might be sharing her, but he still needed that special connection with her, still needed to know he was the guy she was thinking about, loving, through all of this.

After he thought he'd nearly fucked her senseless, he eventually went still, taking a break, for both their sakes. Neither of them spoke, but as he leaned over, resting close to her, skin to skin, and resting inside her, too, he felt what he wanted to: that link that went beyond sex but was strengthened *by* sex.

Once he'd regained some energy, he stood upright, pulled his dick from her sweet body, and then gently turned her over and took her hands, helping her to sit up.

She looked . . . well fucked, her skin shiny and sticky from cheesecake, bits of it clinging to the naughty lavender lingerie he'd bought her, her hair messy, her eyes tired yet vibrant and a little wild. And he thought she was beautiful, as beautiful as he'd ever seen her—maybe just in a different way.

Following the softest urge he'd had in a while, he leaned in for a slow, gentle kiss, just letting his mouth linger on hers.

Then he closed his hands over her hips and drew her to the very edge of the table, after which he slowly spread her legs until they were as far apart as they could go.

He looked down, took in her pussy, still surrounded by butterfly wings.

"Let's take these off you," he said on impulse then, touching the fabric at her hip. They were pretty, and sexy as hell, but in his mind the time for them had passed. He just wanted her naked now, natural. Things had turned raw quite a while ago, and somehow lace and chiffon just didn't make sense here anymore.

She didn't argue or ask why, just put her legs back together and lifted her ass to let him pull them off. When they were gone, he reached for the straps on her faux bra, and she helped by reaching behind her back to unhook it.

"Spread for me," he gently commanded and she re-parted her thighs, as wide as possible, just like he'd had her before.

Yeah, looking at her pussy now—this was what he'd wanted to see a moment ago, all that tender flesh unfettered, unbound. "So pretty," he told her, studying her there.

He kept his eyes on her cunt but sensed her looking, too, maybe wanting to see it in the same way he did.

Leaning in closer, he nudged his still erect dick at the opening in her pink folds and watched—as well as felt—it slide easily in. They both let out heated sighs. Her pussy cushioned his length from all sides, warm and slick.

As he began to fuck her again, this time he did it slowly, letting his cock slide in, then back out, lingering, feeling each languorous inch of the glide. "Watch," he told her. "Watch me going in and out of you."

It was around this time that he became aware of Rogan in his peripheral vision—he stood a foot or so away, and he was watching, too, still part of this. And that was okay. It had to be. Inside, he might want it to be just the two of them right now, but he'd chosen to make it so that there were three instead, and he could deal with it. In fact . . .*you wouldn't be here like this, in this exact place, feeling this exact intimacy with her, if Rogan weren't here.*

And even with Rogan present, he still remained in control of what was happening now—and he liked feeling that. Despite having let Rogan control their sex for a while, he'd still simply . . . never felt closer to her than he did right at this moment, after everything they'd shared so far on this weekend getaway.

"Baby, it was so hot coming in your mouth today," he told her without weighing it. God, she'd really let him do that. Finally. He looked her in the eye, spoke slowly, deeply, from the heart. "I want all of you, every part of you, Mira, in every way."

He continued to move his cock smoothly in and out of her slit at an almost achingly slow pace, but now their gazes were locked on each other instead of what took place below.

"You *have* all of me. I promise." Her voice slid like silk over his skin.

And he couldn't fight the notion that maybe she knew what he was thinking, feeling—that she understood he'd gotten a little jealous of Rogan.

But whether she did or whether she didn't, that promise of hers reassured him, made him relax. And . . . maybe it even served to remind him that this—this weekend, all this sex— was all about her, was supposed to be about her pleasure and nothing else. And that maybe he'd overreacted to Rogan's take-charge attitude.

He had all of her, after all. Everything was fine here.

"What do you want right now, honey? Anything at all— it's yours. Anything you want to do, anything you want to feel—just name it." And he meant it. His little spurt of envy was past. Rogan's personality sometimes just didn't allow for putting other people first, thinking about anyone else's needs. He should be used to that by now, and he shouldn't have invited him to be part of this little threesome if he couldn't handle that.

So now he just kept his gaze on Mira, urging her to tell him her deepest desires, whatever they may be. And he was going to do his best to make them a reality.

His pretty girl—who'd gone from shy lover to wild wanton and back again today, many times already—now blushed a little. It touched his heart in that moment to see that—it reminded him that no matter what happened here, no matter what she experienced, she was still his sweet Mira; they were both still the same people they'd always been. It took more than a weekend of wild sex to change who you were deep inside. And he'd known that from the start or he never would have suggested this anyway.

"Tell me," he prodded her.

And finally, she peered into his eyes and said softly, "I want you both to kiss me all over. I want you both to touch me all over. I want you both to fuck me until I scream."

Chapter 15

Mira lay between them on the bed, basking in pleasures that felt at once simple yet ever so complex. Kisses from two mouths spanned her body. At the moment, Ethan's tongue swirled around her nipple while Rogan kissed his way up the front of her thigh. Ethan's fingertips grazed her stomach as she tried to take it all in, absorb it into her skin.

They'd been kissing her, running their hands over her, for fifteen or twenty scintillating minutes now. Certainly a much softer way of sharing her than many of the others this ménage à trois had brought about. And she loved it all. Right now, in the middle of them, she was back to feeling worshipped again, cherished.

And it would have been perfect if . . . well, if she weren't struggling inside. She kept remembering the way Rogan had fucked her in the woods. The way she'd *let him* fuck her. The fact that ever since then, she'd felt closer to him than before. And the truth they all knew was that she'd felt close enough to him from the start or none of this could be happening. Even Ethan had known that.

Rogan was . . . the ideal bad boy. Always had been. Her mother hadn't liked him. He'd been completely different than any other guy she'd ever dated. And from the start, she'd known he was dangerous. To her heart.

She'd just been at a point in her life when she'd been willing to take a risk, ready to throw caution to the wind. Every girl needed a bad boy once in her life and Rogan had been hers. And he'd broken her heart, as bad boys were wont to do. And she'd pulled herself together and moved on.

But now she had to ask herself—was it really possible for a guy like Rogan to change? At his very core? Could what he'd said in the woods be real, meaningful? If she suddenly gave him her whole heart, what would he do with it? Would whatever they shared last forever? Or would it turn out to be nothing more than pretty words spoken in the heat of passion?

And—God—what was she even *thinking*?

You love Ethan! And she really, truly did.

And . . . mmm, right now he suckled her breast so sweetly, so deeply, as he fondled the other one in his hand. When he twirled the nipple tenderly between two fingers, a hot sigh erupted from her throat. She looked down, watched him delivering the smoldering ministrations, and remembered how gorgeously handsome he was. Not that she'd forgotten—but Rogan was so much on her mind right now, just by virtue of having been thrust back into her life when she'd least expected it, that at moments it was easy to take Ethan for granted, to forget how hot he was in his own right. Any woman would be lucky to have him. *She* was lucky to have him. After all, how many women got a gift as generous as this? Very few, she was sure.

The strange part was that if Ethan hadn't brought Rogan here . . . yes, they'd be rediscovering each other this weekend, having a lovely, hot, sexy romantic time—but she'd never know the astounding depth of his love, trust, and generosity. She'd never have let out the indescribably feral new side of her sexuality—because she wouldn't have quite known about that, either. He'd truly helped her discover, uncover, parts of herself she wouldn't have believed were there—and not only that, but he'd helped her explore them, embrace them, too.

And yet at the same time, in order to do all that . . . he'd had to introduce her old lover back into the picture. The old lover who now kissed his way across her belly while cupping her mound in one possessive hand. Had Ethan had any notion, any clue, that it would bring old feelings bubbling back to the surface? Had he harbored any fear that she could end up feeling attached to Rogan all over again?

She knew that, no matter what he said, he was experiencing some jealousy now. She'd felt it in the way he'd practically pushed Rogan aside at the table a little while ago; she'd felt it in the ferocity of the fucking that had followed.

But then, she'd also understood what had brought that on. Rogan had grown more and more aggressive through the day, and then, after she'd blown out the candles on her cake, his true nature had shone through when he'd pretty much just taken over.

And she'd . . . simply rolled with it. For one thing, Rogan was a hard guy to say no to when he was in full take-charge mode, especially sexually. And for another . . . was it her place to step forward and stop things? No. She hadn't started this. She hadn't brought him here. And yes, once she'd accepted the idea of a full-blown ménage à trois, she'd enjoyed it more than she'd known was humanly possible—but it wasn't her job to control it or run things. She was enjoying it, but at the same time it was . . . more than a little emotionally draining, and so, in ways, she was working as hard just to get *through* it as she was to enjoy it.

Part of her had been glad when Ethan had taken over. And—oh God—to her utmost surprise, she'd ended up delectably aroused by everything that had passed between the two of them once Rogan had stepped aside. She'd never before known she wanted Ethan to be a little rough with her. And maybe, after what she'd secretly done with Rogan by that wishing well, she thought she deserved it. But she'd just never imagined those particular roles working for her and Ethan so well.

Now he kissed her mouth while Rogan sucked her tit, their moves all slow, sensuous. At this moment, she was living that fantasy again, the one where three people could exist like this in harmony, with no particular emotions off limits, where no one was ever at risk of getting hurt.

But that's not real.

Someone's going to get hurt here, no matter how good it all feels.

Yet then she lectured herself. *Damn it, you're not supposed to be thinking, just experiencing.* And at moments, she was able to achieve that. After all, every time she opened her eyes or took in the scene, it felt dreamlike and perfect now. Two men who wanted nothing more in life than to pleasure her—what could be better?

But you know they both want more than that deep down. They both want you to belong to them. They both want you to love one of them more than the other.

She *did* love Ethan—so, so much. She hadn't been lying to him earlier—he truly had all of her, her whole heart.

But she *could* love Rogan again—so very easily. *When the one man you never fully felt you could have suddenly comes back and says he wants you the way you always wanted him* . . . well, the very notion bloomed with a dark temptation that was difficult to fight.

The truth was that now . . . she wasn't sure where this was

going, any of it. Inside, it all felt to her as if it were beginning to spin out of control.

But the further truth was . . . *there's nothing you can do to stop it at this point, or fix it. It's all too deeply in motion—there's no turning back.*

So maybe the smartest thing to do at this particular moment in time was to—once more—stop thinking. *Just enjoy this. The men you've loved most fervently in your life are kissing you, touching you, fucking you—even, each in their own way, making love to you. How often does that come along? How often? But you're in the middle of it, living it.* And it would be downright insane not to relish every second.

She found herself turning into Ethan's arms then, into his kiss, even as Rogan moved up in the bed behind her, spooning her as he began to kiss her shoulder, her neck, his thick cock cradled against her ass. Mmm, God, it felt so good, made her body hungry again for more than just this soft, sensuous foreplay they were raining onto her.

But then, just as deliciously, Ethan's rigid length nestled against her slit in the front, making her moan as it came to rest against her clit. Oh Lord, being sandwiched between them, between those two strong shafts, was to know utter perfection.

She continued kissing Ethan—they traded hot, delicate tongue kisses now—but occasionally she turned to look over her shoulder, leaning her head back to kiss Rogan, too. To be fucked by them both was amazing, but to take turns exchanging kisses with them held its own, quieter erotic joys.

She hissed in her breath as their bodies moved together, gliding back and forth against each other, hers the recipient of the delights from both sides. And as it went on, she did truly relish it all and again pushed the worrisome parts of this from her mind. It was incredible how the pressure of two big, hard cocks against two very sensitive places on her body could make her cease thinking about anything else.

When Rogan reached down between their bodies—his and hers—she wasn't sure at first what was happening, but then she realized he was positioning his erection at the opening between her legs. "Mmm," she moaned against Ethan's mouth at the sensation, then cried out softly as Rogan pushed his way inside. That lovely intrusion just never became commonplace—it was always fraught with startling pleasure.

When Ethan looked at her, clearly wondering what was happening, she said, "Rogan's fucking me."

And before Ethan could even respond, Rogan began to pump smoothly into her cunt and she automatically found the rhythm—which meant meeting Ethan's cock in front as well with each instinctive move she made. "Oh God," she said on a veritable purr, "this is like . . . sex heaven."

She peered into Ethan's eyes and knew he understood that his hardness felt as good to her in front as Rogan's did inside her, only in a different way. "Aw baby," he rasped, still undulating against her, one hand warmly caressing her breast, "it's good?"

He just wanted to hear it some more, she knew. And she didn't mind. "So incredibly, amazingly good." She punctuated the sentiment by slipping her hand down between them to curl her fingers around his erection, massaging lightly, pressing his length all the deeper into her tender flesh.

He moaned and she sighed, and as their gazes met again, she realized this was one of those moments, the ones that did exactly what Ethan had told her would happen when he'd presented this whole idea—bonded them tighter by virtue of experiencing such raw, extreme pleasure together.

Except . . . it wasn't only Ethan she felt close to.

She couldn't deny what a strange, stark, honest intimacy she felt with *both* men just then—different than any other time since this weekend soiree had begun.

Was it some sort of cumulative effect? Or was it about Rogan's seduction and confession in the woods? Or the way Ethan had taken charge of the sex on the table? Was it the turmoil swirling in her heart from knowing she had strong feelings for both of them? She didn't know the answer—all she knew for sure was that despite that turmoil, she'd never felt more connected to either of them as she did right now, at the very same time.

All she could do was continue to let the emotions surround her, cushion her, as lushly as their two beautiful male bodies did. She knew in that moment that nothing she'd ever experienced in her life had ever felt more sublime.

And so when Rogan unexpectedly extracted his wonderfully hard cock from her body, she gasped. And felt . . . a gaping emptiness, physically, at having him gone.

"What . . . ?" Ethan murmured at her reaction.

Her voice came in a broken whisper. "He, um, pulled out."

And she was in the process of turning her head to look over her shoulder, wondering what was going on, why Rogan would stop fucking her at this most blissful of hedonistic moments, when he leaned near her ear to say, "Shhh, babe. No worries. Just relax and it'll all be good." One palm molded to her hip and his slick-from-her-juices cock rested in the crease of her ass, and that alone felt amazing in a different way, so she tried to be patient, tried to calm the hunger inside her. Maybe he just needed a break, or needed to readjust the way he lay or something.

That's when she felt the pressure at her asshole, firm and direct. She sucked in her breath, surprised—but instantly . . . pleasured. It was his thumb—she could feel the rest of his hand, his fingers resting on the curve of her ass. But it felt . . . moist—he'd made it wet somehow, maybe just swiped it along his penis. And now he was rubbing the little fissure in firm, tight circles that made her begin to pant—just before he pushed his thumb inside.

Another gasp left her—this one not about loss, but about intrusion. A strange and welcome intrusion, in a spot where she still wasn't accustomed to being entered. She shut her eyes, instantly entranced by the diverse pleasure. And as he began to work his thumb in the tiny little hole—first in and out, and then, it seemed . . . in circles—her breathing went shallow and she started to tremble, just a little. She pressed her palms to Ethan's chest, trying to brace herself against the unfamiliar sensations.

"What is it, honey?" Ethan asked, voice low.

But she didn't have time—or the wits—to answer before Rogan drew his thumb quickly away. "Oh!" she heard herself say.

But then . . . mmm, oh God . . . the head of his cock was there, nudging at the same tight little opening, now stimulated and shockingly sensitive. She clenched her teeth upon realizing two things: This was going to happen. And she wanted it to.

When he pushed in the thick tip, the physical response stretched through her whole body. "Unh." Her eyes fell shut and the back of her scalp tingled.

"What's happening, baby?" Ethan asked again.

"He's . . . he's . . . starting to . . . to . . ." She could barely get words out. And by the time she mustered the strength, she didn't even consider Ethan's reaction. "He's fucking my ass."

"Shit," Ethan whispered—not in any sort of anger, but just clearly stunned. Then his eyes changed, his brows crinkling slightly as he looked at her. "Is it . . . ?"

"Strange. Overwhelming. B-b-blindingly . . . good." Her lips quivered now as she spoke.

Ethan released a hot sigh at her words, still obviously taken aback—and maybe, like her, a little amazed. But no, on second thought, he couldn't be feeling even *remotely* like her. Because he couldn't begin to know how this felt.

Rogan eased his stiff length into the tiny crevice inch by slow inch, whispering, murmuring, "Aw, damn, you're so fucking tight there," and "I'm gonna give you a little more, babe, and now a little more."

Heat infused her cheeks from the inside out, and sweat oozed palpably from every pore—she felt his cock filling every molecule of her being. It was as if every atom of her body was being gently, tightly stretched the same way her anus was. Sensation radiated to the very tips of her fingers and toes. Her face tingled. Her every muscle was pulled taut with arousal.

And then, after that tiny hole was as full with his erection as it could possibly be, he began to move. Slowly at first, slow and smooth—but soon he increased the pace, the pistoning strokes coming a little faster. It made her wild with pleasure that felt as if it coursed through her very veins, pumping through her like lifeblood.

And through it all, she stayed so very aware of Rogan behind her, inside her in this new way, fucking her in a way that felt . . . almost like possessing her—and yet she was peering into Ethan's eyes at the same time, sharing it with him, too, her every response more for him to see than for Rogan.

The experience was so powerful that she wondered how much more she could take. She felt each thrust everywhere, pulsing through her cheeks, her forearms, her thighs. Small cries of pleasure erupted from her throat with each small, smooth stroke. And all the while, she was leaning into Ethan, drinking in the warmth of his embrace, the passion in his eyes, while his beautifully hard cock slid against her slit again and again.

She knew she was going to come only a second before the orgasm struck, sudden and wild and hard, making her cry out abruptly as it exploded through her clit and outward, fast and engulfing, and she heard herself screaming, screaming, just like she'd told Ethan she'd wanted them to make her do.

Oh Lord—it had to be the best, most intense sensation she'd ever endured. And again she couldn't help be overcome by the knowledge that she'd experienced this most awe-inspiring pleasure of her life with both of them. It had come initially from Rogan—and yet also from Ethan. And she could have sworn she'd come harder somehow just by virtue of looking into Ethan's eyes while another man fucked her so thoroughly. And while it was Rogan's cock in her ass lifting her to that strange new pinnacle, it had been Ethan's against her clit that pushed her over that jagged edge. It had come from neither one of them any more than the other.

And it was only after she'd recovered from it all, resting in the arms of both the men in her bed, Rogan's erection still buried firm and deep in her ass, that Ethan whispered, "Aw baby, I want inside you, too, now."

"Huh?" she whispered. She understood the words, of course, but under the current circumstances, she wasn't entirely certain what he was suggesting.

Until he added, "I want in your sweet little pussy . . . while Rogan's still in your ass. You think you could handle that?"

The concept nearly stole her breath. For more than one reason. It sounded impossible—and a little frightening. But also like . . . the ultimate way of having them both. There had been so many moments since this had started that she'd felt she was achieving that, and yet . . . this still seemed like . . . more. A deeper, fuller way to be shared by the two men she cared for, the two men she lusted for with her whole soul.

"If . . . if you think . . . that'll work." She shivered a little, suddenly nervous, and the tremble made her newly aware of Rogan's hard cock filling her ass impossibly full.

"It'll work," Rogan replied from behind her. Then, answering the obvious question his statement left hanging in the air, he added, "I've seen it in movies." Porn, he surely meant. And though she wasn't entirely sure something was safe and doable just because someone in a porn flick had accomplished it, it reminded her all over again what an extraordinary experience she was having here this weekend, and that she didn't want to say no to anything just out of fear.

So when Rogan's hand slipped between her thighs, cupping the one on top, and he said, "Here, just lift this leg up, babe," she didn't resist. Though the move—any move, she supposed—made her feel Rogan's dick more. And Ethan's attention moved down her body to the area just put on display, and even though the room was half-dark, shadowy, still lit only by the kitchen lamp they'd turned on before lighting her birthday candles, she witnessed the fresh arousal on his face at what he saw. She suffered the urge to see it, too—one thick shaft entering one hole, the other opening next to it waiting . . . for his.

When he positioned the tip of his cock, she tensed, and he whispered, "Try to relax, honey. I won't hurt you. If it hurts, we'll stop."

She gave a short nod, but her body felt as tight as a fully stretched rubber band anyway. So she took a deep breath. Another. Then a third. Then she closed her eyes.

She still gritted her teeth lightly as he began to push his way in—and, oh Lord. It didn't hurt at all. It was simply . . . what she'd thought a moment ago. The ultimate way of being shared. The ultimate way of being . . . filled.

"Aw God," Ethan groaned as he entered her pussy deeper, deeper, and she sensed all three of them practically holding their breath, trying to adjust to this new way of fucking. Ethan was panting when he finally said, "You okay, Mir?"

She nodded. "Mmm." It was the only response she could manage.

His face was flushed, his eyes half-shut, when he cupped her cheek in his palm to murmur, "I'm gonna fuck you now, move in you."

Another nod.

And then he began to deliver leisurely strokes, slow glides of his hard cock up into her, and she had to bite her lip because the utter fullness in that area of her body was difficult to fathom.

And it was only a moment after that when Rogan kissed her shoulder and began to slowly drive his erection into her, too.

At first he found a rhythm that opposed Ethan's, so that as Rogan thrust in, Ethan was withdrawing, and vice versa, and there was never a second when she wasn't taking the full brunt of an inward drive. And it was too much, just too much. "No, no," she heard herself whimpering instinctively. And when they both stopped, Ethan looking concerned, she explained, breathlessly, "Do it at the same time. Together. Can't take it this way."

"Ah," Ethan said, adding, "Sorry, baby," in a rough whisper.

And then they began again—Ethan first, setting a steady, medium sort of pace, after which Rogan joined in, pumping into her ass at precisely the same moment.

"Unh! Unh!" she cried out at the tremendous impact—
stunned, amazed. At how outrageous it felt to be fucked like
this. At the fact that she was able to take it, absorb it, love it.

She'd never felt so thoroughly fucked in her life. And as
she gave herself over to it completely, she shut her eyes, lifted
her arms above her head, and simply soaked in all they had
to give her. Every thrust from every inch of the two perfect
cocks that hammered away at her in hot unison. Every kiss—
on her shoulder or her breast or her mouth. Every touch—
hands explored her skin, brushed over her nipples, ran
through her hair, and she didn't know or even care which
touch belonged to which man now.

And then she realized the front of her body was now connecting with Ethan's, up above the base of his shaft, in just
the right way now—everything was working in perfect unison, and even though having another orgasm was the last
thing on her mind, she was going to.

She even began, instinctively, to move against him, which
meant taking in his plunges with more impact—but pulling
away from Rogan's a little. And then—God, Rogan did
exactly what she'd stopped him from doing a few minutes
ago; he switched his rhythm so that whether she moved her
pelvis forward or back, she was meeting the thrust of a rigid
cock.

"God! God! God!" she screamed—yet immediately realized she *could* take it now, every drive. It filled her with more

sensation than she'd known a woman could handle, but she was indeed handling it.

And then, just like with the last climax, without warning she was tumbling off the edge of sanity into a mind-numbing ecstasy that had her screaming her pleasure as it blasted through her body like a freight train, unstoppable, boundless— until finally the wild roar of it began to recede.

But that was when Rogan muttered, "Aw—aw, fuck. I'm gonna come. I'm gonna come in your ass, babe."

And before he even finished, Ethan let out a low, feral groan of his own that told her he was coming, too. And as they both ejaculated into her, she thought for the first time about how close their cocks were to one another, and she wondered how they looked, side by side, going in and out of her. And would their come somehow mix, would their dicks touch each other when they pulled out of her in a moment? The thoughts, the nearly crushing sensations, poured through her as the culmination of the most intense sexual experience of the weekend so far, which of course also made it the most intense of her life.

But as they all lay there recovering—she and Ethan trading kisses, Rogan nibbling on her shoulder before she turned to kiss him, as well—she couldn't deny that there was much more filling her senses than provocative questions about the two sturdy cocks inside her.

And as she curled up between them both a few minutes

later, ready for sleep after what was easily the most mind-blowing day of her existence, she could no longer push it down. All the emotion. For both of them. Some of it old, some of it new, but all of it swirling together in her head in ways that, even amid the sex-driven euphoria still pulsing through her flesh, left a small knot in the pit of her stomach when all was said and done.

Because all these feelings for them . . . well, here, now, in the cabin, intoxicated with both wine and sex, she'd managed to deal with them, accept them, even appreciate the unique bliss of being between two men who not only aroused her but who she truly, deeply cared for. But tomorrow the party ended. And the wild sex ended then, too. And even if she'd started somehow accepting her confused, tangled emotions over the course of the evening—even on some level finding them acceptable—tomorrow it just wouldn't be that way.

As she lay cuddled cozily between the two men—her head on Ethan's shoulder, his arm wrapped around her, while Rogan spooned her loosely from behind, one hand on her hip—she feared she might really have a horrible question to answer when she woke up tomorrow morning.

What if she really, truly loved them both?

Chapter 16

Ethan woke with the sun. It came beaming in the window, somehow fighting its way down through the tall trees around the cabin as if shining a light into his soul.

He couldn't have imagined all that would take place this weekend; he realized now that it was easy to envision something like this, a ménage à trois, but impossible to predict how it would really turn out, all the directions it could lead. And somewhere along the way, in between all the amazingly hot sex and the joy he'd taken in watching Mira open up and be so free yesterday, he feared this had all become . . . more complicated than he'd planned.

Maybe he'd been naive to think it would be simple. Maybe he'd been downright dumb to involve her old boyfriend. But he'd come at it from a place of good intentions, and he'd . . .

well, maybe he'd just approached it wearing rose-colored glasses or something. It could be damn easy to see only what you *wanted* to see sometimes.

And it wasn't even exactly that he harbored regrets. As he looked beside him to see Mira and Rogan stretched out, asleep and naked atop the covers next to him . . . hell, what they'd all shared here this weekend still aroused him. On more levels than he could even process right now. Yeah, he'd gotten a little pissed at Rogan during certain moments last night, but maybe a little jealousy was worth it when he added it all up.

And damn, couldn't say the whole thing hadn't ended with a bang—their final round of sex last night had nearly blown his mind. Not just because of the intense arousal involved, not just because of seeing Mira experience such startling pleasure—but because something about it had been so very raw, so extremely personal.

It had been utterly strange to peer down between her legs—which she'd obligingly kept apart, the top one bent, for the entire time—and see his own dick next to Rogan's, not an inch between them. And then to push into her, feeling not only the warm, moist tunnel of her pussy, but also Rogan's cock through the thin barrier of flesh that separated it from his. And it shook him up a little to acknowledge that . . . well, it hadn't turned him off. Somehow, in the heat of the moment, it had only added to the new and unrefined lust he'd been experiencing.

Hell, in a way he felt like . . . he'd lost a sort of virginity last night. Even though Rogan was the one who'd been in her ass.

Did that add to his jealousy? It had surprised him, but . . . no, it *hadn't* made him any more jealous.

Only now he wanted to be there, too. He'd never had that particular inclination before, but now that he knew how damn crazed it got her, he wanted to be the one making that happen. And maybe he didn't especially like the idea of Rogan having had a part of her that he hadn't. So he'd have to rectify that soon.

Yep, no doubt about it, he was learning a lot of things about both of them through this little threesome. And mostly things that would expand their sex life, take it in new directions, deepen what they shared. So . . . if a little weirdness had resulted at times—hell, even if he'd wanted to punch Rogan in the mouth a time or two last night—overall, he supposed he'd gotten exactly what he'd wanted from this birthday gift to Mira.

Now, glancing over at her again, her freshly tanned skin looking shimmery and sunkissed in the morning light, he hoped she was happy with what she'd gotten, too.

Though she'd thought she'd felt Ethan stirring next to her a little while ago, when Mira finally opened her eyes, she found both men in her bed, still sleeping. Both men in her bed. Wow, that idea still took some getting used to. And even though the weekend was soon drawing to a close, the memories—the reality that this had truly happened—would always be with her. Maybe someday it would all begin to grow a little fuzzier, the recollections less sharp, like the dream that somehow started all this, but it was hard to imagine. It was hard to imagine, in fact, that life would ever feel quite the same again.

Sure, she'd go back to the shop tomorrow and resume making book baskets for customers like nothing had changed. And tonight, she remembered, she had to attend her family birthday dinner, and even if she remained a little shaken up by all this, she'd walk in with a smile and no one would ever suspect that her entire sexual landscape had been forever altered over the last forty-eight hours. But she knew it would all still be churning in her mind, in her soul.

And it wasn't just about memories. Her body felt different now. Doing something physically, she thought, truly had the ability to change you. It was something you . . . took inside, something that left an imprint that wouldn't wash away. At the moment, she could still feel everything she'd done with Ethan and Rogan in her very fingertips, in her mouth; she could still feel their touches dancing across her skin. She could still feel their presence in her pussy, too—and, well, after last night, now also her ass.

She was understandably sore between her legs this morning, and her anus felt . . . stretched. And she knew those physical sensations would ease, but she still couldn't envision a time when she wouldn't, at any given moment, be simply . . . *aware* of how well-filled and well-used and well-fucked those parts of her body had been on her thirty-second birthday.

Part of her never wanted to leave this bed or her spot between Ethan and Rogan. It felt . . . safe there in a strange way. It was the place where she could love and want them both without guilt or worry.

And yet, with a wistful sigh and a long look first at Ethan, then Rogan, she gently scooted down to the foot of the bed and off, not wanting to wake either of them just yet. She needed to be alone for a few minutes, needed to clear her head.

Padding to her weekend bag, she found a pair of simple black cotton panties and a hot pink cami with black polka dots and black lace at the neckline, and slipped them on. She suffered an urge for coffee, but didn't want to make even that much noise. The only thing she could hear right now was the song of a bird somewhere outside, and it was so peaceful, just that and the silence behind it, that she wanted to keep it that way for as long as possible. Quietly, she crossed the room and stepped out the door.

On one side of the cabin's porch was the hammock where she and Ethan had made love yesterday morning, and on the other an old-fashioned glider like the one she recalled from her grandma's backyard when she was little. She sat down on the long, sofa-like glider but didn't set it in motion, instead leaning back against one side arm and pulling her legs up next to her, knees bent. She hugged them lightly as she looked out into the quiet green surroundings, liking the way the trees almost seemed to cocoon the house. Maybe it, again, made her feel safe, and like as long as she was here, her feelings for both men were somehow okay. Or maybe the woods and the great lake beyond seemed so big, vast, that it made her feel small—in a good way, like maybe her emotions and relationships didn't matter so much in the big scheme of things.

But they did. She knew that. And she needed to weigh things, needed to think.

Because she'd hoped she might wake up feeling more settled, but instead she remained torn. Between Ethan and Rogan. And yes, life would return to normal in ways today—there were family parties and jobs to return to, practical matters to handle—and life wasn't going to just stop, or appear to change dramatically to anyone who knew her. But she couldn't deny that questions, temptations, and confusion all still warred in her brain. She loved Ethan like crazy, but the things Rogan had told her had, that quickly, burrowed their way into her skin, her heart. And the truth was, she had choices. *A* choice—one very big, important one.

God, why can't I have them both?

But she knew the answer to that. It was because life and love just didn't work that way. Sure, you heard about people in shocking arrangements, people who lived with more than one lover and claimed all were content and generous and happy with what they got from the relationship. Other people had open marriages and somehow, miraculously, avoided all the jealousy and conflict that made such a situation sound crazy to her. But for most people, something like that was impossible—and she wasn't sure she believed it was so real and wonderful anyway. People *got* jealous. People wanted to be loved completely and totally—not as part of a set. *She* wanted to be loved completely and totally; she wanted to be her man's one and only, his soulmate. She knew both Ethan and Rogan wanted to be loved totally, too.

Still, when she thought of the two men who she'd shared such profound intimacies with this weekend . . . both offered her such different aspects of life, love, passion. And she longed to have all of it equally.

Then she let out a sigh, upset with her very thoughts. After all, what was she thinking? Would she really consider leaving Ethan for Rogan? *Could* she? What sort of sense would that make? And how could she ever hurt Ethan that way?

Yet then she remembered Rogan in the woods, how she'd tried to fight that heat but failed. That's what Rogan was—

heat, fire. And he'd hurt her in a lot of ways back when they'd been a couple, but he'd never neglected her or made her feel taken for granted the way Ethan had the last couple of years. And Rogan was older now—maybe he'd grown up. Maybe he really *could* be the devoted, committed man she'd wanted him to be five years ago. Maybe she'd spend the rest of her life wondering . . . what could have been, what might have happened, if she'd let herself find out.

But could she even imagine her existence without Ethan now? No, she truly couldn't. He was her life, her love, her companion in all things—from hot sex and naughty lingerie to family gatherings and picking up the dry cleaning. They *worked* together, so well. Like her, he was steady, dependable. And neglect aside, even over the recent past when she'd felt he was so much more into his work than into *her*, she'd never doubted that he loved her, ever. She'd only begun to worry, over time, that she'd feel lonely in the relationship, dissatisfied. And now he was promising to change all that.

One man gave her fire, the other warmth. The two elements were so similar in ways—and yet so very different. And still she didn't want to say goodbye to the things *either* of them gave her—she longed to have it all.

But you can't have it all. No one can. Not really.

Just then, the cabin's front door opened and she looked up to see Rogan.

And—oh Lord—something in her chest sizzled. He

wore blue jeans, unzipped—nothing else, not even under-wear from the look of it. And, God help her, her pussy spasmed at the mere sight of him, his thick hair rumpled, face unshaven, eyes dark as night as they pinned her in place. But it wasn't just sex—it was *him*, all of him. It was wanting to tame him and wondering if she could, if she . . . somehow truly *had*. Wanting to know she was the woman who could win his heart, for real and for keeps. Wanting to soothe whatever hurt him. Wanting him to open up to her and to need the same from her in return.

Oh God, this was . . . *real*, these emotions she was suffer-ing for him. They were old and they were new and they were everything in between, but they were real, not some figment of her imagination by that wishing well. She wanted him in the same way she wanted Ethan. *The very same way.* What the hell was she going to do?

"Hey, babe," he said, voice soft and perhaps tinged with a sweetness that wasn't usually there.

"Hey," she said—though it came out as more of a whisper.

He gave her a playfully chiding look, narrowing his gaze. "I didn't like waking up and finding you not there."

She tried to make light of it. "You probably just freaked out a little when you realized you were in bed alone with another guy, naked."

Still appearing amused, he shook a finger at her, spoke quietly. "Be careful, or you'll get yourself in trouble."

"Is that so?" she teased.

He joined her on the glider. "That's so," he said. But then his expression turned more inquisitive. "Whatcha doin' out here anyway?"

She took a deep breath. She didn't really want to tell him. So she kept it simple. "Guess I had some thinking to do."

"Yeah?" he asked, tilting his head slightly.

She just nodded, aware that both of them kept their voices low as they talked. Neither wanted to wake Ethan, but she wasn't sure that was due to pure intentions.

Rogan took in everything about her—Mira in the morning. It was . . . how he liked her best. They hadn't ever lived together, but they'd certainly spent plenty of nights at each other's place, and when she was like this—scantily clad, hair messy and wild, face so natural—he'd always felt like he saw the real her. He admired the professional woman who ran her own business, always so put together and on top of things—but he loved the girl who was just comfortable and happy sitting around with him half-dressed and sexy as hell without even trying.

"This thinking you had to do—come to any conclusions yet?" He asked it easily, but his heart beat harder than normal against his ribcage. Because he knew damn good and well what she was thinking about. She might have walked away from him after their sex against that old well, telling him they were going to forget it, but all night last night he'd been able to read the struggle in her eyes. And God knew he hadn't come here planning to upset the balance of her life—of *any* of their lives—yet at the same time, knowing how much what he'd said to her affected her had only amped up his lust even more last night. And with every hot stroke of his cock into her mouth, pussy, ass, he'd had . . . hope.

Though not a lot of it. And if he'd let himself think about it very much, he'd have felt damn guilty for Ethan's sake, same as he had yesterday at the well. But maybe he just wasn't a very good person because, when it came down to it, he wanted what he wanted. And he wanted Mira more than he cared about fucking over Ethan. That probably made him a piece of shit, but there it was.

"No," she finally replied, giving her brunette head a pretty shake. "I'm still . . . torn."

And now . . . a little more hope. And a lot more desire. Shit, it burned through his veins like a fast-moving drug at the very sight of her this morning, and it was all he could do not to just take her, right here, right now, on the front porch, Ethan be damned.

And maybe he should be surprised to find her seriously thinking this over, seriously considering the play he'd made for her yesterday—but somehow he wasn't. Yeah, they'd been apart a long time now—far longer than they'd been together in the first place—but for the time when she'd belonged to him, the passion had been . . . fucking electric, magnetic. And that kind of thing might go away for a while, but it never really died.

And even though they both knew good and well what they were talking about here, he discovered that he still wanted to hear her say it. "Over me and Ethan? Me *or* Ethan?"

She gave a light, barely perceptible nod, and her voice came just as small. "Yeah."

And hell—just that one tiny word, whispered as soft as a breath, sent his heart soaring.

Most of the time in life, Rogan let his instincts guide him, and this moment was no different. In response, he leaned slightly closer, facing her, and though her knees— pulled up in front of her—created a barrier between them, he smoothly slid his hand around the back of her ankle, then let it glide up her calf as he said, "Maybe I can help you decide, babe."

Their gazes locked and he fell in love all over again with the hunger in her green eyes. How the hell had he ever let her go? And he didn't know if sex was the way to win her back— but as always with Mira, and especially after the new sides of her he'd seen here, he couldn't push down his urges. And what he was feeling now—it wasn't about the hard, dirty sort of sex he'd had with her this weekend, or even by the well. No, it was just about being close to her, connecting with her—though the drive for it was just as strong as anything he'd felt over the past two days.

Using both hands, he parted her legs—and she let him, lowering one foot to the wooden porch below. Her eyes shone glassy with desire, emotion. He really did feel bad—about putting her in an unpleasant position, about Ethan—but God, she was beautiful, and he just didn't have the strength to fight it.

Easing his arms around her, clamping his hands onto her ass, he lifted her into his lap until she straddled him, the crux of her thighs—covered in black cotton—meeting with the erection that had begun to push its way up and out of his unzipped jeans. He let out a low groan and she emitted a shivery sigh. Then he leaned forward, let his forehead touch hers. "Babe, I don't know how I was ever stupid enough to walk away from you, but it's a mistake I won't make again if you give me the chance."

When he finished, he heard her pretty intake of breath. Wondered if she were really on the verge of putting her trust in him again, of really forgiving him and letting them start over. On impulse, he kissed her, firm and deep, squeezing her bottom in his hands.

And then her fingers were in his hair and she was whispering. "Last night, when you were in my ass . . ."

"Aw babe," he growled, low. Yeah, after all these years, he'd finally gotten there and it had felt . . . fucking triumphant in a way. And like he *belonged* there. "You loved it as much as I always knew you would," he finished for her.

She looked breathless, her cheeks flushed, and simply nodded.

And he couldn't hold in his grin. "God, you were fucking amazing. You blew my damn mind this weekend, over and over."

She smiled, too, though now she looked a little sheepish. Same Mira—as sweet as she was sexy. But hell, after this weekend, he knew that the sexual animal within her was just as ravenous as he ever could have hoped. "I still can't believe some of the things I did."

"I can," he told her. Then he kissed her again, all the while following the urge to push her top up over her sumptuous breasts, the beaded nipples a paler pink than the cami she wore. "I always knew there was a nasty girl deep down inside you, and I'm damn glad I finally got to meet her."

Why did those words affect Mira so deeply? Maybe because it felt so . . . right to have found that nasty girl. She'd been so afraid of that part of herself as recently as Friday night, but now she'd fucked two men, over and over again in every possible way, and the world hadn't stopped spinning. She was at once changed but still the same person she'd always been. Just . . . a different form of herself. A more *evolved* form. And she couldn't deny that maybe Rogan had been right—maybe she *had* held back in bed when they were together before and she'd just never known it, because she'd never realized how much she was capable of letting go until now. It was like . . . like all this time she'd been held hostage by her fears, her ideas of what made a woman good or bad. But no more. Both Rogan and Ethan had set her free.

And then it hit her. Both men she'd spent this weekend with had once been selected to be on a hostage rescue team, the H.O.T. program. She never could have dreamed just how far their skills in that area could extend. But, together, they'd both drawn her out of the protective sexual shell she hadn't even known she was hiding in. Together, they'd somehow released her from her old notions of who she wanted to be sexually and they'd shown her who she *could* be—who she really *was*.

She found herself kissing Rogan back for all she was worth, her arms wrapped tight around his neck, her nipples grazing his chest as a cool morning breeze wafted over them, heightening every sensation. And as always, it felt so intoxicatingly good as she sank deeper and deeper into the moment, into the heat of him.

And was this . . . was this her choosing Rogan?

But . . . no. No, this was only being *seduced* by Rogan. This was still the imaginary, temporary world of the cabin. This was . . . a last hurrah.

Whoa. Was it? The end? The last? She wasn't certain—she only knew those words had come to mind just now. And she also wasn't certain what she was doing here, what she was thinking. Wasn't this just as wrong as it had been yesterday when they'd fucked in the woods? Was she letting herself go down that dark road again? And if so, why?

God, all these questions—they almost threatened to overwhelm her. But she couldn't stop asking them. Because this was big. Important.

Even so, another part of her—the sexual animal she'd discovered inside herself this weekend—truly didn't want to think about them. That part of her didn't want to measure or analyze this right now—that part of her simply wanted to soak up every second of this, every nuance, the dark passion in his gaze, the way his slightly roughened fingertips felt as he ran them up her sides . . . the sensation of his big, hard cock stretching up the center of her right now, making her grind against it.

His voice was a low, sexy rasp in her ear. "You wanna fuck me, babe?"

The heat in the question nearly stole her breath. God *yes*, she wanted to.

But she only breathed, "I can't."

"You can't?" he asked, his eyes asking something deeper. *Do you mean you can't right now, here on the this porch? Or that you really can't, ever?*

She tried to breathe, but it was hard. And rational thoughts were even more difficult to come by. "Not here, not now," she heard herself whisper shakily. Though she wasn't sure what the answer meant—if she was somehow telling him this could go on, this thing between him and her, or if she was just confused and caught in the passion of the moment and didn't know how to deal with it.

And that's when she realized, saw in her peripheral vision . . . oh God.

Ethan stood on the porch with them.

She and Rogan both looked up at the same time to see him staring down. He, too, wore blue jeans—even shoes—and carried a T-shirt in one hand, giving the impression he'd been getting dressed as he'd stepped outside. Lord, he'd been so quiet. Or maybe the loud pounding of her heart in her ears had somehow just drowned out his approach.

She met his gaze—and even after everything they'd shared over the weekend, at this moment, she felt like the sluttiest woman alive. To be straddling Rogan. To be telling him, in effect, that she would love to fuck him and couldn't only because she needed to keep it secret from the man who loved her.

He'd witnessed that part; she could tell. The hurt in his blue eyes ran that deep.

"Ethan, I—"

She stopped, though, when he simply turned around and marched toward the porch steps.

"Ethan!" she called, instinctively reaching up, pulling her top down over her boobs. She remained in Rogan's lap yet was barely aware of it now.

"Leave me the fuck alone," Ethan bit off as his feet reached the ground.

"Wait." She was trying to get disentangled from Rogan's body, trying to get to Ethan.

"Dude, it's not her fault," Rogan said.

But Ethan was still on the move, trudging away from the cabin now as he called over his shoulder, "Fuck you, man. Fuck you both. You can both go to hell."

Chapter 17

Seeing the hurt in Ethan's eyes had been . . . God, like a lightbulb suddenly and brightly illuminating over Mira's head. What was she doing? Why on earth had she risked hurting him—in the woods with Rogan yesterday or now? How had she let herself be so stupidly reckless?

Because in this moment, it all became clear to her. To the very core of her soul, she understood with shocking clarity that Ethan was the man for her, the man she loved and would *always* love, the man she wanted to spend the rest of her life with!

If she hadn't just ruined that.

Finally getting herself apart from Rogan and onto her feet, she said to him, "I'm sorry, Rogan. I'll probably always want you in ways—but Ethan has my heart now."

And with that, she started to dash off the porch after the man she loved, but Rogan stopped her with, "Babe. Shoes."

Oh shit, he was right—she'd learned already that it was dangerous to walk around here barefoot, even when trying to be careful choosing each step, and right now she didn't have that luxury—she needed to run!

Rushing back into the cabin, she spotted her flip-flops and shoved her feet into them. And she thought briefly of clothes, remembering how little she wore, but then decided it didn't matter—it was more important to catch up with Ethan before he got any farther away.

And what she'd just told Rogan was so very true—she did want him, she truly cared for him. Maybe she even really loved him. But it just wasn't on the same level as what she shared with Ethan. This weekend with them both had been beyond incredible, but so confusing, too—and to tempt her with her old lover had just been, well . . . *too* tempting, apparently. Yet now, faced with the idea of really losing her man, and knowing how much she'd just hurt him . . . her heart shriveled in her chest.

She felt bad about the fact that she barely gave Rogan a backward glance as she darted out the door and down the steps, though she still heard him say, "Be careful," behind her. And she truly wished she had time to go back, to make him understand—and maybe give him one last kiss. But she didn't. She'd screwed up her priorities enough his weekend already—now was the time to remember who came first and to put him there the way she should have all along.

From the side of the cabin, she scanned the area and caught sight of Ethan up ahead—he followed the path that led to the well.

God, he has to go there? To the very spot where I first betrayed his trust?

But she couldn't think about that now or let it slow her down—so she moved briskly up the trail after him, as quickly as she could go in her flip-flops, her heart pounding a mile an hour.

"Ethan, please wait!" she called after him. He was moving too fast and she wasn't gaining any ground.

But he ignored her, just kept walking. And for the first time since he'd appeared on the porch, her sense of shock and panic began to give way to something else: *I could lose him. I could really lose him. Right here and now. God, maybe I already have.*

She moved faster, watching her footing, jogging a little when she could, but the path grew more narrow with each step, and like the last time she'd been in these woods, she felt the forest closing around her, becoming more pervasive. She hadn't minded it so much then—but she minded it now. She suffered the sense that the forest might just swallow her and Ethan whole by the time she caught up to him.

Chilled by air that felt cooler, danker under the trees than back at the cabin, she was breathless by the time she began to draw closer to him—he'd reached the trail's end at the wishing well. He still held a dark blue T-shirt wadded in his hand, one she recognized from a Florida beach vacation they'd taken together two summers ago.

Now that she was here, she wasn't quite sure what would happen and thought he might just keep right on ignoring her—but instead he looked up at her approach.

"This your wishing well?" he asked brusquely.

"Yeah." Her voice came too quiet; she barely heard her own reply.

His eyes narrowed on her in disgust. "What'd you wish for?"

"Lasting love," she told him. "For the rest of my life."

He simply made a *pffft* sound and rolled his eyes. She guessed she couldn't blame him.

"I meant it," she insisted anyway. Though she wouldn't explain that the coin she'd used had come from Rogan's pocket—and she had no idea if she should tell him what else had happened here with Rogan, either. Same as when it had taken place, it wasn't that she wanted to lie, but why hurt him further? Why make him think she really wanted Rogan when she knew now that she didn't? Yes, she'd been confused for a little while, but it all seemed so clear to her now. And so she simply spoke from her heart, and was as honest as she *could* be about how she felt. "Ethan," she began, "Rogan is . . . sex. But you're . . . *everything*. You're sex, you're love. You're . . . walks in the park and trips to the doctor. You're paying the bills and running errands with me on Saturday mornings. You're holding me when I cry at sappy movies. You're . . . snuggling while we sleep. Rogan is sex, but you're *my life*.

"What you saw," she went on when he didn't answer, "that meant nothing. This weekend was . . . amazing for me, but also . . . confusing as hell, E. It brought back old feelings for Rogan—and maybe I just had to get them out of my system or something. But I never meant to do anything that hurt you. And I promise it's all in the past—you're the only man I *really* want. You're the one I love."

Ethan simply looked at her. He'd seen so many sides of her over the past two days—and now she stood before him in her underwear in the middle of the woods apologizing for something that . . . despite himself, he still couldn't believe she'd done.

Because even though they'd never actually talked about it, to share her with Rogan, to have a threesome with him, was a damn different thing than for her to go fooling around with him when he wasn't there. And she obviously knew that—all three of them knew it. This weekend had been intended to draw the two of them closer together, not bring about things that would tear them apart.

"It still . . . fucking hurts," he told her. And hell, it was even more than that—it felt like having his damn chest ripped open. Like he couldn't even breathe.

"I know, Ethan, and I'm so, so sorry. I wish I could take it back, but I can't." He couldn't deny that she looked as upset as he felt, her eyes desperate and guilty, her hands clenched into fists at her sides. "Apologizing is all I know to do. Please forgive me."

He found himself thinking aloud, not even weighing his words. "I gave you this fantasy—and this is what I get back in return."

In response, her eyes changed then—shifting from distress to just . . . a replete sorrow he could almost feel dripping off her. "It was . . . a pretty complicated gift," she quietly pointed out. "Generous beyond words, but . . . a lot to handle without much warning."

And shit—something in her words squeezed his heart. He didn't want to feel bad for her right now—she'd fucked up and he wanted to stay mad, hold her accountable—but . . . hell. He'd *brought* Rogan here. To her birthday celebration. And right into the center of their relationship.

And he'd wanted it to be simple—this simple living out of her fantasy. He'd wanted it to be easy and hot and fun. Yet the truth he couldn't reject now was that maybe it all came with . . . a certain darkness, too. A darkness that revolved around sex and lust and pushing boundaries. A darkness within him that he'd . . . shoved on to her, without warning, as she'd said.

And that's when it struck him: He'd actually thought a

threesome could be simple. He was a lawyer, he'd been trained to think in logical ways—and yet that very thought suddenly seemed like a contradiction in terms. *Threesome. Simple.* The two words just didn't make sense together.

So maybe he'd been unwittingly asking for this. Maybe it was ... some kind of cosmic punishment for wanting to bring this kind of forbidden excitement into their lives. Maybe, even though he'd wanted it for her, maybe he'd wanted it even *more* for him. More than he'd ever been willing to admit to himself until this moment.

So maybe it was his own fault he'd just found his girl-friend grinding against another guy's dick.

And still, when he tried to look at it *that* way—remembering the naughty grind, the hot, happy encounter he'd seen taking place—hell, the sting of betrayal came right back, piercing his soul all over again.

And though, both as a cop and a lawyer, he'd gotten pretty practiced at controlling his emotions, showing only what he chose to any given moment—right now he wasn't holding back what he felt. So when he spoke, it came out gruff. "Look, I know I started this, I know it's my own fuck-ing fault he's here, but now ... damn it, Mira, now I just need to fucking know you belong to me!"

She looked a little startled by his tone, and despite him-self, it pleased him. "I do belong to you, Ethan! You know that! I do!"

He drew in a breath, let it back out. Tried to let it calm down the ferocious anger still tightening his chest. It didn't work, but when he replied, his answer at least came out lower, quieter. "That's not enough. I need to feel it."

At which she looked confused, bereft. And pretty as hell still standing there in that bright pink cami and black panties. "How can I make you feel it?" she asked.

As the dense woods seemed to wrap around them a little tighter in lush green isolation, that same darkness he'd acknowledged a moment ago came wafting back, seeming to settle over him in a heavy mist, something he almost felt covering his skin. It was the darkness that had first nibbled at him when he'd come up with this idea, this birthday party for her—it was the same darkness that he'd experienced in a deeper, more direct way last night when it had been Rogan's actions who'd made him feel so possessive and hungry. And now he experienced its power again, forcing him, one more time, to open himself up and accept what he really wanted. Hell, who knew—maybe he'd *always* wanted it in some hidden corner of his soul. God knew *something* inside him had put all this into motion.

Whatever the case, he wanted it *now*. And he couldn't see any other way than to just be honest, put it out there. Despite the new truths he'd just discovered about her still having feelings for Rogan, he couldn't refute that this weekend had been all *about* honesty—sexual honesty to be exact—and here was some more. "Maybe I need . . . to be a little rough with you. Maybe I need to make you beg a little." Something thickened his throat as he spoke—he thought it was lust. "Maybe I need to feel what I felt last night when I fucked you on that table—like you're all mine, no matter what it takes. Like the harder I fuck you, the more mine you become."

At first, he thought she appeared a little frightened. That he could say something like that. But then he realized that, at the same time, she looked . . . excited. Aroused as hell, in fact. Then she said, "Whatever you want."

Whatever you want.

That's what she'd said.

And he was going to take it to heart.

He hadn't come here knowing he could ever be turned on by being so dominant—hell, that role fit Rogan, *was* Rogan, and he saw the two of them as opposites in many ways. But maybe in *this* way they were more alike than he'd ever suspected.

Because right now the idea of having power over her—emotional as much as sexual—had his cock hard and throbbing behind his zipper. He wanted her undying devotion, and her willingness to do anything it took to prove it. And he was still pissed. And putting those factors together made it so he didn't even try to fight it.

"Then get on your knees and suck my cock." It came in a low, firm command.

And though there was a part of him that waited for her to look a little horrified, or maybe even tell him to go to hell—because this was not a game they'd ever played before, and at the moment it didn't feel much like a game—she simply let out a quiet breath, stepped forward, and sank gently to her knees in the soft earth beside the old stone well.

He inhaled sharply as she reached up to undo his jeans, the look in her eyes . . . downright loving, giving.

But when she pulled down his briefs, hooking them under his balls, then boldly took his erection in her hand, her expression changed to one he'd seen many times this weekend—she was suddenly the hungry animal who needed to be fed.

As she lowered her mouth over him in one long, wet descent, a groan rumbled up from his gut.

"Look at me," he told her, and she raised her eyes, and in spite of the gnawing ache still clawing its way down through him amid this fresh pleasure, he knew he would forgive her. *Was* forgiving her, this very moment.

She moved his dick in and out of her tender mouth with a skill and enthusiasm that soon almost made it difficult to keep on his feet. She'd always been good at giving a blow job, but the undeniable fact was—she'd gotten even better at it this weekend with so much practice. "Aw baby, yeah. Don't stop, keep going. You suck me so, so good." And with that, he reached down, ran his fingers through her hair, and held on to her head lightly without controlling her moves. He had enough power already right now and she did a damn fine job without him guiding her mouth. He couldn't imagine it feeling any better.

Mira was nearly overwhelmed with emotion. So much had happened in the past fifteen minutes that she could barely fathom it. And now she was on her knees in the dirt, proving her love after having him demand it of her, and . . . God, to her surprise, she was excited. More excited than she could have predicted or could even really understand.

Lord, this was a new side of Ethan—even more commanding than he'd been for a little while last night. And though she'd never known she wanted anything like this from him, it had her aroused beyond words. She had definitely developed a new appreciation for sucking a man's cock this weekend, but at the moment she truly reveled in bringing Ethan pleasure. She delighted in having submitted to him at his demand. And she felt like just one more wild-growing thing in the forest.

What did it mean that she wanted him to control her a little? She had no idea. But she didn't care. And . . . maybe it was just a little kinkiness. And as Rogan had once taught her, she *liked* a little kinkiness.

Maybe, until this weekend, she'd forgotten that. Ethan had, from the start, always seemed so much more like her than Rogan ever had. Ethan was the guy next door, the one you took home to meet your mother. And after Rogan had led her down a few hot and marginally kinky paths and then broken her heart—well, Ethan's clean cut, aboveboard image had appealed immensely. Especially when she'd learned how drop dead hot and sexy a clean cut and aboveboard guy could be.

But now . . . now that was changing. And as she slid her lips, warm and moist, up and down his erection, she realized that she *loved* the change. That as strange as it seemed in her own civilized mind, she was somehow falling a little more in love with Ethan this very moment.

The longer she moved her mouth over him, though, the more her pussy ached, felt empty, needy. That should have been impossible given how ridiculously much sex she'd enjoyed and endured in less than forty-eight hours, but it hungered to be filled the same way her mouth currently was.

Finally, unable to stand it anymore, she extracted his rigid length from her lips and, peering needfully up at him, said, "Please fuck me now."

For a second, he stunned her, looking doubtful and still demanding, like maybe he wasn't quite ready for her to start calling any shots here. But finally he said, voice still rough, "Turn around."

Okay, she could do that—no problem. And she was so painfully eager right now that she'd truly do whatever he asked. Both to earn his forgiveness and faith—and to get the fucking she so desperately needed in this moment.

So she wordlessly shifted on her knees until she faced

away from him. Before her sat the wishing well that was beginning to feel like some sort of strange magnet to her.

"Push your panties down," he demanded. When she rushed to do so, fresh air struck the sensitive flesh of her cunt, leaving it all the more tingly and ready.

"Now bend over. I want you on your hands and knees. And arch your back to show me that pretty pussy."

Happily, she braced herself, her fingers digging slightly into the soft soil, here sprinkled with bits of ivy. Arching as requested, she felt the opening between her legs growing still wetter, knowing that Ethan was studying it now, and that she was putting it on display for him. She had the sensation that it gaped wide with want.

"Is that naughty little pussy craving my cock?" he asked.

Oh God—she'd thought he would finally do it now, thrust himself inside her! She was going crazy with need. "Yes," she said, nearly breathless.

"Tell me how badly you want to be fucked, Mira."

She let out a shaky breath. She sort of wanted to kill him. But she also felt the arousal inside her climb even higher as she said, "I want to be fucked so, so much, E. I think I want to be fucked more in this moment than I ever have before." Facing the stone well with Ethan behind her, she found herself clenching her teeth as her desperation increased. "I want you inside me! I want you to fill me up!"

"Beg," he said simply then. "Beg me to fuck you."

She didn't hesitate. "Please! Please, please, please, baby. Please fill me with that perfect cock. Please fuck me senseless. I need you so bad! I beg of you to fuck me hard!" Now she only prayed he would finally give in and deliver what she yearned for before she collapsed in a heap of roiling frustration.

And then—oh, oh God—she finally sensed him dropping to the earth behind her, heard the soft *mmmph* of his knees landing in the dirt, and then his hands molded to her hips and she knew hot bliss was near. Yes, yes, almost!

"God, please," she added to her appeals. Now not because he'd told her to beg but simply because she needed it so horribly, wildly much and each second she waited was pure torture.

When the column of stone that was Ethan's erection came to rest on her ass, she shivered with delight. "Please, please," she whispered mindlessly now. Her cunt practically dripped with raging need.

Behind her, she heard him draw in his breath sharply. "Tell me why I should give this cock to such a bad little girl."

She could barely talk through her panting breaths now. "Because I'm sorry and I love you! Because you've punished me enough! Because I need you so bad!" God, what would it take? Was he somehow just teasing her and not planning to follow through? Was this all some sick, cruel game to punish her further still? And if so . . . God, was he really not going to forgive her? Was it really... over? Ruined? Done? "Ethan..." she began helplessly, without quite knowing what more she could say or do now.

And that's when he positioned the tip of his dick at her pussy and drove it into her, deep.

Chapter 18

She cried out at the most gloriously welcome intrusion of her entire life.

And then, immersed in her cunt to the hilt, he went still for a minute, just letting them both savor it, absorb it. She drank in the wonder of how it felt to have him back inside her where he belonged, shadowed by the cool green canopy of the woods.

And then—oh God, yes—he began to thrust, thrust, thrust. Hard, mind-numbing plunges reverberated through her whole body, each making her let out a high-pitched moan that echoed through the trees. "Yes! Yes!" she managed through clenched teeth.

At some point, she shut her eyes, blocking out the forest and the well, the ivy and the path, so that the only thing that existed in the world were the two of them. No more Rogan. No more mistakes. Just their bodies and souls connected the way they should be. She'd never loved him more, and though she was growing weak and couldn't even muster the strength to speak any longer, she just prayed he knew that, could feel that.

And then—oh Lord—she could scarcely believe it, but his thumb brushed across her anus. The touch came feather light but almost electrical in its power. A quick, low sound escaped her throat.

After that, the brushing became more like rubbing—and then a pressure that had her biting her lip even as he continued to pound his cock into her. She couldn't hold in the low whimpers the sensation caused to rise within her.

And then—oh. Wetness, there. Saliva, she thought. Being rubbed in by his finger in a circular motion—until the tip of that finger sank inside. "God," she murmured.

Last night, having both Ethan and Rogan inside her at the same time—one in her ass and the other in her pussy— had been . . . the ultimate filling, overflowing sex. But this . . . this was more . . . intimate. Intimacy between the three of them had been thrilling and new and had led her to express her sexuality in bold ways she never had before. But this— she and the man she really loved, would *always* love, getting closer and closer here on the forest floor without even the need for words—this was the *truest* intimacy. As it should be.

The pleasure was nearly crushing as he fucked her with both cock and finger—she suspected she was writhing and bucking and groaning like a wild animal, but she didn't care. Ethan had seen all of her now; he could see this, too, this rawest of reactions to the hot, naughty delights he sent coursing through her body.

When, panting, hands on her hips, Ethan pulled his cock from her, she let out a cry of loss—she wanted him back—now! And yet . . . deep inside she knew what was coming.

And so she tried to stay patient, her arms growing heavy and weak, her teeth almost chattering with how much she needed him. And Lord, behind her she thought she heard E's breath trembling—and soon the very sensation of it rumbled through her chest.

When the tip of his cock pushed at her asshole, she let out a soft, mewling moan, then tried to relax her body, hoping it would extend to the muscles surrounding her anus, as well.

The initial entry of the head hurt—she cried out, absorbing the pain, then worked hard to come back to the pleasure. And after a moment of stillness, of letting her adjust, he began to ever so slowly ease his length deeper. First maybe another inch, producing a low, heated sigh from her. Then another. And eventually another.

And after that she didn't know, couldn't truly gauge how much of his shaft she was taking into her ass—she knew only that it was a lot, and that the permeating pleasure she'd experienced from the same kind of penetration last night was blasting through her now, wild and consuming.

Her cheeks flushed, her every muscle seemed to vibrate, an intensely deep pleasure echoing through her whole being. As he moved in short but firm strokes in that impossibly tiny passageway, her own cries sounded almost inhuman to her— she had no control over her responses anymore. All she knew was a pleasure that nearly drained her.

At some point not long after this began, her arms gave way, buckling beneath her. Her palms remained flat on the ground, but now her cheek rested atop them, her hair fanning out to one side over the earth and ivy beneath them.

She whimpered and he groaned and her clit ached. She'd been so into different kinds of pleasure here in the woods up to this moment—pleasing him, having him in her mouth, then welcoming the hot, hard drives of his cock in her cunt—that she'd honestly not even thought about coming. This wasn't about that. Except that . . . now it was. Now that sensitive little spot at the top of her cunt hungered—in a way she recognized from every time she'd ever indulged in ass play with Rogan, last night or even before that, times when they'd been together and he'd tried to persuade her by teasing it, touching it.

Now she was wondering why on earth she'd put this off for so long, letting someone fuck her ass—but maybe it had taken the particular dynamic of this weekend to push her there, to push her that far into her sexual self that she could finally accept the things she really wanted to do, the sexual being she really wanted to become. And now she could share that fully with Ethan—*was* sharing it fully with Ethan.

And, oh God, how her clit screamed for attention now. She didn't quite understand why, but the erection in her ass seemed to have a direct connection to the swollen nub just above her pussy. It yearned for—*needed*—attention, pressure, anything.

Her knees had given out, too, and were now bent beneath her, pulled up almost to her chest. And it wasn't a decision so much as an urge, or maybe an instinct, when her thighs parted, just enough—enough that her cunt came into contact with the bed of ivy on which she rested. And that was all it took. That one tiny bit of stimulation to her clit, and for only a second. She exploded into orgasm, lost, wild, screaming her pleasure, wrung out from it even as it spiraled through her like a corkscrew.

"Oh fuck, I'm coming, too, baby! I'm coming, too!" Ethan yelled, and she had to clench her hands into fists to withstand those final few drives, more ferocious than he'd delivered in her ass up to now.

"Oh God, I love you," he said, the words seeming to spill from him in a rush as he curled his body around hers, still buried in her anus.

"I love you, too, E," she breathed, as weak as she thought she'd ever been. She'd never shared such powerful sex with anyone in her life.

And now, now she just had to hope it was all enough. To

have truly repaired things between them. Not just the sex, of course, but her apology, her explanation, and . . . well, yes, the sex, too. It mattered. She'd just given herself to him in a way she never had before, body and soul. And nothing about it had been sweet, or tender. No, this was primal. Gut deep. And something she never wanted to share with anyone else—and she hoped he could feel that.

When he pulled out of her, the opening felt . . . too large at first, uncomfortably so. But as she rolled to her back on the ground, that sensation began to fade. Especially when she looked up into Ethan's eyes. "I love you," she said again.

"I love you, too, Mir," he replied, his body angled over hers, one hand cupping her jaw. And—*oh God, thank you!*—he sounded like . . . well, like his normal, usual, loving self again. Which she thought, at this point, seemed like a good sign.

And even as they began to kiss, she remained turned on, whispering, "That was so hot."

"I know."

"Not that I necessarily want it to be this way every time, E, but . . . well, I think I could go for more of this. If you could. I think I'm glad we, um, discovered this."

His grin was laced with just a bit of naughtiness. "Aw, me too, baby. Me too."

"Are . . . are we good, Ethan?" she asked then. Because she had to. It all *felt* good, and she hated to take them back to a bad place, but this had to be talked about.

He hesitated a minute before answering, his eyes serious and a little sad, until he finally said, "It wasn't your fault."

She peered up at him, let out a sigh. The truth was, some of it *had* been her fault. But a lot of it hadn't. So she simply replied, "I just . . . got swept up in the weekend. But you're *truly* the man I love, Ethan." Then she lifted a hand to touch the stubble on his jaw and knew no words she'd ever spoken had been more accurate.

"I believe you," he said softly, then lowered his mouth over hers for a long, slow kiss. And when it was done, Mira wanted nothing more than to kiss him again and again, and to forget anything bad had happened this weekend—but she still couldn't.

"Although . . . there's something you should know." Oh Lord, she really *didn't* want to tell him this, really didn't want to hurt him further or risk what they'd just repaired, but now . . . now she was beginning to realize the brutal truth: If they were to move forward from this weekend, *really* move forward, she *had* to tell him what had happened between her and Rogan in this very same spot yesterday. She just had to. To leave it unsaid would be like a lie between them, and even as much as she'd been trying to hold this back, even as afraid as she was to say it, she simply had no choice. "Something more," she added, trying to will the difficult words out, "about the walk I took here yesterday."

Ethan just looked at her for a long moment. And she

thought he could almost read the truth in her eyes, or that maybe what she'd just said made the truth clear enough already and that she didn't have to say anything at all. Though it surprised the hell out of her when he finally told her, "Maybe I don't want to know."

She drew in her breath, let it back out. "Are you sure?"

"I . . . I guess I didn't think through all the situations that could arise or . . . the complications that could crop up by bringing Rogan into our relationship. So . . . nothing that happened between you and him matters—I promise. I just want to move forward, me and you, consider this a fresh start. How does that sound?"

She couldn't help smiling. Because he'd just proven to her what a truly amazing man he really was. "Sounds perfect."

They walked back to the cabin without discussing what they would say to Rogan when they got there. Mira thought perhaps they were both on overload—so much sex, so much conflicting, confusing emotion—and it felt a little surreal to be treading quietly up the path in the woods with both of them half dressed. She just wasn't sure there was any room left in their exhaustion-ridden brains for thinking ahead right now.

Yet when they stepped inside, there was no sign of him. The bathroom door was open, the small room empty, so

Ethan wordlessly pulled back a curtain to glance out toward the driveway. "His car's gone."

It was about that time that Mira noticed a note on the kitchen table, still a mess with cheesecake from last night—the corner of the paper held down by an empty wine bottle.

Mira and Ethan,
> *Thanks for a great weekend.*
> *Hope you had a happy birthday, M.*

That simple. Not even a signature.

Part of her felt a little empty inside—for better or worse, she'd shared some shockingly intense intimacy with Rogan this weekend, too, and she just hadn't imagined there wouldn't even be a chance to say goodbye.

But she knew almost immediately that it was best. And that maybe he'd done this for *her*, leaving so abruptly. Maybe Rogan really *had* changed, really *could* love her the right way now. She'd never know for sure. But that probably was best kept as one of life's grand mysteries anyway. She was supposed to be with Ethan—she knew that now without a shred of doubt.

After showing the note to him, she wondered aloud, "Will things be okay between the two of you now?"

Ethan pursed his lips, then let out a long sigh. "They kinda have to be. We live in the same town, we play on the same team and hang with the same people, and he's one of my academy buddies—no matter how ya slice it, he's gonna be in my life a long time."

Now she did start thinking ahead a little. "Is it gonna be weird if I see him at a softball game and say hi? Because . . . it seems like it would be *weirder* if I *don't* say hi."

Ethan gave a small nod. "I'll keep my cool. And it'll be easy, because I won."

She couldn't help slanting him a look. "Ethan, it wasn't a competition." Though even as she spoke, she knew that, in a way, it had become that—but she just couldn't see the good in acknowledging it. She just wanted to let the negative parts of this weekend pass away as peacefully as possible, for all of them.

"And maybe when you go offering your girl up to another guy," he went on, "you're asking for something like this."

"Well, it's over now," she reminded him, and, unable to hide a naughty little grin, added, "And there *were* good parts."

"Damn right there were," he said. "The only problem now might be that if I see you talking to him or looking at him, I might have to take you home and fuck your brains out to make sure you know you're with the right guy."

She smiled up into his gorgeous blue eyes. "I *already* know. I'll always know. But if fucking my brains out will make you feel better, I won't argue."

"Damn straight you won't," he said in that same slightly

commanding tone she'd had a few tastes of now, even though a hint of a grin tugged at his mouth this time.

She bit her lip, thinking through all she'd learned about herself and her relationship with Ethan this weekend. She'd experienced moments when she'd wondered if normal, two-person sex could ever be as great now. But it was. Already. What they'd shared this weekend had made it more exciting, more intimate, more adventurous than she ever could have imagined.

"You know, honey," he said then, "I wanted to believe this weekend was all for you, or at least *mostly* for you, but I know now that it was just as much about . . . letting loose a darker part of *me* I didn't even know existed, about needing to explore that, and . . . I guess, about needing more with you in some way."

She touched a hand to his chest. "I'm glad I know that darker part of you now, E. And I'm kind of loving it, too. And I'm glad we've both now officially met the darker parts of me, as well."

In response, he gave her a smile, along with a warm kiss that moved all through her.

"So," she said, looking around at the cabin that somewhere along the way had begun to resemble a pigsty, "I guess we should get this place cleaned up, then pack and hit the road home."

And she was surprised when Ethan let out a small laugh,

until he said, "You wouldn't believe how good it sounds to me just to spend the day doing regular, normal stuff with you."

She released a soft trill of laughter then, as well, because she agreed. A normal day—from this point forward anyway—would be nice.

"I love the hot-and-dirty you," he told her, "but I love the everyday, normal you just as much."

And she concluded then that, really, that was what this all came down to. Finding the person in life who loved *all* of you—from the purest parts to the kinkiest—equally.

And through the ups and downs of her most unusual and extreme birthday party, even through the jealousy and betrayal that had resulted, she knew they'd discovered new parts of themselves. What they'd done this weekend wasn't about three people—it was about stepping outside the pre-set boundaries, about accepting their true sexual natures and letting their inhibitions go on the deepest level. And now that they'd done that, their sex life would be richer, they'd always be closer, and their passion for one another would run deeper.

And all that aside, it had certainly been a birthday she'd never forget.

About the Author

Lacey Alexander's books have been called deliciously decadent, unbelievably erotic, exceptionally arousing, blazingly sexual, and downright sinful. In each book, Lacey strives to take her readers on the ultimate erotic adventure, and she hopes her stories will encourage women to embrace their sexual fantasies. Lacey resides in the Midwest with her husband, and when not penning romantic erotica, she enjoys studying history and traveling, often incorporating favorite destinations into her work.

CONNECT ONLINE

laceyalexander.net
facebook.com/AuthorLaceyAlexander

Read on for a special preview of the next
H.O.T. Cops Novel by Lacey Alexander,

Give in to Me

Coming from Signet Eclipse in January 2013

April Pediston regretted her business suit the moment she stepped into the Café Tropico, which, she instantly realized, was less a café and more your garden-variety bar and dance club. Not nearly as trendy—or classy—as most Ocean Avenue establishments, the Café Tropico had clearly been here a while, though she got the idea that its heyday had long since passed.

"Table for two," she told the skinny twentysomething hostess clad in a baby-doll tank and ultrashort cutoff jeans. She couldn't help noticing the girl hadn't bothered with a bra, and her nipples jutted prominently against the snug fabric. And the slightly perplexed look on the girl's face as she led April to a table assured her that she looked just as out of place as she felt. But she'd come straight from work, and she was here on business, so she hadn't given it a thought.

Meetings outside the office were generally held at places where . . . well, where she wasn't usually greeted by someone wearing so little.

Warm night air—punctuated with just a hint of soft breeze blowing in from South Beach—permeated the partially open-air restaurant and reminded April that summer was descending on Miami. She'd always meant to move away, to someplace cooler, calmer. Although the feeling was vague and long-since accepted, despite being born and raised here, she'd never felt she fit in Miami any more than she fit in at the Café Tropico.

Across the room, intimidating guys with tattoos and goatees drank beer and shot pool, the clack of the balls cutting through her thoughts, while a band set up instruments and sound equipment at the small stage in the distance. She was just beginning to wonder whether the Café Tropico actually served food—she hadn't eaten, assuming that this was a dinner meeting—when the braless hostess returned with a menu and glass of water to inform her a waitress would be with her in a minute.

"I'm meeting someone," she replied, "so— Oh, here she is now."

She'd just looked up to see Kayla Gonzalez crossing the floor toward her, past one of several potted palm trees that actually gave the place a little tropical ambience. Kayla wore jeans and a tight tank top, her gaze—and entire countenance—as haggard as the last time April had seen her two years ago. Hair that had been black was now platinum blond with dark brown roots an inch long.

As April greeted her, the other woman tried to smile, but the gesture didn't reach her eyes.

"Shall we order dinner before we talk business?" April suggested. She'd been on the run today and had eaten only a granola bar for lunch.

When Kayla looked hesitant, though, April realized dinner *hadn't* been on this evening's agenda for the other woman. "I . . . probably shouldn't."

Thinking maybe it was a matter of money, April smiled and said, "My treat."

As Kayla blinked, April saw some remnants of youthful beauty pass through her eyes. Whereas April was thirty-three, Kayla probably wasn't yet thirty, but she looked far older. "That's awful nice of you, but . . . I was hopin' we could get right down to business. I don't have much time."

April held back her sigh. Dinner could wait—whatever legal matter Kayla had called her here to discuss was clearly weighing on her. "Sure," April said. "What can I do for you?"

Kayla tossed quick, furtive glances back and forth across the room as if to make sure no one was watching as she leaned across the small table and said, just loud enough to be heard above the other noises in the room, "I want a divorce."

April wasn't entirely surprised at this news, and in fact, she suspected it would be the smartest move Kayla would ever make. The last time she'd worked with Kayla—connecting via a women-helping-women group through which she did pro bono work—Kayla had been accused of stealing valuable equipment from the warehouse where she'd worked as a receptionist at the time. April had built a case proving that Kayla couldn't have done it—not only had she had an alibi, but she was physically too small to have lifted and transported the generators and other heavy items taken. And though Kayla had maintained her innocence throughout, April had been torn between believing Kayla had just been a convenient target and worrying that Kayla's husband had been involved in the theft. She'd met Juan Gonzalez only once, but he'd made a terrible impression, striking April as emotionally and possibly physically abusive.

Even so, April tilted her head to explain, "Kayla, I wish I could help you, but I'm not a divorce lawyer. That's not the kind of work I do. Though I can connect you with someone else through Women Helping Women."

Kayla's eyes clouded over so darkly that April felt the woman's response in her gut. "But . . . I want *you*. That's why I called you on my own and didn't go through the service—I didn't want nobody else. You were so nice to me before. And . . . you don't make me feel like . . . trash." She'd whispered the last word as if it were an obscenity.

As a pang of empathy shot through April's core, she reached out to touch Kayla's hand on the table. "Kayla, you shouldn't ever let *anyone* make you feel like trash."

Yet Kayla's expression stayed downcast, and even as April thought of her colleague at the firm who handled divorces for disenfranchised women for free, she knew Ellen did sometimes intimidate her less-confident clients. She never stopped to remember how fragile some of them were. And April clearly recalled how difficult it had seemed for Kayla to even look her in the eye when they'd first met two years ago. Now, since Kayla was comfortable with her but wouldn't have that luxury with someone else . . . Well, she didn't want to be responsible for the poor woman postponing her divorce, especially if her husband *was* abusive.

"Please," Kayla added then. "I really need your help."

April let out a breath and said, "I'll need to get some guidance from my colleague." Though hopefully it would be a simple thing, something cut-and-dried and easy for all involved. "But all right," she said. "I'll see what I can do."

"You'll be my lawyer again?" Kayla asked, her eyes suddenly looking much brighter than they had since she'd arrived.

April nodded reluctantly. "Sure."

After which Kayla thanked her profusely, now reaching out to squeeze April's hand. "That's such a relief," she went on. "I'm strung out enough over this without havin' to get to know somebody new. And like I said, you've always been so nice."

I really don't need this added to my *already stressful life. But if it will get you away from your scumbag of a husband a little faster, how can I say no?* "I'm glad to help," she said instead. "Now, does your husband know you want a divorce?"

Fresh panic seemed to seize Kayla's body—she tensed visibly. "God, no. He'll kill me."

April knew enough about women like Kayla to realize she wasn't exaggerating. So she spoke calmly, hoping to calm Kayla, as well. "We'll come up with a plan for telling him, preferably on the phone, after you have someplace else to stay. But first, as I said, I'll need to confer with my colleague— then we'll talk about how to move forward. Does that sound okay?"

Kayla nodded.

And April felt a little relaxed, perhaps for both of them. Or maybe she was just tired. And hungry. And now that she felt their business had officially concluded . . . "You know," she said, "I'm really starving, so if you don't mind, I'm going to order dinner. You're more than welcome to join me if you'd like."

Like before, Kayla glanced nervously around the bar, which April realized had begun to get more crowded in just the few minutes since they'd started talking. Why was Kayla so paranoid? Did people here know her? Or her husband? Maybe it hadn't occurred to Kayla that April would stand out in the crowd so much in her professional attire, possibly drawing more attention to them than Kayla had bargained for.

"Or if you need to leave," April added, wanting to give her an easy out, "that's no problem at all."

She saw Kayla glance to a clock behind the bar before she said, "Um, I guess I can hang out for a few more minutes."

Rogan Wolfe sat at the bar nursing a beer. The pretty girl behind the bar—who couldn't have been a day more than twenty-two—was making conversation, but she was too young for him. He'd never used to pay attention to things like that, but he guessed he'd gone through some changes lately. Maybe he was finally growing up. Or maybe it was about Mira.

Mira was an old girlfriend whose heart he'd once broken—and she'd returned the favor last summer. It hadn't been her fault, and though he'd never really talked to anyone about it, the truth was that he'd spent quite a bit of time after that pining for her. Another first—Rogan Wolfe, pining for a woman. He'd pined, in fact, until he'd realized he needed to make a change, a big one. He'd needed to get out of Charlevoix, Michigan, the same small lakeside town where they'd both lived—and he'd needed something exciting to take his mind off her. So he'd come down to Miami to visit his friend Colt and he'd applied for a job on the Miami Police Department while he was here. A month later, he'd turned in his Charlevoix badge and started working South Beach.

And the change had been exactly what he'd needed. Miami was hot sun, hot music, hot girls, and action, action, action. But maybe what falling for Mira had done was to help him see that, when it came to women, the time had finally arrived in his life when he needed more than just a pretty face and smokin' body. He needed a little substance. And that fact surprised *him* more than anybody else, but there it was—the next time he got involved with someone, he wanted it to count for something, be someone he could envision a future with.

Though the truth was . . . women, dating, fucking—they hadn't been high on his priority list since he'd come to Miami. Sure, he'd found someone to hook up with a few times—God knew his sex drive hadn't faded after Mira—but mostly, he'd thrown himself into his job. Which was why he was here tonight, working undercover. Undercover and not officially on the clock.

Remembering why he was here, he pushed the beer aside, not wanting to let alcohol dull his senses. He might not always play by the rules—and his partner would be pissed if he knew Rogan was here right now—but that didn't equal being sloppy. In fact, since hitting South Beach, Rogan had felt more inspired by his work than ever before. After spending the first dozen years of his career in small town Michigan, he'd found his calling in Miami. In Miami, things were happening, crimes were being committed—and there were true bad guys who needed to be taken down. A place like Miami, Rogan now knew, was the reason he'd become a cop in the first place.

A few minutes ago, the Café Tropico had been mostly empty and he'd been keeping a low profile at the bar, but now that it was filling up more and the band was getting ready to play, he felt safe to casually shift on his bar stool and take a look around the open-air room. He was hoping Junior Martinez and his sidekick, Juan Gonzalez, would show up tonight. The bar's owner, Dennis Isaacs, who Rogan had gotten friendly with since working this area, suspected the two of selling drugs out of a back room. Dennis had let them know they weren't welcome here, more than once, but he was an older man and the two thugs were comfortable throwing their weight around. The Café Tropico wasn't fancy and had certainly seen better days, but it was a decent place—besides possessing tidbits of old Miami charm if you looked hard enough, it was also one of few places on Ocean Avenue where you could walk in and get a burger without busting your wallet. And Rogan wanted it to *stay* a decent place.

The truth was, coming to Miami had lit a fresh fire under

him, sharpened the edges on what had almost become a dull occupation. And so now he found himself going unofficially undercover, taking a special interest in this situation off the clock, in hopes of bringing down a couple of dealers, even if they were low-level. Best-case scenario—he could end up getting promoted to detective. Worst—well, even if he wasn't completely playing by the rules, if he was successful in taking some drugs and a couple of losers off the streets *and* helped out a local business owner at the same time, he just didn't think his captain would come down on him too hard.

The room was filled with the same people he would expect—a few tourists in shorts ate burritos or cheeseburgers while they waited for the classic rock cover band to start. Some club hoppers—younger and more slickly dressed— had stopped in for an early drink before moving on to the trendier establishments up the block. A middle-aged couple Rogan thought he'd seen here before did some salsa dancing to the Latin music that had begun to play over the loud-speakers a few minutes ago, warming people up for the band. So what if the Latin tunes would clash with the band's songs? It was that kinda place—more about easy grub and alcohol than worrying about sticking to a theme.

The only unpleasant sight was the guys at the pool table in the corner. Some Latino, some white, they sported too many bald heads, muscle shirts, and tattoos for Rogan's liking as a cop—they just looked like trouble. And he knew he'd seen at least a couple of them hanging with Martinez and Gonzalez on previous visits.

That's when his eyes fell on the lady in the navy blue suit. Damn, talk about out of place—what on earth was some starched professional chick doing here, dressed like that, on a Friday night? It wasn't like it was against the law or any-thing, of course, but . . . well, she just looked sort of ridicu-lous. Not to mention far too stiff, even as she lifted a sandwich to her heart-shaped lips.

It was then that it hit him—she was pretty. Almost hard to notice the way she was dressed, and with her coppery hair all pulled back tight in a bun like a librarian would wear. But she had damn attractive lips, that was for sure—and as his eyes traveled downward, he caught sight of a nice pair of legs ending in a pair of pumps that would have been more sexy than professional if they weren't the exact same shade of navy as her tailored suit. *You should let your hair down, honey.* She just looked . . . buttoned up too tight. Didn't she know this was the tropics?

And that's when the shouting started.